MURDER IN MIND

Further Titles by Veronica Heley from Severn House

The Ellie Quicke Mysteries

MURDER AT THE ALTAR
MURDER BY SUICIDE
MURDER OF INNOCENCE
MURDER BY ACCIDENT
MURDER IN THE GARDEN
MURDER BY COMMITTEE
MURDER BY BICYCLE
MURDER OF IDENTITY
MURDER IN HOUSE
MURDER BY MISTAKE
MURDER MY NEIGHBOUR
MURDER IN MIND

MURDER IN MIND

Veronica Heley

severn House

This first world edition published 2012
in Great Britain and in the USA by
SEVERN HOUSE PUBLISHERS LTD of
9–15 High Street, Sutton, Surrey, England, SM1 1DF.
Trade paperback edition first published
in Great Britain and the USA 2012 by
SEVERN HOUSE PUBLISHERS LTD

British Library Cataloguing in Publication Data

Heley, Veronica.
  Murder in mind.
  1. Quicke, Ellie (Fictitious character)–Fiction.
  2. Widows–Great Britain–Fiction. 3. Detective and
  mystery stories.
  I. Title
  823.9'14-dc23

ISBN-13: 978-0-7278-8179-3 (cased)
ISBN-13: 978-1-84751-435-6 (trade paper)

All Severn House titles are printed on acid-free paper.

Severn House Publishers support The Forest Stewardship Council [FSC],
the leading international forest certification organisation. All our titles that
are printed on Greenpeace-approved FSC-certified paper carry the FSC logo.

MIX
Paper from
responsible sources
FSC
www.fsc.org   FSC® C018575

Typeset by Palimpsest Book Production Ltd.,
Falkirk, Stirlingshire, Scotland.
Printed and bound in Great Britain by
MPG Books Ltd., Bodmin, Cornwall.

ONE

Ellie Quicke considered she had more than enough to worry about ahead of a visit from her husband's family, before a couple of murders sent her stress levels right off the scale . . . and her daughter Diana's latest problem came to light!

Monday, after school

'You freak me out, treading on my heels! Angelika will do her nut if she finds you in her own personal gym. You know she doesn't let anyone else use it. Well, apart from me, duh!

'Oh, get out of my way! I want to use the treadmill. Whatever are you like! Don't fiddle with the speedo. I don't like to go any faster than . . . are you deaf as well as stupid?

'I said don't touch the . . . Omigod! I can't . . . not so fast . . . take your hand off so I can turn it down! Aaargh!'

She stepped awkwardly off the treadmill, caught her foot, tripped and plunged across the room, arms flailing. Helped on her way with a kick from a well-aimed boot, she ran head first into the opposite wall. Blood sprayed. She folded down on to the floor.

Silence.

She's dead? Must check. Yes.

Well, that couldn't have gone better, could it?

Now, wipe fingerprints off the speedo.

Leave the treadmill running.

Close the door on leaving.

Wednesday afternoon

Ellie had never considered herself a great brain, particularly where mathematics was concerned, but it did occur to her that allocating rooms for all the visitors she was expecting was like trying to fit a quart into a pint pot. She had inherited a

large sum of money – which she'd put into a charitable trust
– and a spacious Victorian house into which she, her second
husband, Thomas, and their elderly housekeeper, Rose,
fitted without any trouble.

Now that dear Rose found the stairs so difficult and had
moved into a bed-sitting-room next to the kitchen, her original
bedroom and bathroom upstairs could also be used for guests
. . . except that it hadn't been decorated for years and the furniture and furnishings were a hotchpotch of leftovers.

Marrying a widower late in life, Ellie had acquired a second
family who lived in Canada but who planned to visit the United
Kingdom for the first time in many years. Of course it would
be delightful – if slightly intimidating – to meet Thomas's
children by his first wife. Would they like her? Thomas said
that of course they'd adore her, but he was biased, wasn't he?

Thomas couldn't see any problem. He said his family would
go to a hotel and he'd cover the cost, but Ellie felt this would be
wrong when they lived in such a large house.

Only, she couldn't make the maths work.

The guest room had a double bed in it and was en suite.
This would be ideal for Thomas's son and his wife.

They had two children. Now, if Ellie arranged for a second
single bed to be put in the room her grandson used when he
stayed overnight, then that would do for the twins, though
they'd probably quarrel over who had which bed. Well, their
parents could sort that out. So far, so good.

Ah, but where could she find a second single bed? Was
there one in the unused room at the end of the corridor upstairs,
currently filled with junk furniture? Might that room be made
habitable as an extra bedroom in time? She made a note to
herself to investigate.

Suppose she could manage to get that end room cleared
out, would it be suitable for Thomas's daughter and her partner?

Oh dear, Ellie did so dislike this modern trend of having
'partners' but not bothering to get married. She knew that
nowadays people tended to have trial relationships, as if they
could turn their emotions on and off like a tap. They seemed
to think it was perfectly all right to move in with one man
because he had a nice line in chat, then move on to another

when they got fed up with the first one getting legless every night. If there was a child involved before they split up, why worry, because everyone does it and children adapt, don't they?

Well, no; they didn't. Ellie could think of several children, including her own grandson, who had had trouble adapting to the break-up of their parents' marriage.

Supposing she could get that end room cleared and furnished, where could she put their child? Rose's old room at the top of the stairs wouldn't be suitable for a young girl.

Oh dear, oh dear. If only the council had seen fit to approve the plans Ellie had submitted to convert the unused top floor of the house into separate accommodation with its own outside staircase and parking place. Time and again her plans had been rejected because of worries about those very parking slots, of all things.

She told herself there was no sense worrying about something over which she had no control. Which didn't stop her worrying, of course.

Another thing. Rose might very soon need more help in the house. If there was one thing Ellie was sure about, it was that her old friend was not going to be shovelled away into the nearest council home, but would be looked after as part of the family as long as possible.

Ellie had someone in mind who might be enticed to move into the house to help Rose – one of her former cleaners, who'd recently proven herself a trustworthy ally[1] – but the timing was all wrong; Ellie had only got Rose's old accommodation upstairs to offer at the moment, which was not sufficient for a single parent with a child in tow.

In any case, Vera, the girl concerned, might now like to go to college, to catch up on the higher education that had been denied her when she'd fallen pregnant at a school-leaving party. If so, it would be up to Ellie to see that the girl realized her dream.

Ellie smiled to herself; she could well imagine what her avaricious daughter Diana would say to her mother giving

[1] See *Murder My Neighbour*

someone else a helping hand up the ladder of life. Diana would be furious!

Ellie's mind slid on to the ever-vexatious question of her demanding daughter. In the past Ellie had been accustomed to panic whenever Diana got into financial trouble, thinking it was up to her to help out, but her generosity of spirit had finally dried up under Diana's aggressive tactics and there had been a noticeable cooling in their relationship over the past few months.

That being said, even now the thought of Diana caused Ellie to frown. How long was it since Diana had seen fit to honour them with her presence? Six or seven weeks, perhaps?

The leaves on the trees were beginning to turn gold and brown and the sun's rays to lose their warmth. Autumn was upon them. Ellie decided she ought to check that Diana was all right.

Well, comparatively all right. Diana tended to live in the centre of a whirlwind, always in a state about something. Men or money. Or both.

Life had been beautifully quiet without her.

Only, now she came to think about it, Ellie had an uneasy feeling that no news from Diana was not always good news.

When last heard of, Diana's failing estate agency was about to be taken over by Hoopers, a large and thriving business in the town centre. Evan Hooper, who ran it, was a businessman of the old school who had earned the nickname of the Great White Shark. Not the cuddly sort, no.

Ellie grinned. Perhaps those two deserved one another?

Ellie picked up their marauding ginger tom, mis-called Midge, and tried to cuddle him. He objected, and she let him leap down on to the floor. He was a typically self-centred cat who wanted food, not caresses.

The front doorbell rang, and who should be there but Diana. Surprise! Shiny black car. Shiny and enormous black handbag. Black business suit with a touch of white around the collar. Black hair stunningly cut to show off a well-shaped head. Make-up rather heavy around the eyes. Diana had not inherited Ellie's beautiful skin, or the curl in her silvery hair.

Midge the cat disliked Diana, so he disappeared with a flick of his tail.

Ellie wasn't wearing any make-up at all and, as she'd been working in the garden, was wearing a pale-blue long-sleeved sweater, a navy skirt, and useful but clumpy clogs. Diana made Ellie feel frumpish, until she noticed that instead of her usual high heels, Diana was wearing ballerina shoes.

Ellie couldn't remember Diana wearing flatties before, not even when she'd been pregnant with little Frank during her first marriage.

Oh. Surely not?

No, of course not.

'Long time no see,' said Ellie, trying to dismiss thoughts of pregnancy from her mind. 'I was just going to have a coffee. Will you join me?'

Diana marched into the sitting room and stood by the French windows, looking out on to the garden. 'I'm off coffee.'

There are several things a mother – however modern – does not wish to hear from a divorced, single-parent daughter.

'I'm pregnant' must be top of the list. Or perhaps, 'I'm gay'? Now, there was a toss-up. Which would you prefer?

'I'm pregnant,' said Diana.

Ellie ran down a list of possible fathers in her mind and decided that almost any of the one-night stands Diana had enjoyed in the past might be more welcome than the name which leapt to the forefront of her mind. *Please God, let it not be Evan Hooper!*

'It's Evan's, of course.'

Ellie took a deep breath and let it out slowly.

She'd had a brush or two with the Great White Shark when she'd inherited a huge white elephant in the shape of Pryce House nearby . . . and that inheritance was another can of worms, wasn't it? Ellie's mind skittered over that problem and returned to Evan Hooper.

Pryce House was too large for private use without a host of live-in servants, and Ellie planned to turn it into a hotel for visitors who would appreciate its quirky charm. Evan Hooper had had the house on his books for sale for a few weeks and, although the instruction for him to sell had been withdrawn, he maintained he was owed the considerable amount of money his agency would have taken if the sale had gone through his books. He had been unpleasant about it, even though Ellie's solicitor assured her that Hoopers hadn't a leg to stand on.

This was the man whose estate agency had recently absorbed Diana's much smaller business. Not that he'd have had it all his own way, for Diana's chief characteristic – after ambition – was a ruthlessness which wouldn't have disgraced Attila the Hun.

Diana was perhaps not entirely as composed as she had tried to appear, for she started to tap on the window. Rat-a-tat-tat. Rat-a-tat-tat. 'He's said he'll marry me, under certain conditions.'

'Wait a minute. To the best of my knowledge he's paying alimony already to two of his past wives, and the current one is only in her twenties. Plus he's quite a few children to support.'

'Only three now. One died earlier this week. An accident in his private gym.'

'Poor man. I hadn't heard.'

'It'll be in the local *Gazette* on Friday, I suppose.' A twist of the lips. 'He's upset, of course, but he's bearing up, looking to the future. He wants a son to take over the business.' Rat-a-tat-tat. Rat-a-tat-tat.

'Sexist of him. Haven't any of his children inherited his brains?'

'Apparently not. He still has two girls and a boy, but none of them are up to scratch for one reason or another. His current wife is a model, swimsuits and underwear, doesn't want to spoil her figure having another child.'

'So you took a calculated risk that you might produce a son for him?'

'It's just been confirmed, today. A boy. Everything is as it should be.'

'I see.' Ellie didn't see. Not really. She'd often wondered how she and her first husband had managed to produce someone as self-centred as Diana but there it was, and you couldn't send your children back where they came from if they turned out to be a disappointment to you. She'd observed that men could cut their emotional ties with unsatisfactory children much better than women. She wished she knew how they did it.

'If I can produce a healthy boy child, he'll divorce Angelika – which she spells with a "k", believe it or not – and marry me.'

'A son being more important to him than a loving wife? What if the boy turns out not to be interested in the business – will he discard you for someone else?'

Diana ignored that. 'There's one other condition. He wants you to give him the money he'd have earned if the sale of the Pryce house had gone through him – which it was supposed to do, remember. He doesn't want it to go through the agency. He needs a private pot of gold to pay off Angelika.'

Ellie laughed, then sighed. 'You mean he wants me to pay off his current wife so that you can take her place? What rubbish. You know the trustees would never allow it.'

Diana's lips twisted. 'You know that you have the final say in everything at the trust. What skin is it off your nose to let him have his cut?'

'It's the principle of the thing.'

'Huh.'

Yes, quite. What had Diana and Evan Hooper to do with principles? Ellie would take a bet they couldn't even spell the word, never mind explain what it meant. She said, meaning it, 'No.'

'Think about it. I know the plans for converting the place have been approved by the local Council. Evan made sure they went through, so you owe him for that.'

Ellie shook her head. 'A councillor he may be, but he's not on the planning committee. Everyone there thought turning the Pryce mausoleum into a hotel would be good for the borough, so I don't owe Evan Hooper anything. Try again, Diana.'

Rat-a-tat-tat. Diana swung away from the window to sit in Ellie's favourite high-backed chair by the fireplace. 'You might at least pretend to be pleased for me. I'm sure you want to see me happily settled at last.'

'Indeed.'

'I'm only going through with the pregnancy if he gets a

quickie divorce and marries me. Otherwise I'll have an abortion.'

'An abortion?' Ellie gaped. Then recovered. 'No, you wouldn't do that. You wouldn't jeopardize your future with Evan by having an abortion . . . How could you even think of . . .? Oh, this is unbearable. We're talking about a person, here. Not a . . . a *thing*, to be disposed of down a rubbish chute. Someone who will love you unreservedly.'

'Oh my! Are we going to go all soppy and talk goo-goo? That's not really me, is it?'

Ellie kept her voice down, with an effort. 'Someone to love you, Diana.'

'I have you.'

'I love you, yes; but not unreservedly. I don't always like what you say or do.'

A shrug. 'Little Frank loves me unreservedly.'

'He used to. Nowadays his love is mixed with pain because you often find something better to do with your time than spend it with him, and then you brush him aside as if his feelings were of no consequence. You've tried him hard, Diana, and he's growing a tougher skin.'

'It's good to be tough. The world needs "tough".'

'May I remind you that he loves his father, Maria and his three little stepsisters – not unreservedly, because there has to be a balance of what you can and cannot do among siblings – but they love him back and he knows where he is with them. He knows they'd never let him down. He has learned that you often do. So, no; he doesn't love you unreservedly.'

Diana turned her head away. 'I have to look out for myself. No one else will.'

'You think that making a bargain with Evan will ensure you a life of Happy Ever After? You know better than that.'

'It will give me what I want in life. A man I can respect, a son to keep him happy. A nice house and business.'

'I notice you think of the baby as Evan's son, not as your own.'

A shrug. 'He can share his youngest daughter's au pair. I understand the present girl's not much cop: more interested in chatting to her friends than looking after the little one.'

'Doesn't the mother – what's her name? Angelika—?'

'She's off here, there and everywhere on fashion shoots. Her brat needs watching twenty-four seven because she's got some sort of allergy. Peanuts. If necessary we'll employ a trained nanny to look after both children.'

'Your poor child. Born out of ambition, on the wreckage created by divorced parents. What damage will this loveless liaison do to Evan's other children? One has died, you say. That still leaves . . . how many?'

Another shrug. 'Three, but I told you, they're out of it. No use to him.'

'And you want to add to this unhappy family? Oh, Diana.'

A touch of steel. 'Wish me luck, Mother dear. Think about what I've said. Pay Angelika off for me and I'm out of your hair for good.'

Ellie's husband Thomas used his key to let himself into the house and called out, 'I'm back!'

Ellie pushed Midge the cat off the kitchen table – again – and hurried out to give Thomas a welcome-home kiss. His beard and hair were beaded with rain, and his car jacket felt damp as she hung it up for him. She couldn't remember exactly what it was he'd been doing so, she said, 'Was it good?'

'For a funeral, yes.'

'Oh. Sorry. Forgot.'

Thomas had retired from parish work, but occasionally still took a service to oblige a colleague. His appearance was misleading, as he looked like an old-fashioned sea captain – complete with beard and moustache – but was in real life the editor of a small but influential Christian magazine, and one of the kindest and most thoughtful of men. Also, solid in every way.

He gave her a hug. 'I diagnose a need for food . . . or perhaps Diana has paid you a visit?' He picked Midge up, and that perspicacious animal purred. Loudly. Midge knew who would give him titbits from his plate at supper time, and it wasn't Ellie.

Ellie said, 'Dear Thomas. Both.'

He tensed. It was only a slight movement, but she caught

it and sighed. Well, best to tell him straight away. 'She's pregnant. I've always thought of abortion with horror, but I'm beginning to wonder if it wouldn't be better for some children if they'd never been born.' She peered up at him, to see if he was shocked by what she'd said, because it shocked her to hear such words come out of her own mouth.

He absorbed the news with a nod and, with Midge superglued to his shoulder, propelled her towards the kitchen and tea. 'Light of my life, you'll feel better when you've had something to eat.'

As always, he rebalanced her world. 'You're right, as always. And I didn't really mean it about abortion. Or not for very long. It's minted lamb chops with lots of different vegetables but only a few potatoes, because we really must try to cut down on carbohydrates.'

He protested, 'I need carbohydrates when I've just conducted a funeral.'

She managed to smile. 'All right, but not too many, right?'

On which note Ellie and Thomas put their worries behind them and did justice to their big meal of the day.

TWO

Thursday morning

Once upon a time Ellie had been content to look after her husband and daughter in an unremarkable, three bedroom semi-detached house. She'd filled her spare time by looking after her husband's aged aunt, working in the local charity shop, singing in the choir at church and helping out wherever required in the community.

With what sometimes seemed like dizzying speed Ellie had been widowed, inherited money and property, and then remarried. Sometimes she felt like the old woman in the song who'd woken out of a nap to find her skirts had been cut off short, and said, 'Lawks, but this is none of I!'

On the whole Ellie had adapted well to the demands of her new position, though she sometimes found it a struggle to turn her mind to business when she'd far rather be working in the garden.

Rose, their elderly housekeeper, had once loved pottering about among the flowers but had recently found it too much for her to prune and dig, and had concentrated on the care of plants in the conservatory at the back of the house . . . which meant that Ellie could have a go instead.

There was, of course, a gardener; but he couldn't be trusted to deadhead the roses and select fragrant plants for the herbaceous border, or to do much of anything if he could get away with it.

Once a week Ellie had to make sure her fingernails were clean, push a brush through her short, silvery hair, find a lipstick if possible, and put on a decent skirt to attend a business meeting, even if it was only to be held in her dining room.

Ellie had a couple of cleaners who kept the house looking good, but she automatically checked for dust on the big table as she prepared for the day's session.

The dining room would have to be returned to its original purpose when their guests arrived, which meant that a rent in one of the curtains – made by a visiting kitten and not by their own marauding ginger tom – must be mended, soonest. Perhaps the carpet should be professionally cleaned?

She tried to view her house as her visitors would see it and couldn't help feeling it would appear somewhat dark and drab with its old-fashioned, mostly antique, furniture. What could she do about that, in the short time at her disposal?

If only she'd started earlier to transform the unused top floor of the house into separate living accommodation, but even if the new plans were passed this month it would be ages before builders could start work and they wouldn't finish till next summer. If Rose were to fall ill again this winter . . . No, don't think about it. Or rather, think about it later.

At ten o'clock, Ellie's part-time secretary Pat traipsed herself, her laptop and a pile of papers from her office along the corridor into the dining room and set up at one end of the big polished table.

Ellie's ex-son-in-law Stewart – Diana's first husband – was next to arrive with his own laptop, iPad, Blackberry, and goodness knows what else. Stewart now managed Ellie's empire of properties to let. Once he'd recovered from the divorce, Stewart had remarried and was now living locally and happily with his new wife and their three delightful little girls, plus his – and Diana's – son, in a semi-detached house with a garden.

As Ellie's business affairs had expanded, Stewart had taken on more and more responsibility, which meant longer hours and a worry line appearing between his eyebrows. He hadn't complained – he wasn't the complaining type – but Ellie was beginning to think she ought to ease his workload. Only, she couldn't think how.

Today Stewart was accompanied by Nirav, a tricky youngster who had once worked for Evan Hooper but was now making himself useful in Stewart's office.

Ellie wondered why Stewart had brought Nirav. He'd never done so before. The boy had proved himself responsible and meticulous, but she still wasn't sure he was trustworthy. Well, if Stewart had brought him to this meeting, the reason would no doubt emerge in due course.

Ellie's old friend Kate arrived last; in a hurry as usual. Once a month she would drop her children off at the nursery and rush in to update them on the financial matters she handled for Ellie and her charitable trust. Kate was a tall woman, whose heavy eyebrows gave the impression that she was frowning, but she – like Ellie's husband Thomas – was solid gold as a friend and counsellor.

Today Kate had brought news of the trust's latest project to turn nearby Pryce House into a modern hotel. A consortium which operated a chain of distinctive hotels had seen the potential of the turreted monstrosity and, with what seemed like incredible speed to Ellie, probate had been granted, contracts signed, and architects commissioned.

Ellie had no wish to be concerned with the actual running of the hotel when it was completed, but as Kate had arranged for Ellie's trust to be allocated some shares in the company which was to run the development, she found herself more involved with the details of the conversion than she had hoped.

Stewart said, by way of starters, 'I understand we've recently lost another member of the Pryce family.'

Ellie knew what he was getting at but refused to defend herself. Instead, she said with a bland smile, 'Edgar's cancer was so advanced that it was amazing he lasted as long as he did. I'm seeing his widow early next week. Is it Monday morning or Tuesday, Pat?'

'Ten, Monday morning.'

Ellie maintained her smile through the following silence. She knew that neither Kate nor Stewart had approved of the dying man's marrying a single parent and adopting her child, since a condition of Ellie's inheriting the mansion meant she had to provide for the remaining members of the Pryce family . . . which now included the man's widow and her child. She wondered what they'd think of her plan to move Vera and Mikey in to her home, partly, if not wholly, so that Vera could help look after Rose.

Ellie stuck out her lower lip. 'They made him very happy in his last few months. He wanted to provide for them and I agreed that we should do so.'

Stewart raised one eyebrow but forbore to comment in any other way. It was, after all, Ellie's decision how she spent the inheritance Mrs Pryce had left her.

Kate hadn't approved, either. Well, tough.

Kate pinched in her lips, glanced at the heavy watch on her wrist and got down to business. 'May we take the hotel first, Ellie? I've got another meeting later this morning.'

Ellie nodded, not surprised; Kate's time was at a premium.

'The plans for the conversion of Pryce House have been passed by the council, which is good news all round. It was an inspired idea of yours, Ellie, to build a lift shaft on at the back of the house. I don't think we'd have had a chance of getting the plans through if we hadn't sorted that out.

'The consortium that have bought the house have chosen a nationally known contractor, and they in turn have appointed a project manager, whose mobile telephone number . . . Here, Ellie. You'd better keep this by you. He's going to be more or less permanently on site. He'll be responsible for coordinating the teams of workmen who'll be descending on the place from now on.

'The idea is to clear the site of everything they don't want to keep, in particular the old greenhouses and tool sheds. At the same time, they'll dig the foundations for the new lift shaft at the back and set up scaffolding all round to check on the roof and guttering. They're planning to take all the heavy equipment through the yard at the side of the house, which means the covered roof over it goes for the time being.

'Inside, they'll have to tear down some walls in the old kitchen quarters to create a new kitchen, cold store and rest room for the staff. The basement will house a laundry, workshops for the maintenance people, and storage. Teams of plumbers and electricians will move into the parts that don't need reconstruction almost straight away, to rewire and install en suites; and when that's finished, specialists will fit out the kitchen area. A design team is working on decoration, furniture and furnishings as we speak.

'There's a provisional date for signing off on the project of, let me see, they've suggested twelve months from the time they're allowed on the site, but are hoping it will be only nine. Now, there's something you haven't settled yet, and that's what's to be done with the garden.'

Ellie said, 'I'd like to keep the garden much as it is. Oh, of course the greenhouses must go; they're pretty decrepit, anyway. But the basic design of patio, lawn, rose garden and pond seems to me to fit the house and would be an attraction for visitors.'

Kate sighed. 'Ellie, my love; you're dealing with professional hoteliers here, and they won't be impressed by anything but a professional's plan for the garden. I've sorted out the names of two garden designers . . . This one and this.' She handed over some paperwork. 'I've looked at their websites and both come highly recommended. I've sent each of them a brief giving the size of the plot, type of hotel, etcetera, and asked them to come up with a provisional design. They need to be contacted soonest, or they'll be so tied up doing gardens for the Chelsea Flower Show that we won't be able to get hold of them.

'Just remember that though you know a lot about gardens in the suburbs, providing a garden for an important hotel is a rather different matter. You've also got to bear in mind that a lot of the garden is going to have to be torn up anyway while the builders are in. If you meet with the designers now and choose the one you like best, you can have your own input and keep everyone happy.'

Ellie tried not to make a sour face. Another job for her to do. She wanted to say, 'Must I?' but realized this was a childish response and that she was all grown up now. Well, most of the time, anyway.

Kate glanced at her watch again and said, 'Oops, I'm running late. Look, Ellie; tell you what I'll do. I'll see if one of them, if not both, can meet you at the site early next week. If they can make it, I'll leave a message for you with Pat. Now, Stewart; just a quickie. I know it's not your scene, but have you any ideas about how many parking slots we can get into the front garden? Their plan includes forty cars, but I don't think that's realistic.'

Stewart and Kate went into a huddle over the plans for the parking, which would have to be outside as the original coach house-cum-garage would be converted for office space on the ground floor, with a flat above for live-in staff.

Ellie felt useless. Of course she thought like an amateur because that was what she was. Kate was right in saying she must make use of professionals, but Ellie had hoped she'd be able to save at least some of the roses with which the garden had been filled by its last owner.

She opened the dining-room door and rang a tiny handbell to signal to Rose that they'd like their coffee, please. Rose was of the opinion that no one should try to get through a morning without sustenance, which was one reason why neither Ellie nor Thomas ever lost weight.

Ellie sighed. Well, if she couldn't calculate how many square metres each car must have, at least she could minister to the inner man and woman. She poured coffee, handed cake and wondered again why Stewart had brought Nirav to this meeting.

At last Kate said, 'I think you'll have to go up to town to meet them, Ellie. They've suggested – where's your diary? If we can fix a date, then I'll be off and leave you all to deal with more mundane matters.' She kissed Ellie, waved to Stewart, smiled at Nirav and Pat, and disappeared at a run.

'Splendid woman,' said Stewart. 'Makes me feel my age.'

Ellie said, 'She makes me feel weak at the knees sometimes, too. Now, Stewart; how are things your end?'

Stewart was meticulous with his figures. A big, reliable man, his waistline was beginning to thicken and his thatch of fair hair was beginning to recede from his temples. He hadn't much sense of humour, but he did know what the word 'principle' meant.

Ellie wasn't sure that young Nirav did. An eager beaver, anxious to please. A bright boy, yes. But.

At last Stewart shut down his laptop and leaned back in his chair. 'Well, that's it for today.' He didn't move.

'Except,' said Ellie, 'that you have something to tell me. Or Nirav has?'

Stewart looked at Pat, who hastily said she needed to get on, didn't she, and departed.

Ellie sighed. 'It's about Diana, isn't it? Or about Mr Hooper? Or, perhaps, both?'

Stewart nodded to Nirav. 'Tell Mrs Quicke what you've heard, Nirav. I know it's only gossip and we shouldn't pay any attention to it, but when it interferes, or when it might interfere with our work . . . You'd better tell her what you know.'

To do him justice, Nirav looked as if he'd prefer not to speak. 'It's just that . . . it *is* only gossip. Are you sure . . .?'

Stewart nodded.

Ellie concentrated.

Nirav wriggled in his chair. 'Well, it's like this. You know I'm working on the maintenance side of the properties to let? When there's a complaint about a leak or a broken window or, well, anything, and when a property becomes vacant, I go in to take a note of what needs to be done, pass the order on to the builders and then keep track of progress. The other day I found our maintenance team had been so short-handed that they'd had to call in a freelance for an urgent job. It turned out that I knew the man because he'd done some work in the past for Hoopers.'

Hoopers. Ah.

Nirav said, 'He works for himself, doing all right, word of mouth, you know? His cousin still works for Hoopers, though she says it's not the same now and is looking around for another job. She passes all the gossip on to him, he knew I'd worked there at one time, and so we got talking.'

His eyes shifted to Stewart. Stewart nodded at him to continue.

With reluctance, Nirav obliged. 'The thing is, I know she's your daughter, Mrs Quicke, and I'm sure she's a great business woman and an asset to Hoopers, and maybe they were over-staffed, but the atmosphere there now is, well, uncomfortable. At least, that's what I was told. It seems that your daughter has been put in charge of assessing the capabilities of everyone who works for them and she's clearing out those who don't think the way she does. Some of them, well, she's probably right, but then she got round to Mr Abel. I liked him. He was always very fair and straightforward with me.'

Ellie bit the end of her pen. She'd encountered Mr Abel when he showed her over the Pryce mansion months ago, and had formed the opinion that he was conscientious, humourless, and efficient. The word that came to mind was 'worthy'.

Nirav gave a little cough. 'She found out that Mr Abel told an interested buyer the truth about a house he was showing, and the buyer dropped the price by thirty K. She was furious.'

Oh dear. What could Ellie say? 'I suppose my daughter was looking out for Mr Hooper's best interests.'

Nirav hunched a shoulder. 'If you put it that way. The word is that Mr Hooper thinks the sun shines and lets her do what she wants.'

'Mr Abel is thinking of leaving Hoopers?'

'He's resigned, though I don't think he was given any choice in the matter. He'll be leaving when he's worked out his notice. Mr Stewart says he thought you'd be interested, but . . .' Another wriggle.

Ellie leaned back in her chair. 'Nirav, would you like to take the coffee things out to the kitchen for me?'

Nirav scrambled to his feet and retreated.

Ellie looked at Stewart, who nodded. 'I've heard similar stories from other sources.'

'If it's true that Mr Abel is looking for another position, then what do you think about offering him one? The more money and property that drifts our way means that more and more work gets piled on to your shoulders; there are only so many hours in the day, and you have family responsibilities, too.

'Look at today's meeting; in the old days you only had to deal with the properties to let, but now you're being drawn into some of the other aspects of the trust's affairs. Some time soon I'd like to talk to the other directors of the trust about inviting you on to the board, and I think we should make you General Manager of the company that looks after the properties to let.'

He looked both pleased and worried. 'Yes, I can see that . . . but are you sure, Ellie? I'm no financier and—'

'Neither am I. That's what we have Kate for. You'd like it, wouldn't you?'

'Yes, I would. But—'

'So we'll need someone else to do all the nitty gritty of the lettings office for us. Not Nirav; he's too young and inexperienced. We have no one else in the office who could take it on, have we? On the other hand . . .?'

Stewart caught on at last. 'I see where you're heading. Well, I've heard nothing but good of Mr Abel. An estate agent who speaks the truth? As rare as hen's teeth. Hah!'

'We will have to advertise the position, but if we made it known in the trade that we are looking to take someone on, don't you think that Mr Abel might apply? That way, we wouldn't be accused of poaching but we'd acquire someone whom we can trust.'

He ironed out a smile. 'I tell Nirav you're planning to increase my responsibilities, which means I'll have to shed some of my workload, which in turn means we'll be looking for an experienced man to join the firm. Nirav tells his engineering friend, who tells his cousin, and Mr Abel hears about it. How long do you think it would take for the word to get through? A couple of days?'

Ellie smiled, too. 'Tread cautiously. Spread the word but don't make any direct approach because we don't want to upset Mr Hooper any more than we have to. As for little Nirav; how trustworthy is he, do you think?'

'He's got a mind like a corkscrew, but at the moment it's in his best interests to be straight with us. He's ambitious. He wants to move into the lettings side, but so far I've said no. He's desperate for accommodation for himself and his girl-friend, who I'm told is about to become his wife very soon. I'm thinking of offering him a short-term let on a flat which is a bit run-down, but which the maintenance team can't get round to for a couple of months. All right?'

'Brilliant. Now, when may I come to see your beautiful little daughters, and is my grandson playing in a football match this weekend? He told me he's first reserve and hopes to play, and I'd like to come to watch, if it doesn't rain.'

Thursday noon

The children's playground in the park was packed on this bright sunny day. Au pairs chatted to mothers and the occasional house husband, while keeping an eye on the toddlers. Scooters and buggies had been parked to one side, awaiting the return of children who would be cross and hungry after expending their energy on the brightly-coloured attractions.

A clown appeared with a bunch of balloons and a plate of biscuits.

'Roll up! Birthday treat!' The clown was white-faced with a red, smiling mouth. A padded red and black suit disguised its figure as it handed out balloons and biscuits with white-gloved hands.

'More!' demanded a fat-faced child with crumbs around her mouth.

A small boy objected. 'You greedy pig! You've had one already.'

The girl snatched the biscuit he'd been about to eat and ran off, cramming it into her mouth. The clown gave away the last of the biscuits and left the park.

The greedy child's au pair was talking to a friend and failed to notice that anything was wrong till it was too late.

Friday morning

It was not until after Ellie had cleared away the breakfast things, talked the weekend menus over with Rose, made out a shopping list, taken down the curtain which needed repair in the dining room, and done a stint in her office that she had time to sit down with a cup of coffee in the kitchen and reach for the local *Gazette*.

She'd forgotten about the Hooper girl's death and was shocked when she saw it featured on the front page.

'Look, Rose.' She held the paper up. '"Teenager's Tragic Accident. A bright and bubbly girl, the light of our lives." It says the Hooper family's prostrated, but they always say that, don't they? Diana gave me the impression that Evan was shocked but not devastated. Oh, look, it says that her mother was . . . No, that can't be right. The local paper often gets things wrong though, don't they? The dead girl was too old to be the daughter of Evan's current wife, wasn't she?'

Rose reached for her reading glasses. 'She looks a proper little madam. I know that sort. Think they can get away with anything, just because Dad's got money.'

'It says here that her school friends are all in tears and have placed dozens of messages on Facebook. That's the way it takes them nowadays. Fame for a few days on Facebook. Poor thing, what a waste of a life.'

'What I want to know is, what was she doing in the gym in the first place? Trying to lose weight?'

'These young things think they can never be too thin. It says here that she was on a treadmill and set the counter too fast.'

'Catch me getting on one of those things. Instruments of torture.'

Ellie had to smile. 'I suppose I ought to do something about my weight, but . . . yes, I agree. Pretty girl, wasn't she?'

Rose snorted. 'I bet she wasn't naturally a blonde. That's a professional hairdo if ever I saw one. Look at those eyelashes; they're never natural. They retouch all those photographs, don't they?'

'Mm, she does look older than fourteen, or is it fifteen?'

Ellie tried to remember what Diana had said about the girl. 'I expect she was at a private school. Yes, it says here; St Augustine's. There'll have to be an autopsy and an inquest before they can bury her, I suppose. There's a sister, isn't there? It must be dreadful to have a sibling die on you like that.'

'I wonder if Her Royal Highness will attend the funeral.' Rose did not care for Diana.

Ellie put the paper aside. 'Well, we must get on. Rose, no need for you to bother, but I thought I might look at what furniture we've got in the end room upstairs. If we can find enough beds, we could get at least one of those rooms ready for our visitors, couldn't we? Do you suppose we could hire some furniture if we're short?'

'I don't know why you want to bother. You know Thomas said they could go to a hotel.'

'I know, I know. But I'd like them to feel they're welcome here. After all, Thomas has seen very little of them since they went to Canada, and he's only twice been over to see his grandchildren.'

'What is young Frank going to say to this lot coming in and taking over his bedroom?'

'I've talked to him about it, and he understands how it is. He wants to know if they'll bring him an American football jersey. I'd better remind Thomas to arrange it. First things first. I'll go up to see what we've got in the way of furniture. Then I'll take that curtain to be mended and do the weekend shopping on the way back.'

She went upstairs, past the bedrooms in regular use, to the very end of the corridor, where there was a large room which had been unused – save as a dump for spare furniture – for as long as she could remember.

She quailed. There were no curtains, or carpet. Well, that might be a roll of carpet and underlay over there . . . and yes, there was a huge box here which . . . Brilliant, curtains! But alas, sadly dusty and . . . Oh dear, frayed at the edges. They fell apart as she lifted them up.

Some dust sheets had been inadequately draped over a mound of furniture, but lifting up one edge, she spotted a double bed – in pieces and very old-fashioned – some chairs which weren't in bad condition, a small wardrobe and a chest of drawers which needed repair.

She despaired. Leaving everything as it was, she investigated the bathroom next door, which only Frank used nowadays. He liked the solid feel of the cast-iron bath and its claw feet. Terribly old-fashioned, of course. So old-fashioned it was almost fashionable again.

Next along the corridor was Thomas's sanctum. Had she time to spare for a few minutes' peace and quiet? Yes, she'd make time.

She went in. The room was sparsely furnished with a couple of chairs, a small table holding various Bibles and reference notes, and an embroidered Victorian picture of Jesus as shepherd, carrying a lamb over his shoulder. There was a blind at the window and a mat on the shining floor-boards. Despite its lack of luxurious furnishings, it had a welcoming look to it.

Ellie only visited the room occasionally, but Thomas used it every day as a place in which to think, to meditate, to pray.

If she commandeered this room, she could put his daughter and her partner in here and . . . No, she couldn't. This room was perhaps the most important in the whole house to Thomas, and she was not even going to hint that he might move out for a while . . . Even though he was supposed to use the library for his den, and never did.

No, she must make up her mind to it. She could not use that room for guests. She sat down, trying to calm her mind.

Dear Lord, all this fuss and palaver. I fear I'm losing sight of what's important in my life. Sorry about that. But if you could spare a moment to . . . No, I can't ask for help on household matters, that's absurd. Although I am rather worried; have we enough bed linen to go round?

Sorry, sorry. Again. I'm being stupid. I should be asking you to keep an eye on Rose so that she doesn't fall ill again. And on Diana. And on . . . well, you know how many people I have to worry about, and you don't need reminding . . . or perhaps you do? Only, I haven't got the time at the moment.

Yes, I know I ought to make a bigger space for you in my life, but . . . please forgive me. Is that the time? Must dash.

THREE

Friday noon

Ellie descended the stairs, struggling to hold on to the bundle of curtains she'd disinterred from the box in the junk room.

The doorbell rang. She tried to shift the unwieldy bundle under one arm as she opened the door. For a moment she failed to recognize her visitor. When you don't expect the police to call, it's a shock to find them on your doorstep, isn't it?

'Let me help you with that,' said Detective Constable Milburn, deftly relieving Ellie of the bundle as it slipped out of her arms. 'Is it a bad time to call?'

'No, I suppose not,' said Ellie, trying to think why this likeable woman was on the doorstep. She hadn't done anything wrong lately, had she? 'Come in. Time for a coffee? Do close the door behind you. It's going to rain any minute, by the look of it. Thomas hasn't got another parking ticket, has he? It's dropping elderly people off outside the tube station that does it. He can't seem to grasp the fact that he can no longer stop the car there. But you aren't in the traffic department, are you?'

'No,' said the DC, smiling. 'But I did want to pick your brains, if I may.'

'Gracious! Are you sure? I'm not exactly Brain of Britain, you know.'

'Eyes and ears of the world, that's you. And I really do need your help. Shall I put this lot down on the chair here?'

Rose appeared from the conservatory, brandishing her little watering-can. Rose liked Ms Milburn. 'Coffee and cake? Ellie, if you think you're going to use those curtains, you've got another think coming. Phew! The dirt! Shall I put them out with the rubbish?'

Ellie tried to brush herself down. No matter how good your cleaners were, empty rooms attract dust if not attended to at frequent intervals. 'Yes, Rose. Thanks. And I'd love a cuppa. Sorry, Ms Milburn. We're expecting visitors and I'm trying to get the junk room for occupation. There's a double bed up there which might do, but I'm at my wits' end to . . . And these curtains fell to pieces as soon as I picked them up so they won't do, either. Sorry. You wanted to talk to me about something. Come and sit down and tell me what's troubling you.'

'It's the Hooper case.' Ms Milburn followed Ellie into the sitting room. 'I thought you might have heard something, know something. All gossip is grist to my mill. What do you know of the family?'

Ellie felt her nerves tighten, but kept her tone light. 'I read about the death in the paper this morning. Shocking. I'm afraid I don't know really know the family. I've had some business dealings with Evan Hooper in the past, and my daughter's estate agency has been absorbed into Hoopers; beyond that, no.'

'You've never met any other members of the family?'

'No. Sorry.'

'You've heard about them?'

'I think – but this is only gossip – that there's an older boy. Is he at college or something? And another couple of girls? That's the extent of my knowledge.'

'Didn't you think that two deaths in the family was rather odd?'

'You mean that one was an accident but that two looks like carelessness?' Ellie did a double take. 'What do you mean, *two* deaths?'

'Or, murder.'

'Murder?' Ellie sank into her big, high-backed chair by the fireplace. '*Two*? Now, hang on a mo, the paper reported the death of a teenager this morning. Can't remember her name. Oh, Fiona. I think. Electrocuted, was she? Something to do with the treadmill in her gym?'

The DC sat down, only to have Midge the cat landing on her with intent. Midge knew that there was likely to be cake on the tray Rose was bringing in. Midge liked cream, and he knew Ellie wouldn't give him any, but perhaps the visitor would?

'That's right. Fiona. We received a call at twenty hundred hours on Monday evening from the ambulance service. One of my colleagues attended and was met by Mr Hooper, who led the way to their gym in a conservatory at the back of the house. The constable found a fifteen-year-old girl lying there, dead. A doctor was already there, who confirmed that life was extinct. There's a strict procedure to be followed in any case of a fatal accident, you know, and my colleague followed it to the letter.

'Forensics arrived, took photographs, dusted for prints, etc. My colleague took a statement from Mr Hooper, who was shocked, horrified and angry. Fiona was his daughter by his second marriage. Mr Hooper had been alerted to the death by his third wife, a model calling herself Angelika with a "k", who'd found the body and gone into hysterics. By the time my colleague got round to her, Angelika had recovered enough to give him a statement. To give them their due, neither Mr or Mrs Hooper asked for a solicitor to be present, and both said they wanted to help the police find out what had caused the accident.

'Angelika says that she is the only person who uses the gym normally, but she had given her stepdaughter Fiona permission to use it if she wasn't around. Angelika says she had gone into the gym to fetch a sweater she'd left there earlier in the day and found the body. When pressed as to her exact actions, she said she'd gone in, heard the treadmill working overtime and was livid that someone had been misusing it. She turned the speedometer down and switched the machine off. Then she saw the body and started screaming.

'Mr Hooper heard her. He arrived, couldn't find a pulse – which wasn't surprising as the girl had been dead for some time – and called the ambulance. The ambulance people called the doctor. The doctor called the police. The police took statements from everyone in the household: that's Evan Hooper, his wife Angelika, another teenaged daughter and an au pair. Oh, there was a toddler, too, but she was safely tucked up in bed by that time and asleep.'

'Isn't there a son, as well? Or am I imagining it?'

'No son visible. My colleague asked for backup and the DI was summoned, who reassured the family that there would be the very minimum of fuss as it was obviously a dreadful accident. It appears that Fiona had recently been trying to get her weight down. She was allowed into Angelika's private gym to use the equipment without supervision and must have set the speedometer too high. Being alone, and for some reason unable to adjust the rate, she panicked, misjudged her step as she tried to get off and spun out of control across the room. Bashed her head in on the wall opposite.'

'Tragic,' murmured Ellie, worrying where this tale might end up. All roads seemed to lead to Mr Hooper, and she didn't like that, not one little bit.

'There was no reason to suspect anything was other than it appeared to be. But now this other death . . .?'

'I hadn't heard of another one.'

'Abigail Hooper, two years and two months, child of Angelika and Evan Hooper. She died in the play centre at Pitshanger Park on Thursday morning.'

'Oh, that's dreadful. What a terrible thing. The poor parents!'

Ellie knew the play centre well. It had its own small but adequate building in the park and a small enclosed play area laid out for toddlers. It was run by two women with some local assistance. They charged just about enough to keep them going, with a bit of help from the council and local charities.

The DC continued. 'We received notification of a fatal accident at twelve hundred hours on Thursday morning. One of the children attending the play centre had an allergy to peanuts, had eaten a couple of biscuits given her by a clown, and died despite all they could do to save her.'

'A *clown*?'

The DC nodded. 'Imagine that. A clown. Somebody's birthday treat, apparently. Only, no one has owned up to having a birthday that day, or to organizing a visit from a clown. The women who run the play centre are trained in first aid. They kept their heads and did all the right things. As soon as the child was found to be in distress, they asked her au pair for the EpiPen to treat her, and used it. No good. The child was past help. Death comes quickly in such cases, which is a blessing in some ways, I suppose. They rang for an ambulance, a paramedic attended, who asked for a doctor; he pronounced the child dead and passed the buck to us.

'The call came into the station just as the inspector was about to go out on another case, and he told me to take it. He thought it must be a hoax call because a clown was mentioned, and someone at the back of the room asked if the clown had big ears, which made him, er, rather cross. I wasn't laughing, honest, but he caught my eye and said I'd be the best person to deal with it.'

The DC's tone was limpid, but Ellie understood the subtext. Ms Milburn's boss bore the nickname of 'Ears' because his stuck out and turned red when he was upset about anything. Ellie had referred to him as the man with the red ears when she first met him and this unfortunate nickname had stuck – much to his fury and everyone else's secret amusement.

'I never meant to cause him distress,' said Ellie. 'I ought to feel sorry for him, I suppose, and I do try to.'

'Of course,' said Ms Milburn, smoothing away a smile. She knew, and Ellie knew, that Ears disliked Ellie. Of course, he didn't seem to like anyone very much, and he certainly didn't care for his DC, who was considerably brighter than him and a woman, as well. So yes; it would have amused him to send her out on a hoax call.

Only, it had turned out to be far from a hoax.

'I got there within fifteen minutes. The doctor was just leaving, and the parents were in the process of taking the other children away. It was lunchtime, you see; the day was warm, the children tired and fractious. Everyone was in shock. It wasn't surprising that they wanted to take their children away.

'The play centre people were excellent. They'd had the morning from hell, as a toddler had fallen off a swing and hurt himself earlier. It was entirely his own fault, nothing sinister, but everyone was concerned, naturally. You know how much noise a frightened child can make, especially when there's a bump on the head or a cut finger? So all the helpers and some of the adults had been involved, looking after the toddler, arranging for the young mother to take him to hospital to be checked out.

'It was all written up in the Incident Book and everyone was relaxing when the clown arrived shouting, "Roll up, Roll up! Birthday treat!" and passing out biscuits and balloons to all and sundry. Before anyone could ask who'd sent him, all the children had clustered around to be given a biscuit or a balloon, or both. Abigail not only took one—'

'Didn't the child know better than to eat anything offered her by a stranger?'

'She'd been warned, of course. The au pair – who was in floods of tears when I saw her – said so. The play centre people knew of her allergy as well. The Hoopers insisted that everyone knew. They referred to the child as their little angel, the light of their lives, etcetera.'

'The parents were at the play centre at the time?'

'No. I interviewed them later, back at their house. The au pair had taken the child to the park. According to the au pair, Abigail was a monster with a shocking temper who, when crossed, could throw a tantrum and make herself sick with crying. Earlier that day the au pair had refused to buy her a bag of crisps and the child had been furious. So angry, in fact, that she'd thrown one of her famous strops and the au pair had threatened to take her straight home without visiting the park. It was unfortunate that she didn't.

'Abigail not only ate her own biscuit but snatched one from another child and ran off to eat it out of sight of the au pair. She died before anyone realized anything was wrong, by which time the clown had long since disappeared.

'I called to the station for backup, which was rather slow in coming. I mean, you can understand that they thought that I, too, had been a victim of a hoax call. My priority was to ask for an All Points looking for a man dressed as a clown and after that to get statements from everyone who might have seen something. I asked the adults who were still there to stay behind till I could talk to them. Some did stay, but others left.'

She lifted her hands in resignation. 'I was by myself, I couldn't physically stop them and I sympathized with them wanting to get their children away as quickly as possible.' She stopped and looked, narrow eyed, at Ellie.

Ellie obliged. 'So, because you didn't stop them leaving, even though you couldn't physically do so, Ears wants your guts for garters.'

'Which is why I need your help.'

'What can I do?'

'You know these people. I've got a whole list of names to wade through, and I need to prioritize, to find who might be likely to have some information. I need to produce something quickly because Mr Hooper is raging mad and wants to sue everyone in sight. First off he wants to sue the play centre. Even if the case is dismissed – which it should be because I can't see that the play centre people are in any way to blame – but if he does sue, the publicity will close them down, they'll lose their jobs and the community loses the play centre.

'Mr Hooper also wants us to arrest the au pair – who is Polish, by the way, and seems a bit dim but otherwise straight-forward. Yes, she deserves to lose her job because she was talking to a friend rather than watching every movement her charge made. But even if she'd been standing right beside the child, she might not have been able to prevent her eating the biscuits. I'm inclined to believe her when she says there was nothing much she could have done to prevent the tragedy because the child was so fond of having her own way. Mr Hooper wants the police to prosecute the au pair for manslaughter, claiming that it was her negligence which caused the toddler's death.'

Ellie shook her head. 'The Hoopers employed her. If they thought she was so inadequate, they shouldn't have let her take the girl out of the house.'

'Agreed, but Mr Hooper is—'

'A bully, and Ears wants to please him. I do understand that you have to go through the motions. The other adults who were there will be able to back up the au pair, won't they?'

'They might, but they won't want to speak ill of the dead. Especially of a child. And I doubt if they'd want to make the sort of statement which would condemn the au pair to a trial for manslaughter.'

Ellie digested that in silence. From what she knew of Mr Hooper, it was more than likely he would insist on his pound of flesh. Equally, none of the other adults attending the play centre would want to be drawn into his quarrel with the au pair.

'What I thought was,' said Ms Milburn, 'that as you know so many people in the community you might ring around, ask if anyone knows anything? It would save me hours of interviews with people who saw nothing, heard nothing and have their lips zipped tight. You never know, you might even be able to get a lead on the clown for me.'

Ellie laughed. 'Ridiculous. How could I?'

'I don't know. What I do understand is that you have a nose for this business. Won't you at least try?'

Ellie thought about it. She liked Ms Milburn and was inclined to help her if she could. 'You've confirmed there was no birthday boy or girl that day? That no one had ordered a clown's appearance?'

'No one admitted to it, anyway.'

'You got a description of the clown from the adults? Was he wearing a mask, or had he painted his face? Was it a man or a woman?'

'You know how unreliable eye witnesses can be. In fact, I think you're almost the only person I know who can remember accurately what you've seen. I was told he was six foot high, not very tall, had a pot belly, was thin as a beanpole, had a bald head, and a ginger wig. He wore black and red trousers with a white waistcoat. No, a red and black outfit with no waistcoat. He had bare arms and a high collar with an artificial flower in his buttonhole, the kind that squirts water at you. Oh, and he wore highly polished black shoes. That last observation came from the small boy who'd lost his biscuit to the dead girl. I believed him. I think the clown really did wear highly polished black shoes.'

'That boy sounds as if he might be worth interviewing.'

'He'd gone by the time I got round to taking names and addresses. His name was Timothy. There are two Timothys on the list the playgroup kept, and I don't know which one he is.'

'The other people are producing memories of clowns they've seen in the past and making out that's what they saw yesterday?'

'Some of them may be remembering correctly, but I don't know which.'

Ellie thought about it. 'Mobile phones. Most of them have cameras nowadays, don't they? An adult waiting around for a child would be interested when a clown arrived unexpectedly. Wouldn't they have taken the opportunity to photograph him?'

'I thought of that, too. By the time I got round to questioning the adults who remained, there were only three left. One was on a business call at the time of the incident. He said his wife was at the dentist's and he'd taken the morning off to look after the child. One of the women said she'd thought of taking a photo but the battery on her phone was getting low so she didn't bother. The third was talking to someone else when the clown came in. She had thought of taking a photograph but at that point her little boy ran up to her in tears because Abigail had pushed him off the slide and he'd hurt his knee, so she forgot about it.'

'One or two of the adults who left early might have a picture on their phones.'

'True. The play centre people had a list of everyone who'd signed in that morning, and they gave me a copy in case I needed to follow it up. It's going to take a while for me to get round all of them. Meanwhile, Mr Hooper is on the warpath.'

'And you want to drag me into the line of fire?'

'You're fireproof.'

Ellie shook her head. No, she was far from fireproof and she was worried that Diana was going to be drawn into this. 'Two incidents, both from Mr Hooper's family. Is the first one still being treated as an accident?'

'Yes, of course.' The DC didn't sound convinced. 'If the clown hadn't disappeared and Mr Hooper wasn't so anxious to sue everyone in sight, we might have written this death off as misadventure, too.'

'How did he disappear? Into a waiting car which was waiting for him outside the park gates? Was he driven off by an accomplice?'

'None of the people I interviewed saw him leave. One moment he was there; the next, everyone was clustering around Abigail, and I suppose that's how they missed his exit. Of course we could divert personnel from other duties in order to question everyone coming and going in and out of the park, to see if anyone saw the clown leave, but that would mean the expenditure of many man hours and put a strain on the budget. Authority is considering whether it's worth it.'

Ellie reflected. 'I suppose it would be easier all round to let Mr Hooper place the blame on the play centre people and the au pair, and to forget about the clown?'

'Well, it would, wouldn't it? That is, unless your imagination started working overtime, and you woke up wondering where this sequence of events might lead. The boss says I'm inclined to let my imagination run away with me. What do you think? Is it possible that someone is targeting the members of the Hooper family?'

Diana.

Diana would gain by these two deaths because those children were expensive and likely to be more so . . .

Ellie assembled a smiled and pinned it on to her face. 'They tell me that all the best policemen and women let their imaginations work for them. If you're right, well . . . I believe Mr Hooper's upset a lot of people in his time.'

'Let's hope I'm wrong. I shudder at the thought of having to investigate a man who dines with the Commissioner of Police.'

Ellie realized she must try to help the DC or spend the next week or so in a state of acute worry. *Could* Diana be responsible for these deaths?

Her heart said no. Diana wouldn't.

Are you sure?

Yes. It would never occur to Diana to target Evan's children. She hadn't got that sort of mind. A bash over the head; possibly. A sneaky visit by a clown; no.

Who could she get to play the clown for her, anyway? No, it was not Diana.

Set aside the first incident because that must have been an accident, surely; concentrate on the clown.

Ms Milburn handed Ellie a sheet of paper on which she'd written down a long list of names. On one side there was the name of the child, and on the other the surname of the person who had brought him or her to the play centre. 'They keep good records. I wondered if you might know any of these people and could find out for me quickly if they'd taken a photo of the clown. It would save some time.'

Ellie looked. She read the list, twice, and put it down. 'The name "Topping" rings a bell. I think I know someone called Topping, but why and in what context . . . Not at church, I think. Was she a volunteer at the charity shop where I used to work? No, I don't think so. Sorry, I can't think where I've met her. I don't know any of the other names. Was this Topping person with a little boy or a girl?'

'A boy. She's a small woman with a big personality. Dark hair cut short. She didn't stay to be questioned.'

Ellie shook her head. 'Doesn't ring a bell. It may come to me later.' Her mind churned with awful possibilities, of Diana being arrested and charged, of the possible fate of Diana's unborn child, of Mr Hooper's anger. Which reminded her. 'You say you interviewed both Abigail's parents? What is Angelika like?'

A shrug. 'The powers that be think a woman handles those matters better than a man so I've had to deliver bad news about accidents and even death to parents several times. If they care for the victim at all, the parents are horrified, disbelieving, shaken to their core. Quite often they tremble visibly. Some hyperventilate. Some collapse, physically and mentally. Some are calm on the surface, but you can see the whites of their eyes and know they'll give way later.

'Angelika with a "k" is quite beautiful. Young, tall and thin, with expensively treated long blonde hair. Beautifully made up. She models for swimsuits and underwear. Long legs, tan all over, expensive clothes. An expressionless face. She held a tissue to her eyes, couldn't speak, except to say how much

she'd miss her little angel, and how there was now a gap in
her life which could never be filled.'

Ellie caught the subtext. 'You don't think she was devastated,
then?'

'I really don't know. She's not that easy to read. I thought
at first that she might be acting the part of a bereaved mother,
but . . . I really don't know.'

'And Evan?'

'A powerful bull of a man. Much older than her but still
handsome in his own way. He kept saying how shocked he
was, that he couldn't believe it. No tears. Then the phone rang,
a landline phone. Most people, if they've just received such
bad news, let the phone ring, or take it off the hook. They
can't cope with an outside call. Or they give the caller the
brush-off, say they'll get back to them later. He was lucid,
calm, able to explain what had happened and then to say he'd
ring back next day. It was a business call from his office.
During this phone call she picked up her handbag, got out her
mirror and touched up her make-up.'

'Ouch. That's shocking.'

'I am prepared to believe they loved and would grieve for
their child, but . . . I suppose they did, but . . . I'm not sure.
By the time he got off the phone, he'd moved from shock to
anger. Within minutes he was casting around for someone
to take the blame. There was no more talk about what a lovely
daughter he'd lost. He strode about the room, projecting
violence.

'Tell the truth, I thought Angelika seemed afraid of him.
When she'd done fiddling with her lipstick and hair, she sat
like a statue, beautiful, emotionless. But her eyes kept flickering: to Evan and back; to the rings on her fingers and then
to the phone. She was thinking about . . . what? Ringing
someone?

'It crossed my mind to wonder if she'd resented the child,
because Abigail had interrupted Mum's all-important career.
I wondered – again, this is only my imagination at work – if
she'd want to put herself through another pregnancy.'

'You thought she was putting on a performance?'

'I'm trying to give her the benefit of the doubt.'

Ellie thought, but did not say, that Angelika had probably lost more than a child when she'd lost Abigail. She might also have lost her husband. Now that Ellie knew the importance which Evan placed on having a son, it was possible to wonder if he'd married Angelika because she was pregnant with his child. And now? Would her beauty be enough to keep her husband, now that Diana was on the scene and carrying his son?

Ellie told herself she had no right to think like that. For all she knew, Evan Hooper might well have been head over heels in love with his beautiful young wife. Well, he might. Perhaps it would be interesting to find out.

FOUR

M s Milburn said, 'Mm,' in appreciation as she laid her empty coffee cup down. She sighed. 'When I interviewed the au pair yesterday afternoon she was barely coherent, not fit to make a statement. So this morning I went back to the Hoopers to see her and was informed Mr Hooper had thrown her out of the house last night. He gave me an address for her; she's moved in with some friends up in Greenford, sleeping on their settee with all her belongings around her in black plastic sacks. A world away from the luxury of the Hooper household.

'She made a statement without any pressure. She feels guilty because she didn't spot what was happening in time, but defends herself by saying it wouldn't have done any good once the child had set eyes on the biscuits. I believe her.

'She says she tried to love the child, but that Abigail made it impossible to care for her. She says she took Abigail to the play centre almost every day, so that the child could get some exercise and meet other children. Abigail was tall for her age and carrying too much weight. I can confirm that. The play centre people agree that Abigail could be difficult.'

'Does the au pair resent being given the sack?'

'She's scared. The Hoopers paid her a pittance and she's no money saved. She's afraid of him, and afraid she'll never get another job with this hanging over her. Even if the police decide not to take the matter any further, she'll be in a difficult position. She's no money, no powerful friends. If I read her correctly, she's in two minds about cutting and running back to Poland. I warned her not to, but I can't help sympathizing with her, poor creature.'

'She is a poor creature?'

'Enormous eyes, thin little thing. Unsure of herself. Perfect victim for Evan Hooper . . . or his daughter.'

'Not grief-stricken?'

'I may be wrong, and they may all three of them be covering up a deep grief which will only manifest itself later, but no one in that family seems to be sorrowing for Fiona or for Abigail.'

'There's another girl in the family, isn't there? What about her?'

'Frozen faced. Shook her head when I asked if she had anything to say. She was at a sleepover with a friend when Fiona died, and she was at school when Abigail ate the biscuits.' Ms Milburn stood up. 'So, here's my card with my mobile phone number on it. Would you ring me if you hear anything about the clown or that might clear the au pair and the play centre?'

Ellie saw Ms Milburn out. Her hand hovered over the telephone in the hall. Should she ring Diana and ask . . . What could she ask her? Whether or not Evan was heartbroken over the deaths of two of his children?

She took her hand away. No. Better not open that can of worms.

She thought back over the conversation with Ms Milburn. Was Ms Milburn really so scared of Ears that she would welcome an outsider's help? Did Ms Milburn really believe that Ellie could supply her with the name and address of the clown? Surely not.

Thomas emerged from his study down the corridor, humming something from a Gilbert and Sullivan operetta. He knew all the words to the patter songs. This time it was something about being a model major-general.

Ellie found herself smiling.

He gave her a hug. 'Are you free for half an hour? I've had it up to here with work, and the computer's running slow. I need fresh air. What about you? If you're free, I thought we might take a walk, go for a coffee in the Avenue.' His eyes were round with innocence.

She patted his impressive frontage. 'I know what you're aiming for, which is more than a coffee. A walk, yes. Coffee, yes. But we're not going to Café 786 for cake, are we?'

The look of innocence intensified. 'I never remember what those numbers mean.'

'You know perfectly well what they mean; they're open seven days a week, from eight in the morning to six in the evening. And they do the best carrot cake in the Avenue.'

'I suppose they do, now you mention it.'

She had to laugh. 'Well, all right. We'll go there, but we'll have just one piece of cake between us, right? I have to watch your weight, even if you don't.'

He grinned. 'Half a piece of cake is better than none.'

'I'll get the shopping list, and you can help me carry the stuff back.'

The pile of curtains slipped off the chair, and he, being nearest, hauled them back. 'What's this?'

'I thought I could get the end bedroom ready for the family's visit, and I found a box of curtains but they're too fragile to rescue. I asked Rose to dump them, but I suppose she's forgotten. But I'll take the torn curtain from the dining room in to be mended on the way.'

He gave her a look. 'Ellie Quicke; anyone would think you had nothing better to do than fuss about curtains and carpets. For one thing, your poor overworked husband requires time out and needs your soothing hand on his brow, not to mention coffee and cake. I've told you before; my family can go to a hotel—'

'No, I really do want them to come here. It'll be so much nicer.'

'If you say so. But only if you get the wonderful Maria and her cleaning agency to sort the house out for you. Let her find men to move furniture, and take curtains down to be mended. If we need new carpets and curtains then get her to organize it. I am more than prepared to foot the bill. In fact –' and he knew this was a clincher – 'I'm enthusiastic about paying her, for it'll cost me far less than sending everyone to a hotel.'

'But . . .' said Ellie. And then smiled and sighed. 'You're right, of course. I have much more than housekeeping to worry about, don't I?'

'Stop right there. We're taking time out, right? Now, the immediate question is: will it rain while we're out? Let's take umbrellas, and then it won't even drizzle.'

She opened the front door and checked on the weather. 'Just wait while I tell Rose we're going out. By the way, you haven't ever come across a Mrs or Ms Topping, have you?'

'Doesn't ring a bell. Is it important?'

'Probably not.' She bustled out to the kitchen with the rejected curtains and put them out with the rubbish. Rose was dozing in her big chair so Ellie collected the shopping list, which looked a little on the thin side, but never mind; she could pick up some more things as they occurred to her. Yes, it would be really good to get out and feel the breeze. Blow the cobwebs away.

Thomas had the umbrellas ready and the front door open. 'Out you go, woman, on pain of feeling my deepest displeasure!'

She laughed and obeyed. What a blessing this man was!

Tea and cake. No conversation. Excellent coffee. Wonderful cake.

Topping . . . She knew the name from somewhere. She asked the owner of the café. He shook his head.

Thomas gave her a look. 'No work for at least half an hour, right?'

She nodded and thrust her worries to the back of her mind. On her return she would ring Stewart's wife Maria, who ran an excellent cleaning service . . . and she would look through her old telephone address book, to see if she could find Mrs or Ms Topping, which did mean something to her, though she couldn't think what.

'My treat,' said Thomas, paying the bill. 'Shall we go back the long way? Do we visit the Co-op or Nisa on the way back? Where's the shopping list?'

It was an even greater blessing to have a husband who'd help you carry the shopping home.

They walked along, content with one another's company, keeping in step with one another. Ellie stopped abruptly outside the new pet shop.

Thomas said, 'You want a toy for Midge? Is he into toys? I thought he preferred living toys. Mice, frogs . . .'

'Birds,' said Ellie, 'and other cats. I've just remembered that someone called Caroline Topping had cats. Four? One had only three legs. She's a friend of a friend whom I met some years ago. She had a baby or a toddler called . . . Can't remember. But surely he'd be too old to go to the play centre now, wouldn't he?'

'You've lost me completely.'

'She – or someone of the same name – was at the play centre when the youngest Hooper child ate some biscuits given her by a visiting clown. The biscuits contained peanuts; the child had an allergy to them and died. Ms Milburn called on me today to ask if I could find the clown for her, which is not reasonable. She wants me to contact everyone I know who might know anything about it, but I don't see why she's asking me to do police work for her. Why doesn't she go round and see Caroline Topping herself? She said I could save her time by whittling down the number of people who were at the play centre when the child died. Does that sound reasonable to you?'

'Depends how busy she is, I suppose.'

'Let me carry some of those bags. There's something lurking at the back of my mind about this whole nasty affair, though I can't think what. Can you bear to listen while I tell you what's happened so far?'

Thomas grinned. 'Anything to avoid work for another half an hour or so.' Thomas was a good listener.

When she'd finished, he said, 'Two deaths in one family. I don't like the sound of that.'

Diana, she thought. But no, it's not her style at all. And yet . . .

She said, 'I really don't want to poke my nose into police business. Only think what Ms Milburn's boss would have to say about it! "Stupid woman," he'd say. "Who does she think she is?" And rightly so. Besides, the Caroline Topping that I remember may not be the same person as this Mrs Topping, if you see what I mean.'

He looked at his watch. 'It's not a common name. Put your mind at rest; give her a ring as soon as we get back, and after supper I'll run you round there in the car. I need to fill up with petrol, and I can do that while you have a chat with the lady.'

'But,' she said, and stopped. 'Oh, this is ridiculous. Why should I go around doing the police's work for them?'

'Ellie? What's the matter? You're usually only too eager to get involved. It's the hunter in you.'

She tried to laugh. 'A hunter? Me? Oh, no. I can see you as a hunter, but not me. I'm just a housewife who's been promoted above her capabilities but, God willing, and with help from friends and neighbours – and from Him above – I muddle through. I am not a hunter.'

'You could have fooled me. What's wrong, Ellie? You're really worried about . . . Is it something to do with Diana?' He stood directly in front of her, so that she had to face him.

She dropped her eyes. 'Of course not. How could it be?'

'If you say so, but . . . you'd tell me if . . .?'

She swung round to continue their walk. 'It's nothing to do with Diana. It's just that I don't like being used by Ms Milburn. I feel I'm being manipulated. I don't like that, and I've too much on my plate already to bother with anything else.'

He nodded without comment. 'What's for supper? Oh, and don't let me forget, I'm supposed to be on Skype to my daughter this evening some time.' He'd recently added the Skype camera to the computer in his study so that he could see his children and grandchildren during their weekly phone talks.

As soon as they were back, Ellie checked that Rose had in fact got out of her chair and was putting the supper on to cook, which might or might not be the case nowadays. This time all was well and Rose was preparing to bake some mackerel for supper with diced courgettes, spring onions and a few potatoes. Rose had been reading recipe books and thought they'd try a mustard sauce with it. It sounded odd, but would probably be delicious.

Ellie unpacked the shopping and put it away before she phoned Stewart's wife Maria at the cleaning agency, to ask if she could think of someone who could sort out the beds and bedding and, well, everything for the forthcoming visit.

'Mm,' said Maria. 'Let me think. I might have been able to do it myself, but we're very busy at work, and it's half-term next week. I wonder if someone in Stewart's office might . . . No, that won't do, they're all working flat out as it is.'

Which led to a discussion about Ellie wanting to promote him and get someone else in to take over some of his work-load, which Maria said was not before time, though she quite understood how Ellie was placed. That was nice of her, but made Ellie feel she ought to have done something about it earlier.

'Moving on to something more important,' said Maria, 'the children and I are going to my parents for the weekend where they will no doubt be horribly spoiled, but little Frank has been asked to play in some football match or other tomorrow morning. He was only a reserve before, so it means a lot to him to have got into the team. Stewart's taking him, and I gather Thomas said he'd try to get along too.'

Ellie hit her head. Of course, the all-important football match. How could she have forgotten? Well, if Thomas went, it wasn't necessary for her to have to stand at the side of the pitch watching muddy boys get muddier as rain fell unrelent-ingly around them. Watching a football match was not high on her list of priorities. Frank could have the pleasure of telling her about it later.

Maria had an idea. 'Ah, I think I know who could help you out. An old friend of mine, recently divorced, empty nest syndrome, has a business as an interior decorator. A bit of a bossy boots, but you could do with someone to take charge, couldn't you? She uses our cleaning agency now and again, and in return I recommend her to suitable people.'

'Er, yes, I suppose so,' said Ellie.

Maria had a laugh in her voice. 'Of course it's wrong to gossip, but you might be interested to hear that she is called upon to redecorate the Hooper house whenever there is a change of, er, mistress.'

Ellie grinned. 'Ah, now I understand.'

'Shall I ask her if she can pop round to see you tomorrow morning? Her name's Betsey, but the name of the firm is "Harmony in the Home".'

'Bless you. Tomorrow morning. Wonderful.'

Ellie dutifully attended to some of the paperwork which her secretary had left for her to sign, and read her telephone messages. One of the garden designers would be around to look at Pryce House early next week . . . Please remember to send a cheque to . . .

Ellie wasn't putting off the phone call to Caroline Topping. Just dealing with more important matters. Only, there was still ten minutes before supper would be on the table, so she reached for the phone book and found a number for a Mr Topping, who lived on the other side of the park.

They were probably out. Or not the people she remembered at all. The phone was picked up, to the accompaniment of a toddler's wail.

'Caroline Topping? This is Ellie Quicke here; I don't know whether you remember me, but . . . Is this a bad time to call?'

'My neighbour's just collecting her son and returning mine. Mrs Quicke, is it? Of course I remember you . . . Excuse me a moment, I'll just let her out.' Pause. A door slammed shut. The phone was picked up again. 'I'm looking after my neighbour's little one for ten days while she recovers from an operation – she can't lift him at the moment – and in exchange she collects my son from school. He then plays with her boy till supper time. Helping one another out.'

'Ah, I thought your little boy must be too old for the play centre now.'

'Hold on a mo.' Caroline put her hand over the phone again. Ellie waited. Caroline returned. 'Sorry about that. My son's just reminded me he has to be at Cubs in less than an hour, and my husband won't be back till late. So I'm going to have to rush. How can I help you?'

'It's the police, really. They're trying to find someone who might have taken a photo of the clown at the play centre on their mobile phone before he disappeared.'

'Yes, that was a tragedy. Really shocking. It makes one think how your own child might have died in the same way if . . . Terrible, terrible! I did take a picture as it happens, though it didn't come out very well. Look, I'll run a copy off on the computer and drop it in to you when I've taken Duncan to Cubs. Is that all right?'

'Well, actually, it's the police who—' But the phone had gone dead.

Ask a busy mum for something . . .

Mrs Topping didn't know where Ellie lived nowadays, did she? This wasn't destined to turn out well.

But, as they were clearing up after supper – the mustard sauce had been delicious with the baked mackerel and Thomas had only grumbled twice about the limited number of potatoes on his plate – someone rang the front doorbell.

There was Caroline Topping, small, dark and only a little plumper than Ellie remembered her to have been. She was flourishing a piece of paper. 'Got it! I remembered just in time that my friend told me you'd moved into a big house, and of course it's in the phone book, but I'm not sure that this photo is any good.'

Ellie ushered Caroline into the big sitting-room at the back of the house and offered coffee, but Caroline was in a hurry . . . Had she always lived life at this pace? It appeared that her son Duncan had returned home wearing someone else's jacket, and she had to drop it back to its owner and collect his, which she sincerely hoped he'd taken home instead, but you never know with children, do you? So if Ellie didn't mind, she'd just leave the photo with her and be off.

'Well, thank you; but it's really the police who need it, not me. Couldn't you take it in to them tomorrow?'

'Sorry, no can do. Half-term, and we're off tomorrow, sharing a rented house down in Cornwall, right by the beach, I do hope the beds are all right, for my husband complains something shocking if they're too hard or too soft. So I won't be here. Look, I took a chance on a quick snap of the clown with my mobile phone and it hasn't printed off very well. I think my printer needs a new colour cartridge, but you can see what he was like, a bit.'

'Was it definitely a man? How could you tell?'

'Oh. I don't know. I assumed he was male because clowns usually are, aren't they? Quite young, I thought. Someone doing work experience, clowning for the play centre, you know? That's what I thought, if I thought at all, which I didn't because it was all a bit chaotic that morning . . .'

She burbled on, but Ellie concentrated on the photo, which showed the clown in profile. A tallish person to judge by the way he/she towered over the children. Thin, to judge by a spindly neck, though wearing bulky clothing. A rubbery clown's face with a wide, smiling mouth. A mask? Ginger wig, with longish hair all over the place. Red coat, wide lapels, huge buttons. Baggy black trousers. Caroline hadn't got all of him or her into the frame, and the polished black shoes were not included.

One white-gloved hand held a plate stacked with biscuits while the other hand clutched the strings of a number of brightly coloured balloons: red, blue and yellow.

Caroline pointed to the clown's right hand. 'The end of each balloon string was tied round into a loop, so that they could be given out quickly. Quite clever, really. The clown said, "Roll up for a birthday treat!" or something like that. All the children ran up and took a biscuit and a balloon each in orderly fashion, except that that one child pushed everyone aside to get at the biscuits. She wasn't interested in the balloons, only in the biscuits.'

'Abigail, I assume?'

Caroline pulled a face. 'Everyone knows Abigail. Knew. She was more often there than not. The kind of child your child avoids, you know? Although I shouldn't speak of her like that, not really. Dreadful, dreadful thing!'

'I think it's important that the police get a clear picture of Abigail, because her father wants to sue the play centre for failing to stop her eating the biscuits. Oh, and he's sacked the au pair for the same reason.'

'Has he?' Mrs Topping looked at her watch. 'That's a bit over the top, isn't it? I must keep an eye on the time, because—'

'What was the au pair like?'

Caroline screwed up her face. 'Couldn't say "boo" to a goose, as my mother used to say about a girl who lived down the road from us. Turned out the girl was being abused by her father but none of us knew that at the time. This girl was Polish. Nice enough, but not really up to Abigail's weight. There was always a scene when she wanted to take the child home, but a lot of children get like that when they've overdone it, and no one takes much notice. It's best to be firm with them and not let them upset you, but the au pair always tried to reason with Abigail. Waste of time.' She looked at her watch again.

'Did you see the child eat the biscuits?'

'Um. Well, they were all milling round the clown, and I looked for my mobile to take a picture and the child I was minding ran back to me, offering me half his biscuit, which was sweet of him, he is a nice child. And then . . . they all scattered, in different directions, and I snapped the clown just as the last of the balloons were given out. So no, I don't think I actually saw her eating it. I was thinking about leaving, the time was getting on – which reminds me, I must be off – and then the au pair was calling Abigail's name, and people were starting to leave because it was near lunchtime, you see. And the clown disappeared—'

'Did you see the clown go?'

A shake of the head. 'I was strapping my little one into his buggy. Someone said that Abigail was hurt or been taken ill or something. We were amused, you can imagine, thinking she'd been greedy and made herself sick. Only, then we realized . . . and after that everything went quiet.'

Silence.

Caroline shook herself back to the present. 'It was quick, they say. The play centre people were brilliant, asked us all to stay until the police came, and I had a drink for my little one in the buggy, so I did stay, but then time went on and I had to get back, the television man was coming to fix it because one of my cats had clawed the wire out of . . . But you don't need to know about that. So I came away. I suppose I understand why Abigail's father should be so angry, but really, that child! I mean, it's terrible, what happened, but she did know she oughtn't to eat snacks. I've heard the au pair tell her so several times. And the play centre does such a good job. It's the only place around with an outdoor play area which has permanent equipment, and it's good inside on wet days, as well. If it closes . . . Oh dear; it doesn't bear thinking about. And I must go.'

'Thank you,' said Ellie, but Caroline Topping was already on the move. Ellie held the front door open for her. 'I remembered you because of your cats. Do you still have four?'

'The oldest one died, but I have a new manic kitten, J-peg we call her because the first we knew about her was when someone sent us a picture . . .' And off went Caroline, still talking, chugging away in her little Volkswagen.

So now Ellie had a picture of the clown, and much good it might do her.

At least it wasn't Diana. Quite definitely not.

FIVE

Saturday morning

Was this a good time to kill another of the hateful tribe? The sooner they were all underground, the better.

What about using the clown get-up again? No, better not. True, it only took a couple of seconds to tear off the mask and wig, and to shrug off the red coat. A white T-shirt hardly raised an eyebrow, and though the black trousers were baggy, they weren't outrageous.

But perhaps it wouldn't be necessary to use it for this one.

So; be prepared. Gloves, yes. Thin, disposable ones. And one of her own syringes, pinched on the earlier visit when all she'd done was laugh. The plan hadn't been thought through then. But now . . .

A glance around. No one in sight.

Most shops – even in a street at the back of the bus station – were busy on a Saturday morning, but this one was so dimly lit that it repelled rather than attracted attention. The window display consisted of a few curling pamphlets, a stack of books on alternative lifestyles, and a selection of weird and wonderful charms claimed to ensure well-being and happiness. The paperback which advertised recipes for everlasting life sported the corpse of a bluebottle. Everything needed a good clean, including the prisms which dangled in the window.

Ting! An old-fashioned doorbell.

The fug inside assaulted the nostrils. Scented candles and incense.

She lived above the shop but at this time of the morning she was usually downstairs, waiting for non-existent customers. Yes, there she was, sitting behind the counter on a high stool, a silk turban wrapped around fading, hennaed hair. She had draped what looked like an old lace curtain over her black dress, stained with her last meal. Or several recent meals. She'd been drinking something from a mug. Probably not straight coffee, though. Her tipple was gin, and she'd probably put a couple of shots in her morning pick-me-up, though with her diabetes she ought not to touch the stuff. Her eyelids were at half mast.

There was another scent here, apart from the incense. Marijuana?

Just her style.

She blinked. 'Back again so soon, you silly thing? I should tell the police about you and your mad ideas, shouldn't I? Were you responsible for Abigail's death?'

Temper flared. One punch and she fell off her high stool, catching her foot in her draperies. Crash, bang, wallop. Over she goes. She hit her head on the edge of the counter and went down. Flop. Flip flop. Out for the count. Snoring.

No need to shift her. She was too heavy to move, anyway. There was a quick way to help diabetics shuffle off this mortal coil. Pull up her dress – ugh – nasty sight! She always injected herself in her thigh. Another needle, another pin prick. Easy does it. And . . . leave the needle there. Clasp one podgy hand around it. And let it fall away.

Confused diabetic overdoes it.
Turn the 'Open' sign on the door to 'Closed'. Drop the latch
on the door.
Perfect.
Exit.

Saturday morning

Ellie stooped to pick up the newspapers which Thomas had strewn about the sitting room. Thomas was a 'horizontal filer', who covered every surface in his study with papers, claiming to know exactly where everything was. The same applied to the weekend newspapers with their supplements. One went this way, another went that; most of them ended up on the floor.

As she arranged the newspapers in a pile, Ellie came across the print of the clown which Mrs Topping had given her. Should she phone Ms Milburn about it? It was the weekend and surely the girl would be off duty? On the other hand, leaving it till Monday might lay Ellie open to a charge of, well, not caring.

Well, she did care. Of course she did. And the clown was certainly not Diana in disguise.

The clown person might well be some student wanting to break into acting, who'd been hired to appear in costume at the play centre and give out balloons and biscuits . . . which had been supplied by whoever it was who'd employed them.

So, you could argue that Diana might have done it, through someone else.

But no; because as soon as an innocent person realized that his actions had led to the death of a child, he'd surely want to confess.

Or would he? Perhaps he'd prefer to keep mum when he realized he'd been responsible for the death of a child?

Ellie dialled the number Ms Milburn had given her and was told that the person she was calling was on the phone already. Of course. Please leave a message.

'Please call Mrs Quicke. I have a picture of the clown for you.'

End of.

She looked at the clock. Time was marching on, and the decorator person would be arriving in a minute. Ellie reached for the nearest piece of paper to make notes for her. So many adults. So many children. So many rooms to spare. A shortage of beds. Had Maria said Betsey could let Ellie have a bed or two? Bunk beds, perhaps, for two of the children? Or would the other child then feel jealous and want a bunk bed, too? Or, worse; suppose the twins decided they couldn't sleep in bunk beds? Really, there was no end of things that could go wrong when you invited people to stay.

A ring at the door, and there was a tall thin blonde – bottle blonde but an expensive job – dressed in a trouser suit in an expensive material which looked like leather and might just be that. High heeled boots. Her figure was excellent.

Ellie sighed, knowing she'd never be a size zero again; not that she ever had been, come to think of it.

'Betsey?'

'Harmony in the Home.' Ms Betsey was armed with a laptop and a briefcase to show that she meant business. And an inquisitive eye.

Ellie liked her straight away. 'Coffee to start with?' Where was Rose? Pottering around in the garden, deadheading roses. Best not to disturb her. 'If you don't mind coming into the kitchen while I make it?'

'A pleasure.'

Ellie led the way. 'We have mutual acquaintances, I believe. Maria, of course. And I believe you know Mr Hooper, too?'

'Indeed. We go back a long way. The Hoopers do seem to have suffered a run of tragedies recently.'

'My daughter Diana is working for him now,' said Ellie, putting a cafetière, china mugs and the sugar bowl on a tray. 'I had some contact with him in the past over a property deal and Diana has linked up with him emotionally, if that's the right term.'

'I had heard, yes.'

Could Betsey be trusted? Ellie rather thought she could. Perhaps it was worth probing further. 'Milk with it?' She switched the kettle on.

'Black for me. I like to keep sharp when I'm working.'

Ellie pushed the biscuit tin Betsey's way. Betsey shook her head. She was sizing Ellie up, just as Ellie was doing to her. The kettle boiled. Ellie spooned coffee grounds into the cafetière and poured on the boiling water.

'Let's take it into the sitting room and make ourselves comfortable. I must admit I'm concerned for Diana. Being a happily married woman myself, I can't help worrying when my daughter is seeing a man who has three marriages to his credit already.'

Betsey sipped her coffee, eyes everywhere. Thoughtful.

'I even had a visit from the police,' said Ellie, 'asking if I had any information about the deaths in the Hooper family.'

Betsey seemed uneasy. 'It's none of my business, but if I were your daughter, I might think it a good idea to cool things with Evan . . .'

'I wish she would.'

Betsey considered her fingernails, pale polish, professionally done. 'If she knew some of the background . . .?'

'Can you bear to tell me?'

Betsey made up her mind to be frank. 'Mrs Quicke, I've known the family for ever because my mother was at school with the first Mrs Hooper, Monique. The word was that he'd married her to get the business, which was owned by her father. Evan's own family wasn't much to write home about; father had a job at the town hall, mother didn't work. Nerves, apparently.

'All right, Monique wasn't exactly a pin-up. She wore glasses and her figure wasn't good. She'd never had a boyfriend but worked in the business and expected to take over when her father retired. Then one day she upped and married Evan. My mother said that it would end in tears, and it did. Monique was in her forties when they married. She produced a son, but his birth left her an invalid, and she couldn't have any more children.'

Ellie sympathized. She'd suffered several miscarriages throughout her first marriage, and the only living child had been Diana. She understood the hunger women had to produce children. Poor Monique.

Betsey continued. 'The boy wasn't up to much. Nerves. Stammer. Dissolved into tears if you so much as looked at him. Sent away to boarding school; not wanted on voyage, if you see what I mean. Neither was Monique after a while.'

'What happened to her?'

'Paid off. She was older than Evan and probably thankful to be out of it. She moved away, set up in business for herself and we lost touch.'

'The boy went with Monique?'

'No, he stayed with Dad. Evan wouldn't let him go, the only son and heir, that sort of thing. My mother died, I got married and started up my little business. Right out of the blue, Evan rang one day and asked me to quote for redecorating the reception rooms in his house, as he was about to get married again.'

'The boy . . .?'

'Not there. I did enquire.' A frown. 'Something about an accident? I think it was about that time he went to boarding school. Anyway, Evan wanted a clean sweep. Out went everything that Monique had done to the house, furniture, curtains, kitchen, everything. In came Airy Fairy Fern.'

'His second wife.'

'I *think*, though I can't be sure, that there was some sort of agreement that Fern would provide him with a son and heir who was up to scratch, because she produced a couple of children as soon as she'd got his ring on her finger. I can tell you she led me quite a dance, changing her mind every five minutes, wanting stripped pine one minute, and all white the next.

'She was a hippy type, you know. Glastonbury, flowing locks, dancing in the nude. I would be summoned to meet her to talk about wall hangings and walk in on her, naked except for some floating scarves. She had a good figure, I'll grant you, for her age. I don't know what it was about Evan. You'd have thought he'd have gone for a sensible woman in her late twenties for a second wife, but Fern was knocking thirty-five then and she drank! And smoked! She had a good hollow cough even in those days. No, I did not understand Evan then, any more than I do now.'

'Fern must have had fun redecorating the house.'

'She went in for rowdy parties, getting drunk and being thrown out of functions, being caught with a toy boy, collecting speeding tickets, crashing her car. Oh yes, she had fun, if you can call it that. But she put on a lot of weight and, what with this and that, began very soon to look older than she really was.'

'Ah, she lost her looks? Now let me see, she produced two girls in quick succession.'

'Freya and Fiona. Think "F" for Fern, and "F" for both her daughters. I was called in to redo their rooms at regular intervals as they grew out of bunny rabbits and fairies. I was asked to decorate one of their bedrooms with black walls, if you please. Actually I persuaded the girl to accept slate grey instead, which looked all right. The other always wanted everything pink. I honestly don't know which was worse.'

'What happened to Fern?'

'Evan got rid of her. I suppose he woke up one day to the fact that her behaviour wasn't exactly helping his reputation as a good, solid citizen. And there'd been no more pregnancies.'

'He divorced her?'

'Uhuh. He bought her the freehold of a shop somewhere in the back streets, set her up as a mystic, all crystals and scented candles, with the lights turned low so that she still looked good. I shouldn't think she's a good insurance risk, what with the smoking and the drinking, and I think she had some other health problem. High blood pressure? Not sure.'

'So marriage number three. This time to a young girl, a model, who calls herself—'

'Angelika with a "k". Much, much younger. She wanted the house redecorated to suit her own taste when she moved in, and who can blame her? She wanted shiny walls and huge mirrors everywhere to reflect her beautiful image, plus the kitchen had to be brought up to date. It cost the earth, as you can imagine. To give her her due, Angelika did ask her step-daughters to stay on when their mother left, rather than sending them off to boarding school. I don't think she really cares about them, but she does see that they're fed and clothed and have more or less everything they ask for . . . in the way of money, I mean.'

'So long as she isn't required to stir a finger?'

'That's it. Angelika has produced yet another girl child. I suppose there was some mistake over the scan. I wouldn't have thought Evan would have bothered to marry her if she hadn't promised him another boy. But who can say? Maybe he really did fall for her beauty.'

'You've had a good opportunity to observe them in their native habitat, so to speak.'

A shrug. 'To my mind Angelika is another disaster. Arm candy. Looking for a sugar daddy, so that she could pursue her career in modelling. Total concentration on me, me, me. Lazy. Dirty underwear left around for someone else to pick up. She either ignores her daughter, who isn't exactly a cherub, they say, or shouts at her.'

A hesitation. 'I don't know that I should repeat this, but on my recent visits – she now wants the dining room redecorated and a wet room put in – anyway, I wondered if she weren't perhaps getting tired of a much older husband and starting to look elsewhere. She always seems to be on her mobile phone when I call, talking lovey-dovey to someone, and I don't think it's her husband.'

'I almost feel sorry for Evan Hooper.'

Another shrug. 'A bad picker.'

'You knew his name has been linked with my daughter's?'

'He introduced us when we met by chance at the golf club. She was dining with him and I was with a customer. Also, I've heard the gossip.'

'You think that will end in tears, too?'

A wry face. A searching look at Ellie to see if she really wanted an honest opinion. A shrug. 'I think she's tough and knows exactly what she's doing. If she's pregnant with a boy . . . Well, the best of luck to her.'

Ellie winced.

Betsey raised her eyebrows. 'You asked.'

Ellie nodded. Sighed. 'Yes. Diana is carrying Evan's child; she's had a scan and it's a boy.'

Betsey nodded, but had the good sense not to comment. 'So, what would you like me to do for you? I gather you've got a load of visitors expected, but don't know how to fit them in. Did Maria tell you that I could rent you whatever extra furniture and furnishings you might require?'

'Bless you. There's a spare bedroom upstairs which I'm pinning my hopes on, but it's full of junk, and oh . . . I started to make some notes on a spare piece of paper. Now . . . where? Ah, here it is. We'll have a quick tour downstairs first, because I have a problem with the curtains in the dining room. One got torn and needs to be repaired. And yes, I know it won't look as good as new. Also, the room is a trifle gloomy. Perhaps it's time to think of having a new set made?'

Ellie led the way to the dining room. 'We have business meetings in here once a week but will have to use it for its original purpose when our guests come, because we can't all fit round the table in the kitchen, except perhaps for breakfast.'

Betsey snapped her briefcase open. 'I'll measure the existing curtains. I may have something that might do for you, a set made up for someone else. You could rent them for the duration of the visit and then put up the old ones again if you wish.' She got out her tape measure and made notes.

Ellie led the way out. 'Now, after the dining room, the first room down the corridor is Thomas's study, not to be touched on pain of death.' She threw open doors as they went along, so that Betsey could see in. 'Opposite is my office. And the room at the end of the corridor is the library.'

Betsey was appreciative. 'Nice big room. Good light.'

'Yes, but somehow we never get round to using it. That's all there is downstairs.' Ellie led the way back to the hall and up the stairs to the first floor. 'I'll show you the bedrooms and let you decide how to fit everyone in. We'll start with the bedroom over the kitchen, which has a bathroom attached. Our housekeeper used to sleep there. She didn't want anything changed, liked it as it was, but it seems very tired and dull to me. She's moved downstairs now . . .'

As they descended the stairs half an hour later Thomas came

out of his study, struggling into an ancient but much-loved anorak. He said, 'Hello,' to Betsey, and to Ellie, 'Ready, then?'

Ellie couldn't think what he meant.

'You can't have forgotten that we promised to watch Frank playing in his football match? Diana can't come, of course.'

Ellie *had* forgotten. Did she have to go? Oh dear. She supposed she must. Diana wouldn't be going; she never did. Especially on Saturdays. 'Just let me . . . Is it raining again? Where did I put my heavier shoes? Oh, so sorry, Betsey. Our grandchild is playing in his first big football match and—'

'I know what it's like.' Laughing. 'Look, if you'll let me stay on a while, I'd like to go round again on my own and take some more measurements.'

'Our housekeeper, Rose, is around somewhere if you need anything.'

'Will do. I'll ring you on Monday morning if I've got any queries, and I'll let you have my suggestions within a couple of days.'

Thomas hustled Ellie into her heavy raincoat. 'Boots, not shoes. Wellington boots. An umbrella. Now, if you can't remember the offside rule—?'

'I understood it perfectly when you showed me using mugs as players and the salt and pepper pots being the goalposts, but—'

'Rose has made us a flask of coffee. So . . . off we go?'

Saturday afternoon

After the match, Stewart took a muddy and tired but ecstatic little boy home for a bath and a late lunch, while Thomas and Ellie retired to the Carvery in the Avenue for massive helpings of roast beef and Yorkshire pudding, with as many vegetables as they could fit on their plates.

Thomas had almost lost his voice from shouting encouragement to the winning team, which made Ellie worry that he wouldn't be able to take the service at a neighbouring church next morning. At least there was nothing wrong with his appetite.

It was well after three when Thomas and Ellie returned

home to find a message on the answerphone to the effect that
DC Milburn was calling round at two o'clock. Well, they'd
missed that, hadn't they?

As they shed their wet clothes Rose bustled to and fro,
getting some tea on the table. 'I told that policewoman you
might be late but she came again at three, and I suppose she'll
be back again any minute.'

Ellie groaned, sitting down to ease off her wellington boots.
'Can you make some honey and lemon for Thomas? He had
such a good time shouting for Frank and his team that he's
lost his voice.'

The doorbell went. It was still raining, but Ms Milburn –
unlike Thomas and Ellie – looked bright and perky as she
shook out her umbrella and left it in the porch. 'At last. I
couldn't wait till Monday. You've got the picture for me?'

Of course; the picture of the clown. Ellie pushed her fingers
back through her hair. Where had she put it? 'Mm. Caroline
Topping brought it round. She's going away, half-term at her
little boy's school, though it doesn't seem to be half-term for
everybody. If only the schools would get the holidays to co-
incide, it would be a lot easier for parents, wouldn't it? Especially
if there is more than one child and they're at different schools.
Come on in. Have a cuppa. Rose, another cup for our friend?'

Thomas went after Rose, attempting, in a hoarse voice, to
give her a rundown of the match.

Ellie found some soft slippers and put them on before leading
the DC into the sitting room. 'Take a seat. Now where did I
put it?' She gazed distractedly around. 'I was in my chair by
the fireplace. Caroline sat over there, on the settee.'

The room looked neat and tidy. Rose must have been in
while they were out, to tidy up and renew the chrysanthemums
in the vase on the table by the window.

The picture of the clown wasn't immediately apparent. Ellie
went over to the bureau. 'I left it here. I'm sure I did.'

Rose came in with two mugs of tea. Nice and hot. Wonderful.

Ms Milburn was fidgeting. 'It's so important, I thought that
even if it was the weekend, I'd come and get it. I told Ears
. . . that is, I mean—'

'Your boss, yes. What is his real name, anyway? I really

must write it down. Now, I had the picture in my hand when I phoned you this morning, didn't I? That would be in the hall.' She looked. 'It's not there now. I'll ask Rose if she's seen it.'

'It is rather important.'

'Of course.' Ellie went out to the kitchen. Thomas had disappeared, and Rose was liquidizing leftover vegetables. 'Rose!' She had to shout to make herself heard. 'Rose!'

Rose stopped the liquidizer, which was making a noise like a cement mixer. 'What?'

'Have you seen a picture of a clown anywhere?'

'A clown? Like in a circus? No. In the newspaper, was it?'

'Separate. Not from the paper.'

Rose shook her head and switched the liquidizer on again. 'Making soup for supper. Cold nights. Nothing like it.'

'Have you—?'

Rose switched the liquidizer off again. 'What is it?'

'Have you thrown away any papers from the sitting room?'

Rose shook her head and started the liquidizer again.

Ellie retired, defeated. Back in the sitting room, she began to take the pile of newspapers apart, shaking out each supplement, leafing through the magazine.

Ms Milburn fidgeted. 'You haven't lost it?'

'No, of course not. It was here, on the bureau.' Ellie finished looking through the pile. 'I'll ask Thomas if he's seen it.'

Thomas was in his study, stabbing at his keyboard, grumbling at the computer in a voice which was fast fading away.

'Thomas, have you seen a piece of paper with a picture of a clown on it?'

He shook his head, concentrating on his work.

Ellie threw up her hands in despair. How to tell Ms Milburn? She went along the corridor to her office. Had she by any chance left it there? But no, she hadn't been to her office since the previous morning, had she? Anyway, she could see at a glance that the picture of the clown hadn't been laid down on top of the usual pile of mail on her desk.

She'd have to confess. And did.

Ms Milburn paled. 'That's . . . too bad. I haven't been able to track down everyone who was at the play centre yet. The weekend, you know. If I can't convince Ears . . . He wants to write it off as a prank that went wrong, that some student perhaps wanted to make a few quid as a children's entertainer, but when it went wrong . . . No, it was meant, I'm sure it was.'

Ellie thought so, too. 'Mrs Topping will be back in a week's time. We can get another print then.'

'If she hasn't deleted it from her camera in the meantime.'

'Yes. Sorry. I can't think what's happened to it.'

Ms Milburn was restless. She went to the window. Rain was sheeting down outside. 'The boss says I'm imagining things. He says that it's all a coincidence, and that I'm pushing myself forward, trying to make out I'm a better detective than . . . Well, you know how he can go on.'

Ellie dreaded to think where this was going. Had they got on to Diana's involvement already?

'The thing is,' said Ms Milburn, 'there was only one set of fingerprints on the speedometer.'

Ellie's brain clicked over slowly. 'You said that Angelika walked into the gym, found the treadmill working overtime. She turned the speedometer down, switched the machine off and only then saw the body. So her prints should be on the speedometer and the on/off switch, overlaying those of her stepdaughter, who'd presumably switched it on and turned the speedo up high. So when you say that the only fingerprints on the speedometer were Angelika's, are you suggesting . . .? I'm not quite with you.' Ellie didn't want to face what this might mean.

Ms Milburn rammed her point home. 'It wasn't easy to get prints from the on/off switch, because it's small, but yes; there were smudged prints around and underneath Angelika's, showing her stepdaughter had turned the machine on, and that Angelika had turned it off. But the speedometer was very clean, with only one set of prints on it . . . Angelika's. If Fiona had turned the speedometer up too high, surely her prints ought to have been visible, even if smudged, under those of Angelika?'

'Perhaps a cleaner . . .?'

Ms Milburn gave Ellie a look.

Ellie shook her head. 'Someone wiped the speedometer after it had been turned it up high. Not Fiona. And not Angelika.'

'That's what it looks like. Also, the pathologist has found a bruise on Fiona's left buttock, consistent with her being kicked just before she died. We think someone helped her on her way to her death.'

Ellie thought: Diana. And then: no, not Diana. She'd bash someone over the head, but not adjust a speedometer to run too fast because . . . because . . . adjusting the speedo wouldn't necessarily lead to Fiona's death, and Diana wouldn't leave anything to chance, if she did decide to commit murder. She might perhaps have lashed out with a cricket bat to Fiona's rear, if one had been handy. Mm, yes. Perhaps.

'You think someone else was there, someone who tampered with the speedometer, perhaps for fun? When the prank went wrong, they wiped the speedometer clean and scarpered?'

'I could accept one prank that went wrong. But two?' Ms Milburn shook her head. 'I don't think so, do you?'

SIX

Ellie said, 'I see what you mean. If it's a prankster targeting the family, then he's caused two deaths with his silly nonsense and has to be stopped. But if he intended murder, then it's much more serious.'

Ms Milburn threw herself into a chair. 'I thought perhaps a student might have been playing around—'

'Yes, I'd got as far as that, too.'

'It would hold up as a theory in the case of the toddler, but—'

'Not for Fiona. Someone knew her. Knew how to get into the house, and into the gym—'

'Or perhaps followed her there? The conservatory-cum-gym is at the back but accessible from the garden either by walking around the house on a gravel path or by going through the garage, which isn't always locked and shut. Angelika was out in her car that day and so was Evan, so the garage doors might well have been left open. I rang this morning and asked about that, but they can't remember, don't think it important.'

'They still maintain that Fiona's death was an accident?'

Ms Milburn nodded. 'The child's, too. They claim someone was playing the part of a clown and poisoned their little one in error. They blame the play centre and the au pair, especially as she's gone missing.'

'She's fled back to Poland?'

'We assume so, as she's not to be found where she's supposed to be. We're checking the airlines as we speak, but she may have got a lift in a friend's car going by ferry and road, in which case there's very little hope of tracing her departure. I did warn her to stay put, but I suppose she thought the Hoopers wouldn't pursue a case against her if she disappeared.'

Ellie gave Ms Milburn a look. In her book Evan Hooper could be vindictive enough for anything.

'Evan Hooper is going to make an official complaint on Monday alleging that I ought to have placed the au pair under arrest, and that I have been culpable in letting her slip out of the country.'

'They don't see that the two "incidents" are connected? Two down and . . . how many of the family to go? Doesn't it seem most likely to you that someone is targeting the Hooper family?'

'That's my gut feeling, yes; but feelings aren't evidence. That's why finding that photograph of the clown is so important.'

Ellie raked her fingers back through her hair and held on to her head with both hands. 'I can't think where it's gone.'

'You've got a good memory. Tell me exactly what the picture showed.'

'Yes, at least I can do that.' She closed her eyes, visualizing the greyish print, and talked it through. 'It doesn't show him—'

'Or her?'

'Caroline Topping said that it was a man, going by the way he walked. I think she'd have known if it had been a woman.

The picture doesn't show his feet but, judging by the way he towered over the children, he was tall. Thin, because his neck was thin. A white face with huge, smiling, red lips. Big eyes and long eyelashes. A ginger wig which came right down to the eyes. I think it was a mask and wig, all in one.

'A bright red coat, padded or stiffened, which stood out from his body. Black trousers, baggy. White gloves. He held a china plate with the biscuits on in one hand and the strings of the balloons in the other. Did you see any of the balloons yourself?'

'A dead end. You can pick up a packet of them anywhere, in stationers, toy shops. They weren't helium balloons. Just the ordinary kind you blow up for kids' parties.'

'What about the plate? A thick china plate. I wonder where he got it. It's not the sort you see for sale in shops nowadays. It's the sort of plate my mother used to stand plants on if she ran out of proper containers. I'm thinking soup kitchens, church suppers. It's the sort of plate you find at the back of a cupboard which you've kept because it might come in useful, except that you never have had a use for it. We used to get plates like that dropped in to the charity shop in the Avenue, sometimes. I wonder if that's where he got it.'

'A young man setting up in a flat or a bed-sitter might find such plates provided by his landlord.'

'True. How about the biscuits?'

A gesture of frustration. 'They'd all been eaten before anyone realized anything was wrong.'

'The boy who noticed the polished black shoes might be able to tell you what make they were. I mean, he could say if they were foil-wrapped or loose on a plate; Waitrose or Tesco.'

'I started to work down the list given me by the play centre this morning, but hardly anyone was at home.'

'It's half-term. Try again on Monday.'

'Meanwhile . . .?'

There was silence in the room, except for the ticking of the central heating as it warmed the bones of the old house . . . and the susurrus of Midge the cat, as he pushed his way into the room and made for the hearth rug.

'Here, kitty,' said Ms Milburn, who really knew better than to try to divert Midge.

He gave her a look of disdain and turned his golden eyes on Ellie, who interpreted the command correctly by switching on the gas log fire so that he could stretch out in front of it. And purr.

'Oh, to be a cat inside a warm house,' said Ms Milburn.

Ellie stroked the fur on Midge's back with the toe of her soft shoe. 'A well-fed cat. He's only just eaten, judging by the fishy smell he's brought in with him.'

Midge began on his toilette. Thoroughly. Both women watched his progress from paw to ear, to mask and back again.

Ms Milburn said, 'Things could go either way. If there's no more incidents, my guess is that the two deaths will not be followed up. Evan Hooper will try to get the police to find and prosecute the au pair, and to ruin the play centre. The prankster will sink out of sight and try to forget what happened.'

Ellie nodded.

'On the other hand, if I were Evan Hooper I'd be lying awake, worrying who I'd offended enough to make him or her want to kill members of his family. Or, perhaps, who might have paid some youngster to do it for him. Or her.'

Ellie nodded again. Ouch. Not Diana, please not Diana!

'Could you ask around? You know people he knows, don't you?'

Ellie was taken aback. Did Ms Milburn know about Diana? 'A family friend of the Hoopers has given me a rundown on the family. Would you like me to write down the names and relationships for you? Just in case there is another "incident"?'

Ms Milburn gave her a dark look. 'How long have you been sitting on that information?'

'I only got it this morning. Now, where's a piece of paper? There's some in the bureau. Right. Here's Evan at the top of the page. First marriage was to someone called Monique. Older than him. She produced a son. Name unknown. He may be educationally subnormal, or whatever they call it nowadays. Sent away to school. I get the feeling he's not the brightest spark in the fireplace. Did someone say something about him suffering from nerves?'

'Son. Unknown.' Ms Milburn was making her own notes. 'Address?'

'No idea. You didn't see him at the Hooper home, did you? I don't think he lives there any more. Next marriage was to someone called Fern. Divorced, paid off, runs a shop dealing with airy fairy fancies, possibly with books on the occult. Don't know where. Here in Ealing? She produced two girls; Fiona – who's dead – and another girl called Freya. You saw her when you took statements from the Hoopers, didn't you?'

'I did. Sulky teenager, could hardly bring herself to speak to me. She didn't seem all that upset by Fiona's death. Walked out while I was talking to them. Said something about having to do her homework. No reason to suspect her of involvement but I suppose I can check up. No address for Fern?'

'No. Then there's the third wife, Angelika, whom you've met. Mother of Abigail—'

'Deceased.' Ms Milburn considered the list. 'Who would you guess to be the next target?'

'Assuming there is another incident? Oh dear; how dreadful this all is. I have no idea. Monique or Fern, I think.'

'Why?'

'I'm not sure. The names just popped into my head. No reason.' Because Diana might consider them an obstacle to her plans on Evan. But we don't say that out loud, do we?

'Fern. Monique. I'll see if I can find out where they live. Meanwhile, you will ask around, won't you? See if anyone has any other information?' She glanced outside. 'Still raining.'

'Yes,' said Ellie, getting to her feet. 'I'll ask around. You left your umbrella in the porch, didn't you?'

'If you find that picture of the clown?'

'I'll ring you straight away.'

Sunday morning

Ellie went to an early morning service with Thomas, who got through it with the aid of throat pastilles. His voice faded out again on the way home. Perhaps he was going down with another of his winter colds?

The rain had stopped for the moment, but the clouded sky looked as if it might release another downpour any minute, so Ellie installed Thomas by the fire in the sitting room with the Sunday papers, and went off to see about lunch.

Rose was having one of her busy times, flitting from larder to table to gas stove, and back again. She had no less than three cookery books out, trying to decide what cake she should make for tea, talking through the merits of each as she turned from one to the other.

Ellie got on with peeling potatoes and putting the joint in the oven.

A long, persistent ring of the doorbell.

Ellie and Rose looked at one another. They knew only too well who leaned on the bell like that. Someone who wouldn't be easily put off.

'I'll go,' said Ellie, taking off her apron. 'Will you put the potatoes and a couple of onions into the oven in five minutes' time?'

'We're not offering tea or coffee, then?'

'I hope she's not staying that long.'

Ellie opened the front door, and in swept Diana.

At least, the height and figure and face looked like Diana, but Ellie hadn't seen her daughter wearing anything but fashionable black since she left school.

This woman was wearing a superb suit in what you couldn't call white exactly, because it displayed other colours as the light shifted. Mother of pearl?

The suit jacket was cut with a peplum, allowing one to imagine a slight swelling of her stomach. The skirt was long but narrow. Kitten heels on her shoes. A pearly handbag on a gilt chain hung over her shoulder.

What was all this about?

Diana shivered. 'You took your time. It's cold outside.'

Ah well, her manners hadn't changed for the better, had they?

Diana would have swept through to the sitting room, but Ellie stopped her. 'I think Thomas is in there, asleep. He's getting one of his colds. Let's go into the library.'

The library was supposed to be for Thomas's exclusive use, but in fact he only used it on rare occasions and it looked more or less as it had for the past hundred years, with books lining every wall, a huge kneehole desk and three large leather chairs for relaxation. The morning had turned darker so Ellie switched the lights on and checked that the central heating was doing its job.

Diana went to look out of the window at the rain-sodden garden.

Ellie waited.

'I've just been to church,' said Diana.

Ellie blinked. Since when had Diana shown any interest in Christianity?

'Not that I believe in it. But it seemed politic.'

Ellie let herself down into one of the big chairs. She supposed it was a good point in Diana's favour that she never acted the hypocrite. 'You decided to go to church because . . .?'

'Don't be obtuse. I'm carrying Evan's child. I'm going to marry him. He's never been married in church so there's no reason why we shouldn't do it properly.'

Properly? Hm. Well. Was Diana about to take on the colouring of middle-class morality to please Evan? Hence the new look, and the attendance at church? Was this a good thing? Well, only if it meant she'd had an equivalent change of heart, which seemed unlikely . . . though one could always hope for the best, and being Ellie, one did.

Diana tapped on the window pane. Rat-a-tat-tat. Rat-a-tat-tat. Irritating.

Ellie said, 'What do you want?'

'There's a fine greeting to your only daughter, who's about to become Mrs Evan Hooper.'

'Have you managed to get rid of Angelika already?'

Diana snorted, amused. 'She's been asked to go on a photographic shoot to Japan, lasting three weeks. After that she's hoping for a fashion show somewhere, Italy? Paris? Both? Evan was so shocked that she should wish to go through with her commitments after what happened to Abigail and Fiona that he—'

'He's using it as an excuse to get rid of her?'

'You don't understand.' Diana seated herself opposite Ellie, drawing a tiny pill box from her handbag, extracting and popping a tablet into her mouth. 'Indigestion. I can't remember suffering so much when I was pregnant before.'

'What don't I understand?'

'Evan feels Angelika ought to show more consideration for the family. Everyone thinks he's a strong man and of course he is, but this has knocked him sideways. He looked to Angelika for support, but she thinks only of her career. She's only cried once for her little girl. She says the best way to get over her grief is to get on with her life.'

Ellie nodded.

'She's never once tried to comfort Evan for his losses. He feels it keenly.'

'I'm sure you've tried to make up to him for Angelika's lack of response.'

Diana didn't recognize irony. 'I've done what anyone with even a small amount of charity would have done. He is aching for love and understanding.'

'Both of which you are happy to supply.'

A tinge of pink in the pale face. 'You may find this difficult to believe, but I do love him, you know.'

Ellie did find it difficult to believe, but she tried to do so. She didn't like having cynical thoughts. It was foreign to her nature. But she did fear that Diana loved Evan for his wealth and for his position in life, rather than for himself.

On the other hand, what did she know about it? Maybe Diana really had fallen for him and was deeply affected by his losses.

Diana's head drooped. 'I feel . . . I know I've made many mistakes in my life . . . but I do feel that I've been given a chance, at last, to love someone who loves me back unreservedly.'

Oh? Ellie didn't comment.

Diana extracted a tiny handkerchief from her bag and touched it to the corners of her eyes. 'I didn't know either of the girls, really. I met Fiona at the office one day, when she called in for something. Probably wanting money. Those girls . . . Ah well, mustn't speak ill of the dead. It's a great help for Evan that I can take over the running of the office while he's so distressed.'

'Of course.' Again the irony slid past Diana without registering.

A deep sigh. 'I have to keep going for his sake and for the sake of our child.'

Ellie said, 'Do you have any influence on him?'

A stare. 'What a ridiculous question!'

'Does he still intend to sue everyone in sight for the death of Abigail?'

Diana's face hardened. 'Why shouldn't he? They were negligent, and it is his duty to put the play centre out of business, or someone else's child will suffer. As for the au pair—'

'Scarpered. Disappeared. Didn't you know?'

'The police will have to find her and bring her back, then. She must be prosecuted. She was criminally remiss.'

'Evan still thinks his family has had a run of bad luck?'

'I wouldn't call two accidental deaths—'

'Suppose they weren't accidents?'

Diana put her hankie to her mouth and did a good imitation of a shocked and vulnerable woman. 'How could you!'

'There weren't enough fingerprints on the speedometer. Only Angelika's.'

Diana put down the hankie. Frowned. Gnawed at her lower lip. 'Are you sure?'

'Yes. The police would very much like to write Fiona's death off as an accident, but there's a certain detective there who thinks otherwise and is going to push the investigation further. What of the disappearing clown? Was he a student hired to stage a stunt, or was he there with intent to poison Abigail?'

'What you're saying is—'

'Who gains by these deaths?'

Diana's eyes switched to and fro. 'I do. But I didn't. Wouldn't. I didn't need to. Angelika was on her way out. Fiona and Freya were a pain, but I didn't need to kill them because Evan had already planned to send them off to boarding school.'

'Costly.'

'Mm. He can afford it. As for Abigail, Evan thought she'd

be Angelika's responsibility, that she could hire a full-time nanny for her or something. He wasn't – isn't – a hands-on father.'

She could say that again.

'It will be different when he has a son.'

'You're sure about that?'

'Of course. He's a bit shell-shocked at the moment, but as soon as I mention the baby, he perks up no end. He's had a bellyful of tragedy in his life, never been able to feel that he was supported by his wives, any of them.'

Ellie forbore to comment. 'So, what brings you here this morning? Perhaps it was to ask how well your son did yesterday when he played in his first match for the football team? You will be pleased to know that he did very well indeed. Stewart, Thomas and I all went to cheer him on. He scored a goal, too. He would have loved it if you'd felt able to come.'

'I was working.' Diana's mind was elsewhere. 'No, what I came about, it's a bit awkward, but I want you and Evan to make up and be friends. He's so low at the moment that he needs something to make him feel better. Apart from the new baby, I mean. His household is all at sixes and sevens. One minute he had a wife and three children under his roof and now he's only got Freya, and she's in a sulk most of the time. His housekeeper has walked out and Angelika's permanently at the beautician's.'

'I suppose you're planning to move in?'

'Not yet. I want all their stuff cleared out of the house first. I've asked Evan to get rid of the gym machines and he's promised to get a decorator to return the conservatory to what it ought to be. Then the kitchen will have to be ripped out and modern fitments installed; not that I intend to be chained to the kitchen sink.'

'Naturally not.' More work for Betsey, then.

'All the reception rooms will have to be redone, and the master bedroom. I'm not sleeping in *her* bed. Then we'll need one of the rooms decorated and furnished as a nursery. I'm leaning on Evan to send Freya off to boarding school straight away, which is the best place for her, nasty little madam that she is. No, I'm not moving in – yet. But I'll make sure no one else does, and I'm running the office for him until he feels he can cope again.'

'You want me to play Happy Families with him?' Ellie thought about it. 'I'm not sure I could. He'd want to talk business, and I'm not prepared to do so.'

'I can promise you he wouldn't. He respects you.'

Ellie thought Evan respected her millions, not her. He'd tried to patronize her in the past. He'd tried talking down to her as if she were a silly little housewife and she'd taken some pleasure in cutting him off at the knees. He'd remember that, wouldn't he, and want his revenge?

Both Ms Milburn and Diana reported that he was in shock at what had happened, but Ms Milburn had observed that a business phone call had taken Evan's mind completely off the tragedy. So how deeply did he really feel the deaths which had ravaged his family?

It might be interesting to find out.

On the other hand, to sit down at table with this man would take some doing. He didn't seem the 'forgive and forget' type. More like someone who nursed a grudge.

'Please,' said Diana.

Ellie's eyes widened. Had she heard correctly? Had her daughter actually said, 'Please?' If so, then perhaps . . . What would it cost Ellie to sit down to table with him? Nothing except a little pride.

Oh, and a suspicion that he must know more about the murders than he'd admitted. Surely he couldn't be so naive as to think these killings were just bad luck?

'Tell me; has Evan upset any of his clients lately? Has he had any hate mail?'

Diana shook her head. 'That did cross my mind, but I accessed his computer at work, all the deleted mails, everything. There's a couple of threatening letters from a client which he'd dealt with, offering to settle. There's the usual complaints about the cut he takes, but no more than everyone gets. No, there's nothing to indicate any sort of vendetta. There've been no unpleasant phone calls, as far as I could tell. Some flack from a man I've had to sack, dead wood, got to be cleared out . . .'

Mr Abel, of course. And not exactly 'dead wood'. More like 'too honest for Diana'. Possibly even 'wouldn't cut corners'.

'Everything's been done by the book. The threatening letters were ancient, anyway. Nine months, a year old.'

But Diana had thought it worthwhile to look. Hm.

'Mind you,' Diana said, 'I haven't asked him if he's received any hate mail at home. Surely he'd have told me if he had? You're right; I'll have to check that out. Before you ask, he hasn't mentioned having any enemies, or tried to lay the blame on anyone except the play centre and the au pair.'

'Yet he might well have made an enemy or two, the way he does business. You know his nickname is the Great White Shark?'

A shrug. 'Amusing, isn't it? He operates under the usual rules, normal business practice. Who'd kill for that? Even if someone had got it in for him, why kill members of his family and not him?'

'Have you considered that if someone is targeting the family, they might not stop with two deaths? What about other members of his family? He has a son, I believe. What of him?'

'Oh, him. Philip. Evan says he's not all there. Nerves or something. Left home ages ago. Evan makes him an allowance, and I think he does voluntary work for a charity. Gardening for old people? I suppose I could have a word with Freya, ask her to be careful . . . but I don't think she'd listen to me.' Diana reverted to her original request. 'So, will you kiss and make up? For my sake, if not for his?'

'No kissing, but if he were to ask Thomas and me to dine with him some evening, I suppose we'd accept.'

'Excellent. The golf club? This evening at eight o'clock. Will you make your own way there, or shall I collect you? Oh, do we really need Thomas?'

'I won't come without Thomas.' Ellie did not wish to face Evan and Diana on her own.

Diana shrugged. Pushed herself off the chair, sighing. Perhaps this pregnancy really was taking its toll on her. 'Let me know if you need a lift. You'll dress up a bit, won't you?'

'I suppose so,' said Ellie, conscious of wearing soft slippers and a slightly bedraggled skirt. All that rain. Yes, it was still raining, but no doubt Diana had brought a large umbrella with her to shield her outfit from the weather, and had parked her luxurious car right up by the front door.

Yes, she had.

Bye bye, Diana.

Rose called out, 'Lunch is ready.'

Ellie went into the sitting room to call Thomas . . . who had fallen asleep in his chair.

'I'm ready for it,' he said, jerking awake. His voice was coming back. A bit.

Ellie was annoyed with herself. 'I'm so stupid. I didn't think quickly enough. Diana and Evan Hooper have invited us to dine with them at the golf club tonight, and we've got roast lamb and all the trimmings for lunch. Can you eat two large meals in one day?'

'Do you have to ask? Of course I can. Do we really have to go?'

'Mm. Afraid we do. She says Evan's in shock and is being deserted by Angelika . . . I'll tell you all about it over lunch. Just don't eat too much now, that's all.'

Thomas laughed and patted his substantial frontage. 'Can't you see I'm fading away for lack of food? Lead me to the table, woman.'

SEVEN

Sunday afternoon

It went on raining. Thomas dozed in his La-Z-boy chair after lunch, while Ellie attempted to read the papers, fighting off sleep.

She woke when the phone rang and went on ringing. Thomas stirred but didn't wake. She stumbled into the hall in the early twilight.

Diana. Sounding tense. 'Sorry to wake you, Mother—'

'I wasn't asleep.' Well, she'd been dozing, that's all.

'There's been a change of plan. The police have just been round. They found Fern. That's—'

'Evan's second wife?'

'Dead. Since yesterday. Some stupid accident with her insulin. She's a diabetic, you know. Was.'

Ellie yawned, rubbed her eyes. 'So this evening's off?'

'You don't sound surprised.'

'I've never met the woman. Have you?'

'No. Evan can hardly believe it. He keeps saying, "It's a blast from the past." Whatever he means by that.'

'How did they find her?'

'She had a "gentleman friend". Used to go to the pub with him every Saturday night. Do a Karaoke turn. He couldn't get a reply when he called for her. She lived above the shop but had never given him a key. He saw the lights were still on inside the shop, which was odd as it was way after closing time. So he called the police. They broke in and found her. She was diabetic and there was a needle sticking in her thigh. She was very dead.'

Ellie was silent. Thinking. Another 'accident'?

'She'd been drinking. It looks as though she'd forgotten what time of day it was and given herself an extra injection. Her gentleman friend was inconsolable, said he'd warned her many a time to be more careful.'

'The police believe it was an accident?'

'I don't know what they believe. Evan refuses even to . . . He's in shock.'

'Diana, this is worrying.'

'Very. The gentleman friend told the police that Evan ought to be informed, so that he could break the news to Fern's daughters.'

'One remaining daughter. Freya, isn't it? How did she take it?'

'She asked if she'd inherit the shop. Then she disappeared. Went up to her room to sulk, I suppose.'

'Does she inherit?'

'Evan said he wasn't sure. He'd paid for the lease on the shop and flat above as part of the divorce settlement. If Fern had made a will, then maybe the lease would become Freya's property. But who knows if that kookhead will have done anything as sensible as making a will. The solicitors will have to sort it out. Complications . . .'

Silence.

Ellie said, 'Diana, have you considered—'

'That I might be next? Thanks, Mother. Yes, I had. But I don't think I'm at risk. I'm not married to Evan, yet.'

'But you still intend—'

'Oh yes. He's in shock.'

Ellie thought that if she heard that once more, she'd scream. 'Well, thanks for telling me. I assume the golf club is off.'

'Well, we can't be seen to go out and enjoy ourselves at the moment, can we? Evan isn't fit for it, anyway. He'd like you to come over here instead.'

'Why?'

'It was my idea, really. I don't know how you do it because the Lord only knows you weren't trained to use your brain, but call it luck, or whatever, people do talk to you and tell you things, and that's not my strong point.'

No, indeed. 'What do you want them to tell me?'

'It's more . . . I'm not the best person to deal with them at the moment.'

Deal with who? With Freya or Angelika? 'No, Diana. I don't think that's a good idea, particularly if someone's bent on killing off the Hooper family one by one. Get the police on to it, give them your file of complaints.'

'I'm going to do that. In the meantime, I really would like it if you could come over. There's a situation here that I really can't . . . Neither can Evan. He's at his wits' end.'

'What situation?'

'Well, someone needs to talk some sense into Angelika. She only ever reads *Hello* and *OK* and *True Stories* magazines, and today she wondered if they might be interested in her story. She wasn't serious about it but Evan blew his top as soon as she was out of the room. If she were to do that, she'd make out, oh, I don't know, that he pressured her into having his child.'

'Did he?'

'No, of course not. That wouldn't be at all like him.'

Ellie was silent, thinking that it was very like what she knew of him.

Diana continued, 'It's absurd, of course, but she's in a highly nervous state, and if he as much as frowns at her she runs off in tears. I asked her what she planned to cook for supper and she screamed at me like a fishwife. Her chief complaint seems to be that no one's paying any attention to her. What does she expect, at such a time? I'd like to slap the make-up off her silly little face, but I can't do that, can I? She's driving Evan mad. If you could make soothing noises to her and let her cry on your shoulder, then everything will quieten down. Come as soon as you can, right?'

She clicked the phone off.

Ellie wasn't sure whether to laugh or cry. So she took the problem to Thomas, who was awake – just – and channel-surfing on television.

'Thomas, please. I need your advice.'

He turned a wary eye on her. If she hadn't known him better, she'd have thought he had a guilty look about him. But he did turn down the volume on the television.

She explained the situation and he looked relieved. 'That's all right, then. I'll drop you round there and go on to take the evening service at St Matthew's. They rang me on my mobile a few minutes ago to ask if I could do it, and of course I said I would.' His voice was coming back, and he looked pleased with himself.

She knew him too well to accept this at face value. 'You planned this. You accepted so that you could get out of the evening at the golf club.'

'No, no. The golf club serves wonderful food.'

'But an evening with the Hoopers plus Diana would be too much for you?'

He grinned. 'You don't need me to sort that lot out. You'll have them eating out of your hand in five minutes.'

'Aren't *you* supposed to be the one trained to deal with people in mourning?'

'Hm.' He switched the volume back up. 'I wouldn't want to push my nose in where it's not wanted.' In a saintly tone.

'Thomas, I could shake you.'

Which was funny, seeing as he was twice her size. So they both laughed. Thomas patted her hand. 'Light of my life, if you really feel you can't deal with that pack of jokers, then of course I'll come with you and tell them at St Matthews to get someone else to take the service. But this is right up your street. Go and make soothing noises to those who are truly bereaved. Inject some common sense into those who are flying off the handle. Warn Diana not to move too fast. Give me a bell on your mobile when you're ready for me to pick you up again.'

Sunday evening

The Hoopers' house was a substantial, ugly, red-brick mansion in a quiet road lined with trees. The building itself looked to be Edwardian, but had been well maintained. There was a burglar alarm box above the front door, and the driveway had been recently tarmacked. There was a double garage at the side, with what looked like living quarters for staff above it. Diana's car was parked near the front door.

Ellie tugged on a knob marked 'Pull' and an old-fashioned bell tinkled inside. No battery to run down. No expense spared.

Diana let Ellie into a large, oblong hall with a tiled, patterned floor. Doors led off it in different directions. A couple of three-foot-high pottery Dalmatians guarded an imposing flight of stairs. The staircase had been painted white, which was a crime in itself as the wood beneath was probably oak, but at least an oatmeal coloured carpet muted sound.

The walls of the hall had also been painted white. No, not white: something which looked white but had a tinge of pink in it. There were hunting prints on the walls on either side of a grandfather clock which was a reproduction and not a genuine antique. A large framed photograph of a sensuous young blonde hung nearby, flanked by huge mirrors.

Decor by Harmony in the Home, to please Angelika?

Everything could do with a dust. Diana had said that the housekeeper had left, hadn't she? A landline telephone was ringing, but no one seemed to be in a hurry to answer its summons.

Diana said, 'You're letting the cold air in. Come in, do.'

Ellie went in. Stared at Diana, who had changed into a mid-blue, long-sleeved top, fastened asymmetrically à la Mao, over darker blue jeans. Ellie had never seen Diana in such garments before. What on earth was the girl playing at now?

Evan Hooper appeared in the doorway of a room to the right. 'Who is it, Diana?' Casually dressed, big and beaky. He looked all right at first glance. An imposing figure of a man. The Great White Shark . . . Only, perhaps not quite as formidable as he had been?

Diana gestured to Ellie. He nodded. 'Oh yes. You said.' Without saying a word to Ellie he went back into the room he'd just left. The phone stopped ringing. And started again. Still no one answered it.

'He's in a bad way,' said Diana in a soft voice. 'Hardly knows which day of the week it is. Go in and have a word with him while I see if I can find Angelika.'

A large room filled with islands of off-white modern furniture, all of it giant-sized. Carpets and curtains echoed the too-pale theme. Another portrait of Angelika – it couldn't be anyone else, could it? – hung over the largest of the settees, which must be twelve foot in length. At least. Mirrors. Shiny walls.

A huge television set over the fireplace had been switched on, featuring a game show. Fortunately, the sound had been turned down low, but Ellie found the flickering images distracting. Beside the fireplace was an operational bar, complete with optics and refrigerator.

There were signs of the usual Sunday disorder of papers and a couple of nasty stains on the off-white carpet. More dust. A mishmash of a room. Not a room to receive guests in. Too large for a snug. If Ellie sat on one of those giant chairs, her feet wouldn't reach the floor. Also, the room was beginning to lose its air of being ready for a photographer to drop in – by appointment, of course – to be featured in the next *Homes & Gardens* magazine, because there were mugs and dirty glasses here and there, even on the carpet. And some takeaway boxes.

The phone stopped ringing. Good. It had been doing Ellie's head in.

Evan poured himself a drink. Double scotch, and not the first of the day by the look of it. He was using a cut-class tumbler.

He swallowed. Shivered. Took another gulp. Lifted his glass to Ellie. 'Care for something?'

She shook her head. 'I'm sorry to hear of your loss.'

He threw himself in a chair, gestured to her to seat herself. 'She'd been living on borrowed time. I ought to have expected it. I suppose it could have happened any time these last few years. But to do it now, on top of everything else! She'd let herself go, you know. I insisted the girls visited, but they used to make excuses. Well, Freya did, but you can't really blame her for that. Fern passed out in the middle of the meal, last time she went. Fiona got on better with her mother, saw her more often. Perhaps Fiona's death helped to unsettle Fern . . . But there, in all the years I've known her, my ex-wife never considered anyone but herself. It's all just too much.'

Ellie nodded. The phone started to ring again. She said, 'Shall I answer it?'

'What? Oh. No. Ignore it. I do.' He crossed to the door and shut it. The phone went on ringing, but at least the sound was muffled now.

Ellie tried sitting back on the chair, and her feet lifted off the floor. She perched on the front edge. 'Is there anything I can do to help?'

He sipped. Swallowed. Passed one hand across his brow. 'We've just got to sit tight, ride it out. I've got to get back to the office, decisions only I can make, you know how it is, the buck stops here, etcetera. Expectations. Can't let the side down. There's at least two deals pending which . . . But I must admit I'm . . .'

He took out his Blackberry, swiped at it a couple of times, concentrated on something. Sat up straight. Started to work on a reply. Hesitated. Sighed. Put it down on the glass-topped table in front of him. 'Can't think straight. Deal with it tomorrow. I'll have to get back to work then. Everything depends on me, you know. Diana's marvellous, of course. But . . .' He finished his drink with one last swallow.

Diana appeared in the doorway, with a bottle of pills in her hand. 'Darling, I've switched the landline through to the answerphone. Is that all right? And it's time for . . . you know?'

'Oh. Yes. Forgot. Ellie, make yourself at home . . . At least

. . .' He glanced around, seemed to see the disorder for the first time. 'Diana, where's that no-good housekeeper?'

'She left, remember?' Diana went to the bar, poured out a glass of water and handed it to him with a tablet.

'Oh. Did she?' He shook his head at himself. No, he didn't remember. He took the tablet with the water and poured himself another scotch.

Diana gave him a peck of a kiss on his cheek and beckoned Ellie to follow her from the room.

Now Ellie knew what Diana's outfit reminded her of: a nurse. Maybe that was what Evan Hooper needed at the moment. He had slipped a long way back from being the confident – perhaps overconfident – man at the top of his world that Ellie had met earlier.

Was it an improvement? N–no. Possibly not. She couldn't help but be sorry for him – a little – as she followed Diana into the hall.

Evan came after them, glass in hand, still talking, leaving the television on. 'When I remember how she used to be . . .' He paused to take another gulp of his drink. 'When I first met her, great heavens, what a creature of fire and passion . . .!'

Diana pushed through a door at the back of the hall, and they followed her into an enormous kitchen-cum-dining-room which had been built on to the side of the house. Windows on three sides. The very latest in modern living . . . except for the dirty plates and pans piled into the sink. Didn't they have a dishwasher?

And where was the gym?

Someone – a tall blonde, slender except for a prominent pair of breasts – was poking around inside a walk-in fridge.

Evan ignored the blonde. 'Fern used to run about the house naked, you know? She was built like . . . like an Amazon!'

'Yes, yes,' said Diana, soothing him. 'You know the doctor said you should rest or you'll be fit for nothing tomorrow.'

'Three funerals! Three!'

Diana took him by the arm and led him – still mouthing the word 'three' – away.

The blonde slammed the fridge door and shook back her long hair. She was wearing a cropped top over jeans, and her feet were bare. She was a size zero, except for the boobs which pertly pushed up above her tank top. 'Thank God for small mercies. I don't know what you're going to find to cook for us tonight, but you'd better get on with it.'

She had a hard, green stare. Contact lenses?

Ellie looked behind her and realized that Angelika had mistaken her for an agency cook. 'Oh. I'm Diana's mother. Ellie Quicke.'

'I don't care who you are, so long as you can put something on the table quickly. I don't suppose *he'll* eat much, if anything. I'm Mrs Hooper, by the way. Then there's my stepdaughter, if she's still around, which she may not be. Don't bother about getting anything for your daughter. I'm sure she'd prefer a diet of toads and snakes.'

Ellie suppressed a giggle, partly from shock and partly out of genuine amusement. So the current Mrs Hooper thought Diana a witch? Well, well. 'When did you eat last?'

A shrug. 'I had some fruit and yogurt at lunchtime. That was just before the sky fell on my dear husband. He's been on a liquid diet ever since. Freya disappeared when she heard the news. Who cares, anyhow? The sooner I'm out of here, the better.' There were tears in her eyes. Perhaps she was not as hard as she tried to pretend?

Ellie gently moved Angelika to one side in order to investigate the contents of the fridge. Soya this and that. Minced meat, cheeses, sliced ham, salad stuffs, all still in their plastic wrappings just as they'd come from the supermarket. And rapidly deteriorating. They should have been removed from the plastic as soon as they were brought home. 'Is there a freezer somewhere?'

'Mm? That door there.'

The freezer was packed with ready meals from the supermarket, heavy on cholesterol and E-numbers. Cupboards to left and right slid out from the wall on rails, to reveal well-stocked larders.

Angelika seated herself on a high stool beside a giant cube decorated with dark glass insets . . . Was this the latest in ovens? It reminded Ellie of an X-ray machine.

Angelika produced her Blackberry and tried a number. 'Why

can't he be there when I need him?' She threw the Blackberry down; it skidded off the table top and landed on the floor.

Ellie retrieved it and put it on top of the cube. 'A friend, or a member of the family?' She went back to foraging in cupboards.

'My agent. Doesn't like me having to turn down jobs. Says he won't be able to fix me up with anything else for weeks. My family? Don't make me laugh! I'm the one that got away, the black sheep, the only one that's worked for a living in three generations. They only contact me for handouts, and that's . . . that's not going to be . . . Sorry, I'm somewhat . . . you know.'

Ellie remembered Diana saying that Angelika needed a shoulder to cry on, and it looked as if that might well be true. However, Ellie was not going to push it.

'How about a spaghetti bolognese with mushrooms and tomatoes, sprinkled with Parmesan cheese? With a green salad on the side?'

'It's Sunday. He'll expect a roast. I'll have a salad, of course, but he doesn't eat salads.'

'There's not enough time for a roast.'

A green stare. 'You can use a microwave, can't you?'

'As I tried to tell you, I'm not a professional cook. I'm here because my daughter asked me to help you out at this very difficult time. Now I *am* here, I'll throw some supper together, if you would like me to.'

She thought: *say 'please', and I'll do it.*

Another hard stare. 'Mrs Quicke. I remember. Aren't you married to some sort of Holy Joe?'

'Thomas. Yes. He's a good man. Would you like to talk to him?'

'What about? Oh. The Precious Infant. Well, I'm not going to pretend. That's not my style. She was not exactly what . . . I've heard of mothers not being able to bond with their daughters before now, and that's what . . . I suppose it didn't help that I had that swimsuit commercial so soon afterwards. I'd signed up for it before I realized, and then . . . I had to go on that crash diet to get back in shape, and I swear she liked her food more than she liked me. The way she used to look at me . . .'

She wrenched a can of Diet Coke from the fridge, popped the top and drank without bothering to pour it into a glass. 'I suppose I wasn't the best mother in the world.'

Ellie found a large saucepan, half filled it with water, and wondered which dial on which surface of the cube might operate the cooker. She pressed buttons and turned knobs. Ah. Result. Now to find a heavy-bottomed saucepan for the minced meat. She said, 'You were very young. Was the baby a mistake?'

A glitter of tears, swiftly wiped away. 'I hadn't intended, it's true. I thought he'd said . . . But it turned out he hadn't taken any precautions and of course *I* hadn't because I trusted him, being so much older. I wouldn't have dreamed of having a baby so soon. Why am I telling you this?'

'Because I had four miscarriages. Or was it five? Those years tend to blur in my mind. Having a baby changes you in more ways than one.'

'That's true. Did you really have so many misses? That's awful. It's so difficult to get your figure back afterwards, isn't it?'

'It was after we'd had Diana, of course. The last one I carried nearly to . . . Well, it was all a long time ago.'

Ellie went to and from the fridge and the larder shelves, preparing and cooking onions and then mince, chopping mushrooms and tomatoes, popping spaghetti into the boiling, salted water, looking for a cheese-grater.

'Sorry,' said Angelika, making wet rings on the cube's granite top with her can of Diet Coke. 'The funny thing is that I do miss the brat; though she was a brat, you know? I thought that she'd grow out of it. If she'd been a pretty little elfin thing, which is what I'd always imagined I'd have, I'd have been able to love her more easily. Or to show it more easily. As soon as I knew I was pregnant, I dreamed of us doing commercials together, mother and baby, you know? But she was so like Evan that that was never on the cards.

'I suppose you think me a selfish cow, but I imagined I was set for life with Evan to look after me and some modelling on the side, because I'm not trained for anything else. All of a sudden she's not there and everything's changed. I've got to rethink my life and . . .'

Her face screwed up, and she hunched herself over.

Ellie pushed the pans off the heat and put her arms around Angelika, who sniffed and mumbled and cried. And cried.

Ellie said, 'There, there.'

Angelika cried some more.

Someone opened the door behind them, said, 'Oops,' and retreated.

Angelika said something inarticulate and prised herself off Ellie.

Ellie found a box of tissues, handed it over and went back to her cooking.

Angelika got off her stool, sniffing. 'I must look awful.' Without another word she went out, shutting the door behind her.

Ellie stirred mushrooms and tomatoes into the mince and tested it for seasoning. She grated the cheese. She thought that Angelika had loved her child after a fashion and would grieve for her more every day. Yes, Angelika was self-centred and had probably been more grateful to Evan for marrying her than in love with him, but she was definitely in shock, and she had not caused her child's death.

Evan was also in shock, though in his case he was having to worry about the business as well as the effect these deaths were having on his family. He hadn't been responsible for the child's death, either.

So who was killing off the clan, one by one?

Or were the three deaths purely accidental?

EIGHT

Sunday evening

'Well? Did you tell Angelika not to contact the magazines?' Diana; impatient, laden with dirty plates and mugs, which she dumped on to an already cluttered work surface.

'Sorry,' said Ellie, testing the spaghetti. Was it done? Y–yes. 'We didn't get round to that.'

'But I brought you here purely to—'

'There was nothing pure about your motives, Diana. Angelika is not the total bitch you made her out to be, and she is grieving for her child.'

'Humph. Could have fooled me.'

'Probably. But she knows what you're up to, and she's deeply unsettled, to say the least of it. Have some consideration for her. She's young enough to be your daughter, her baby's died, and you're about to take her husband off her. She's looking into a future without a husband or a home. All she knows about is modelling.'

'She's not top model material.'

'I know. Too much bust. Swimsuits and underwear for her—'

'Until she starts to show her age. But if she gets the press interested she can write her own cheques, employ a ghostwriter and produce a misery memoir, get it serialized in the tabloids, go on celebrity-watch shows. Evan can't bear the thought of all that publicity. You've got to stop her.'

Ellie drained the spaghetti, tested the mushrooms. A touch more salt? 'Food up. You're overreacting. Angelika hasn't thought that far. She doesn't strike me as being overly intelligent. If she were to go down that road, she'd need help. An agent, perhaps. What do you know about her agent?'

'Less than nothing. She understands money all right. I suggested Evan made her a good allowance if she agreed to a quickie divorce and doesn't go down the publicity route.'

Ellie started to ladle the food on to plates. 'Would it be so wrong of her to cash in on a spot of notoriety? Perhaps she could do it under her maiden name.'

Diana liked the sound of that. 'Her maiden name? I suppose . . . Yes, that's a possibility. But we'd still have the tabloids battering down the door, asking for our version of events and hinting that Evan was unkind to his little waif of a wifey, and that I'm the wicked witch of the west.'

Ellie smothered a smile.

Diana said, 'What?' catching her mother's amusement but not understanding the cause of it. 'Well, see if you can talk her out of it. I'm sure Evan would be prepared to give her a good deal so long as she keeps his name out of the limelight. That food looks good. I'll take mine and Evan's through to the snug. Horrible decor, isn't it? All those mirrors and pictures of Miss Acton Town. That's the first room I'll change.'

Exit Diana, carrying a tray laden with food and cutlery.

Enter a nubile teenager, a true honey blonde this time, clad even more skimpily than her stepmother in a cropped top and jeans. No waif, she. A buxom but real bosom, a shapely behind, thick fair hair in a single plait down her back, bright blue eyes and a determined expression. No beauty. The likeness to Evan was startling.

'Hello; are you the new cook? I hope that's vegetarian. I don't eat meat.'

'You must be Freya. I'm Mrs Quicke, Diana's mother, and not a professional cook. I'm just helping out this evening.'

'Yuck. What's all that? I totally hate mushrooms.'

'Just spaghetti and cheese do you?'

'I hate spaghetti. It's so . . . thick.'

'Ah. Well, in that case I think you'd better find yourself something you can eat from the freezer.'

Freya blinked. 'Aren't you going to get it for me?'

'Why should I?'

'I'll tell my dad and he'll find someone who'll look after me properly.'

'Fine. You do that. Although he might have some difficulty getting someone in on a Sunday night.'

Ellie dished up a plateful for herself and began to eat it. Quite tasty, though she said it herself.

Freya tossed back her plait and took a seat. 'Well, I suppose I could try it. If it makes me sick, I can always blame you.'

'You're not allergic to cheese, are you?'

'Like Abigail was to peanuts, you mean?' Freya helped herself to spaghetti and cheese and lifted a tiny portion to her mouth. Smelled it. Tasted it. With a face full of doubt, she chewed and swallowed. 'I suppose it's not bad. You can always phone for the ambulance if I fall to the floor writhing in pain.'

Ellie grinned. 'Does food often affect you that way?'

Freya actually laughed. 'Sorry. I was out of order, wasn't

I? I mean, well . . . sorry. Things have been a bit, you know? I mean, total yuk.' This was no carefree adolescent but a girl who thought for herself. She hadn't been crying, but she was as tense as an iron bar.

Ellie said, 'Understood. Want another helping? I'd better leave some for Angelika.'

'Why bother?'

'She's very upset.'

'Nothing upsets Angelika for very long. She can't allow herself to get upset, or she'll get spots or frown lines. She's completely synthetic. Like her boobs. You've noticed her boobs, have you?'

Ellie had. 'I suppose she thinks it's necessary in her line of work.'

Freya checked on her own natural boobs, with satisfaction. 'When I've got my A levels I'm going to uni to get a business degree. Then I'm going into Dad's business.'

Ellie's eyes opened wide. What would Diana say to that?

'Dad doesn't think women can cut the mustard, but he doesn't see what's under his nose, does he?' She hit the table. 'Diana, under his nose . . . heehaw!' Tears were restrained with an effort.

'Er, quite.' Ellie got the point. A crude young lady, Miss Freya? Or one driven to uncharacteristic comment by events? Let's get away from the difficult subject of Diana. 'So you won't be upset when Angelika leaves?'

'Can't wait. When's she off, do you know? Although I suppose the new one's going to be worse. Oh. Your daughter, isn't she? Sorry. Slap on wrist. I suppose you're pleased with the way things are going.'

Back to Diana. 'No, my dear. I'm not. Not at all.'

'Families, eh? Who'd have thunk? I mean, Angelika moping over that kid who was, like, the most ghastly infant you could imagine. Spitting and spying and spoiling things. Telling tales.'

'Attention seeking?'

Freya looked sharply at Ellie. 'I suppose. Like me, you think?'

'I don't know you, dear, but I wouldn't have thought you were like that.'

'You called me "dear".'

'I can see you're hurting.'

Now that was a chance hit, for it might be rage and not grief that Freya was hiding. The girl bent her head, intent on demolishing the rest of her plateful. No tears. When the last mouthful had been eaten, she pushed the plate aside and faced Ellie with defiance. Rather brave, really.

'I'm not hurting. Not at all. I'm not sad, either. Of course people who didn't know any better would expect me to be sad, losing my mother and two sisters, but if they'd known them, they wouldn't be sad. Do you know what my nickname is in the family? It's "try again". When Mummy presented Dad with me, he said, "Try again." So I never had a chance. Rejected from birth because of my sex. "Try again."'

'That's awful. Was it the same for Fiona?'

'You'd have thought it would be, wouldn't you? You'd have been wrong. She could wind Dad round her little finger, and she hadn't half my brains. She didn't want anything from him except money. I got used to it. You can get used to almost anything if you try hard enough. I'm always top of the class, and the teachers say I should try for Oxford or Cambridge University. So one day . . . Yes, one day I'm going to show him that I'm as good as any man.'

Ellie nodded. 'I believe you can do whatever you set your mind to, but—'

'You don't think he'll listen?'

'Your father is of the old school. He's been brought up to think that men rule the world and women exist to continue the species. You've inherited a lot of his drive and personality—'

Freya's mouth wobbled. Tears threatened, but she refused to let them fall. 'Thanks for that.' In a muffled voice.

'But – I'm stepping right out of line here, Freya – why limit your horizons? I do believe that you have the brains and the sticking power to be a success in whatever line you decide.'

'Become a nuclear physicist, you mean?'

Ellie had to laugh. 'Or an explorer in the Arctic—'

'Or an Olympic swimmer—'

'Prime Minister?'

By this time Freya was laughing too. She picked up their dirty plates and added them to the piles on the work surface. 'I've never thought of doing anything else but following Daddy into the business. I don't know if I . . . You've given me something to think about.'

Ellie opened the freezer door. 'What do you fancy for afters? Ice cream?'

'All right. It's made with soya, but it's not bad. Angelika won't have any other kind in the house.'

'Let's put some maple syrup on it, to buck it up. I think I've seen some somewhere. This is definitely the day for carbohydrates.'

Ellie rummaged in cupboards, while Freya scooped ice cream out into bowls.

Ellie said, 'You didn't have a good relationship with Fiona, then? Even though she was close to you in age?'

A wry smile. 'I'm the odd one out in this family. Dad used to say to Fiona, "Does Oo want another prezzy, then?" And she was always Mummy's favourite. I never counted. Who got the best bedroom? She did. Who got her allowance increased regularly? She did. Who got all the hugs and kisses when we were little? She did. She was Mummy's Little Precious and it never worried her that Dad treated her as if she were a pet poodle. I mean, he shouted at her if her school reports were bad – she wasn't all that bright, you know – but it never bothered him. Or her, really. Water off a duck's back.

'I was the one who was supposed to look after her and see that she didn't come to any harm. I was responsible for taking her to and from school, and making sure she did her home-work. A laugh a minute, I can tell you. Especially after Mummy left.'

'That must have been a difficult time for you. Did you want to go with your mother?'

'She didn't want us. I could see that, even if Fiona couldn't. Fiona was in two minds, going or staying, but in the end she plumped for staying here and having someone cook and clean for us. Mummy wasn't exactly house-proud, you know. And the arguments! The mess! I like order. I like peace and quiet and things in their right place. It may sound horrible, but I was glad when she went and we could get the house really clean.'

'Didn't you have a cleaner?'

'We had cleaners, all right, one after the other. But Mummy smoked. You understand?'

No, Ellie didn't. And then she did. 'You mean, smoked something illegal?'

Freya wrinkled her nose. 'Marijuana. Horrid smell. The cleaners objected and refused to come back, or else she sacked them for what she called their impudence. Daddy hasn't much sense of smell. Fiona liked to try everything, too. Then, I don't know when it started, but one day Fiona made a joke about men coming in to see Mummy when Dad was at work, and Mummy walloped her, which was such a surprise because she'd never laid a hand on Fiona before! Mummy swore us to secrecy but after that I worked out what was going on. It had never occurred to me before that . . . I suppose I was a late developer. Dad found out eventually, of course. He couldn't take that.'

No, he wouldn't, would he?

'So . . .' A shrug. 'She left. It was good for a while. Quiet. Daddy got a housekeeper in, a Filipino who lived over the garage with her husband who did the garden. We got on with our lives until one day Dad brought Angelika home and we had the decorators in again, and . . . Well, she isn't unkind or anything. She leaves us alone. That's all I ask; to be left alone.'

'Did Fiona like it when Angelika came to live here?'

A shrug. 'She was rude to her till Daddy put a stop to it. Fiona thought Angelika had pushed Mummy out, but I don't think she did. I think he's a serial monogamist. That's the right word for him, isn't it?'

Ellie nodded. 'Coffee? Tea? Chamomile or something herbal?'

'Nothing else, thanks.' A short laugh. 'You wanted to know what Fiona was like? Well, I'll tell you. She used to try out all Daddy's booze and blame it on the help, so the housekeeper left and we had to get another one. I told Fiona if she did that again I'd tell on her, so she started going out with boys who'd take her to clubs. She'd tell Dad she was having a late night with a school friend or a sleepover, and he never checked.

Sometimes she'd stay out all night, and at other times she'd come back in the early hours of the morning, wobbling around all over the place.'

'But she was only, what, fourteen or fifteen?'

Freya pulled a face. 'She looked older. I told Mummy, but she said Fiona was just having fun. Fun! Do you know what I did first thing when I heard my sister was dead? I went through her room and got rid of all her drugs and the contraceptive pills that poor dear Daddy had no idea his daughter had been taking.'

'Where did she get them from?'

'Mummy dearest, of course. Fiona was growing up to be just like her. I could see it happening, and I couldn't do anything about it. Fiona said she knew exactly what she was doing and that she wasn't giving up sex just because I was a po-faced virgin. I know she took the morning-after pill a couple of times.'

'You might have told your father.'

Freya gave her a weary look. 'Then what? I hinted once or twice, but he doesn't see what he doesn't want to see, and Angelika thinks of nothing but her career. I did think Fiona's last boyfriend might turn out to be a more stable character, but then she had a row with him and broke up because he said she was getting fat. Which she was. That's when she went on a fitness binge.'

'Hence the session on the treadmill?' Ellie polished off the last of her ice cream and sighed, replete. 'I'm always talking about going on a diet, but . . . They used to say that if you wanted to please your husband, you made sure to feed him well.'

'What's your husband like?'

'Overweight.' Ellie smiled. 'A good man. Trustworthy. Comfortable.'

'Like old shoes?'

'If they're ones that keep the rain out, yes.'

'That's . . . nice.' And very unlike her own family.

Angelika drifted in, looking lost, hooked up to some music. She didn't look at Freya, and Freya didn't look at her. They walked around one another like two cats, aware of one another, careful not to touch. Freya dumped their pudding plates on one of the piles of crockery waiting to be washed and departed without another word.

Ellie said, 'Angelika, would you like something to eat?'

Angelika might have heard, or might not. She looked as if she were thinking about something – or someone – a long way away. She opened a high cupboard door and lifted a key off a hook inside. 'I'll be in the gym, if anyone wants me. Which they won't.'

The gym in which her stepdaughter had died. Of an accident. Or an incident. Whichever. Ellie was interested. 'Is that the only key to the gym?'

'Of course. I can't have just anybody traipsing into it and using the equipment.'

'Would you like to show me?'

Another voice. 'Show you what?' Diana, bringing back the dirty dishes. 'What's for pudding?'

'Ice cream and maple syrup,' said Ellie.

'Nothing hot?'

Angelika and Diana ignored one another, just as Freya and Angelika had done. Diana hesitated, not finding a space to dump her dirty dishes. She opened the dishwasher. 'It's full. Why didn't you start it?'

Ellie shrugged. 'Diana, why don't you and Angelika decide who runs this household? Count me out. I've got my own house to run and –' looking at her watch – 'it's time I rang Thomas to come to fetch me. Unless, of course, you're going to give me a lift home.'

Diana froze. So did Angelika. Unexpectedly, Angelika began to laugh. 'It's up to you, Diana. If you don't like the heat, stay out of the kitchen.'

Diana went pale with fury, and then red. She said, 'Evan will have to get another housekeeper in. I can't look after this house as well as his business. Where are the pudding plates kept?'

Angelika continued to laugh. 'Find out.' She unlocked an unobtrusive door at the back of the kitchen and disappeared through it. Ellie heard the key turn in the lock on the other side. So that was where the gym was to be found?

Diana rummaged through cupboards. 'All the good china's in the dishwasher. Where did you find your plates, Mother?'

Ellie pointed. 'Top cupboard, to the right of the freezer. I think we used the last two.' She bent to open some other cupboards. There were a lot of them. Some held pots and pans. Some swung out to reveal racks of Pyrex dishes. A carousel of spices.

'Ah. Will these do?' A miscellany of china, odds and ends of plates, some old-fashioned soup plates, which nobody seemed to use nowadays. A stack of thick white china plates, crazed from long use.

China plates. White. Thick. Pottery, rather than china.

As used by the clown to carry a load of biscuits into the park. Biscuits which contained peanuts.

With intent to kill.

Diana swooped on them. 'I suppose they'll have to do. Give me a couple and I'll take some pudding through to Evan, though I suppose he might prefer cheese.' She scooped ice cream on to the plates and found some spoons. Put the maple syrup on her tray to take in with her.

'You're not going to give me a lift home, Diana?'

'Can't you see I'm busy?'

Diana left the kitchen with her loaded tray, and Ellie looked despairingly at the mess in the kitchen. She hated mess. Like Freya, it made her uncomfortable. If this had been her own house, she'd have set to and got it cleared up. As it was . . . She pulled out her mobile phone and asked Thomas to come to fetch her.

He'd been waiting for her to phone him. 'Five minutes,' he said.

It was still raining.

All the way home she was thinking that Diana hadn't killed those two girls, or Fern. Neither had Angelika. Nor Freya.

And certainly not Evan.

Those plates. Old stock, donkey's years old, placed at the back of a cupboard. Not in use. They hadn't been thrown away because they might be useful in an emergency, for standing house plants on to drain, for feeding a visiting dog or cat.

Of course, such plates might be found in many a household

hereabouts, or in a charity shop. There was absolutely nothing to prove that the plate which the clown had used came from the Hooper kitchen.

Diana hadn't reacted at the sight of them. But then, Diana hadn't seen the picture of the clown, which had been taken in the park.

Diana hadn't killed Abigail. Definitely not.

Angelika was in the clear, too. She had not been responsible for killing her child.

The gym was kept locked, and the key was kept in a cupboard in the kitchen. You'd have to know where it was, to get into the gym.

Who would know where the key was kept, apart from members of the Hooper household?

They all would know. But, none of them had killed Fiona. Or had they?

Round and round and round we go . . .

NINE

Monday morning

*T*ime to ratchet up the terror.
    A phone call to a couple of the seedier tabloids should do the trick. If they get the merest whiff of infanticide, the whole boiling lot will be banging on the front door, asking which member of the family did away with the little chick and begging neighbours for interviews.

Then . . . what about taking it one step further?

Suppose I mix and mingle with the reporters? That way I can point them in the right direction.

There'd have to be a different look. Perhaps long hair, a padded bra, a black jacket and jeans. A camera.

Knowing my way around the neighbourhood, I could get in through the back door before they realized what was happening. And then . . . who should be next? Angelika or Freya?

Ellie woke up feeling tense with anxiety. Surely she didn't need to worry about the Hoopers, of all people! No, no. She could put them out of her mind with a clear conscience. Or try to.

Nag, nag . . . three members of the family down and how many more to go?

Nonsense. Think about something else. Lots to do. A bright sunny morning for once. Good.

Rose chattered away at breakfast time about restocking the conservatory with plants for the winter. Neither Thomas nor Ellie listened. Thomas grunted over the newspapers. Ellie tried to concentrate on anything but the Hoopers. Would the remains of the roast do for supper tonight? Mm, yes.

There was something at the back of her mind . . . Something she'd forgotten to do, or promised to do?

She wondered, smoothing out a grin, how the Hooper household had got on that morning at breakfast. Would they eat their cornflakes out of ancient and unmatched pudding bowls, or had someone actually managed to switch the dish-washer on?

Again, Ellie turned her mind away from the Hoopers. What had she done with that picture of the clown? She felt guilty about mislaying it. It wasn't like her, and it was an important piece of evidence.

The phone rang. Thomas slid out of the kitchen and into his study, leaving her to answer it.

Diana. Oh.

'Mother, I rang Evan just now and he said you hadn't turned up this morning. You could at least help me out for a few days. You know I have to be in the office today. Evan said he might try to come in for a few hours this afternoon, but there's no one there to look after the house for him.'

'You didn't really expect me to—?'

'Who else?'

'I have my own work to do.' She'd just remembered who she'd arranged to visit that morning. She looked at her watch. She had half an hour to get organized and get there. 'Diana, I have people to see this morning. Why don't you get a cleaner in?'

'At such short notice? Don't be ridiculous.'

Ellie was silent. The obvious thing was for Diana to ring Maria's agency and arrange for a team of cleaners to descend upon the Hooper household, but Maria was married to Diana's ex-husband Stewart. Happily married, with children. Diana wouldn't call Maria if she were dying.

Ellie sighed. 'You want me to call Maria and organize something?'

'Get someone good.' The phone clicked off.

Ellie growled at the receiver, but dialled Maria's number. It was half-term, so Maria might not be there, though she had a good assistant. Luckily, it was Maria herself who answered the phone.

'Dear Maria; Ellie here. I'm so pleased to have caught you. I thought you might be off with the littlies. Half-term and so on.'

'I know. It's difficult. My assistant has children too, so she and I are working half the week each. The children are all at my parents', including Frank. He's happy as they are going out for the day. Legoland? Something like that. So I'm working Monday, Tuesday and Wednesday and taking the rest of the week off. What can I do for you?'

'I've got a job for the Archangel Gabriel. Can you find a couple of good cleaners straight away, and a man and wife housekeeper/gardener to live in as soon as possible?'

Maria was amused. 'That might be difficult. A lot of my customers are away, but so are many of my cleaners. Why do you need an archangel? Won't an ordinary angel do?'

'Well, no. It's for the Hooper household. You may have read in the papers about the accidental deaths of a teenager and a toddler. A previous, divorced wife was also found dead at the weekend. There are questions which need to be answered, though so far the police are treating the deaths as misadventures. Their housekeeper and gardener have walked out, and the household is at sixes and sevens and rapidly descending into squalor. The Hoopers are all very upset and finding it difficult to come to terms with what's happened. I must warn you, though. Diana has plans to become the next Mrs Hooper, even though Evan's current wife is still living there.'

'Diana's living there?' Amused.

'No, but she's in and out. Taking over at the office while Evan Hooper recovers his wits.'

'Mm.' Maria didn't sound happy about sending someone to work for Diana.

'Yes, I know. Can you find a pair of experienced workhorses who'll go through the place like greased lightning and give Diana as good as they get?'

'Not this week, I shouldn't think. Next week, let me see . . . Yes, next week, with luck. I'll have to ring around, maybe switch . . . But this week? I'm not sure. Listen, Ellie, I'll see what I can do, ring around, get back to you, right?'

Ellie put the phone down, picked it up again to order a minicab, darted into Thomas's office to say she'd be out most of the morning, collected her handbag and an umbrella – because you never knew in October – grabbed her jacket and . . .

The landline rang. Ellie ignored it. She sang out to Rose that she was off, and then slipped out of the front door before anything else could happen.

Ellie had long cherished a plan regarding Vera, her one-time cleaner, but had put it on hold when the girl had moved on to nurse and then marry Edgar Pryce, a man who had only a few months to live.

The Pryce fortune – including the house which was being turned into a hotel – had been left to Ellie on condition that she kept the remaining members of that feckless family from poverty. Edgar had been the best of the lot, and before his death he had passed responsibility for his wife Vera and her son to Ellie. He had left Ellie a letter in which he asked her not to give them an income but to help Vera to a decent job and, since he lived in a rented flat, find her somewhere to live.

Ellie had kept a watching brief since the funeral, but now that Vera had asked to see her, perhaps the time might be ripe to mention her own idea for the girl's future?

Some time soon, perhaps this winter, Rose would need more help just to stay where she was. Rose, being Rose, had said she must go into a home when the time came, but Ellie and

Thomas hated the thought of it. Rose had a daughter but, alas, not one who would put herself out for anyone, let alone her mother.

And there was Vera who, after her short-lived marriage to Edgar, was now at a loose end. Vera had been one of Maria's star cleaners. She was dependable, bright-eyed, strong, and devoted to a son with behavioural problems. And, there was the empty top floor of Ellie's house.

To Ellie, it seemed that the answer to both their problems was obvious, but she realized that Vera might think differently. Also, Ellie still hadn't got permission to convert the top floor of her house into separate accommodation.

It was time to see what Vera had to say for herself.

Ellie got out of the cab to survey Vera's flat, on the ground floor of a terrace of Edwardian houses. Tiny front gardens. Red-brick. Large bay windows. Trees in the street. Quiet. Perhaps a little depressing? Or was that only in Ellie's mind? The bright promise of the early morning had given way to a clouded sky.

Vera let Ellie in. Superficially, marriage to Edgar Pryce hadn't changed Vera, who still wore her hair pulled back into a ponytail, and her clothing – a plain black T-shirt over jeans – was no more expensive than the clothes she'd worn when cleaning people's houses. But she'd lost the 'bounce' which had once characterized her. Even her blue eyes looked washed out.

The sitting room was shadowy as heavy curtains, though looped back, obscured much of the daylight. Behind them were nets. Ellie disliked nets because they needed so much attention in the grimy air of a city. These were clean, because everything Vera had about her would be clean, but they added to an atmosphere of quiet desperation in the room. The furniture was good and solid. Nothing new; about what you'd expect in a downmarket furnished flat.

On the plus side, the central heating system worked.

There was a framed photograph on the mantelpiece of Edgar in happier days. A radio was playing something cheerful nearby, but there was no sign of Vera's child.

'No Mikey?' said Ellie.

'Edgar introduced him to computers and he's never looked back. I'd never been able to afford a computer for him, but Edgar suggested we both went on a beginner's course, so we did. I know how to do this and that now, but Mikey left me far behind. The tutors say he's got some sort of kink in his brain, means he can understand things much faster than normal people. They say that's why he was always in trouble, before. He was frustrated. He's a different boy now. You'd hardly know him.'

'So that's where he is now?'

'He's signed up for an advanced course today. The tutors say he's one of only two pupils who can run rings round the rest of us.'

'How is he, nowadays?' said Ellie, not wanting to refer openly to Mikey's famous tantrums.

'He's all right. The doctor said he'll get over it. Children do, don't they?'

Ellie remembered what Edgar had said about the boy in his letter. Edgar had loved Mikey and believed that the boy had loved him in return. Edgar had been worried how the boy would cope after his death, and perhaps he was right to worry. 'What's wrong?'

Vera reddened and shifted on her chair. 'Nothing. Mikey was really fond of Edgar, you know.' A slight hesitation? 'It's just that, well, sometimes he refuses to eat.'

No tears. Very composed. Subdued.

How awful. How like Vera to keep on keeping on, not complaining. Expecting nothing. Ellie let the silence roll around them. Was this the time to mention her plan for Vera's future? No, it was too soon.

There was, however, something else Vera might do, if she felt up to it. No, no. The timing was all wrong.

Vera started. 'I'm so sorry. Would you like a cup of tea? Or would you prefer coffee?'

'Coffee? I don't mind "instant".'

'Come into the kitchen. It's brighter there.'

It was brighter. There were house plants on the window sill and a small radio playing something lively. An ironing board had been set up, with a pile of clothes waiting to be dealt with.

There was a Formica-covered table with three chairs around it. Vera produced coffee and biscuits, and they sat at the table.

Ellie said, 'You asked to see me, and I'm really glad to have the opportunity to catch up with you. How are you coping?'

'I can't seem to think straight. I mean, it wasn't a great love match, or anything, but I was terribly fond of him. We both knew he hadn't much time, but he'd been so much better that I thought, and he thought, he might go into remission, and we began to think maybe we'd have Christmas together, and he'd be able to teach Mikey to play chess and even, possibly, take him to football matches.

'He was wonderful with Mikey, you know. I was so worried, I warned him about Mikey's moods, but as soon as I saw them doing weird and wonderful things on the computer together, I knew it would be all right. Do you know, Mikey didn't have but one tantrum all the time . . .' She swallowed. 'We were lucky, I suppose, that we had those months together.'

Ellie reached out to hold Vera's hand.

Vera was dry eyed. 'We never slept together. I offered, he said "soon". But I held him in my arms when I found him, sitting in his chair with the telly on and the newspaper on his lap, fallen asleep. So I held him till he was quite, quite cold. And when Mikey realized, he came to sit on his other side and stroked his hand.'

'Edgar was a fortunate man.'

'Not that I was ever his equal socially, of course. I came to look after him, and then he took to Mikey, and Mikey took to him, and when my rent was due and going up, he said would I like to move in, and Mikey said it would be a good idea, because then he could work on Edgar's computer, so we did. And Edgar bought Mikey a brand-new, state-of-the-art computer, and, well . . . I cooked and cleaned for them and listened when they talked about gigabytes . . . Is that the right word? I've never been able to understand what they were.'

Ellie nodded. 'Me neither.'

'Then we had those three days at the seaside, not waiting

for half-term, and the teachers didn't like it one bit, us taking Mikey out of school, but if we'd waited, we wouldn't have been able to go, would we? Edgar sat in his chair on the beach, and Mikey scrambled around, collecting shells and wanting to look them up on his laptop, and me falling asleep in the sun, would you believe? I even got a tan. He got up out of his chair one day and went along the shore with Mikey, looking for some rare shell or other. I never did work out what, but that didn't matter, did it?'

'No, it didn't.'

'And we thought . . . we hoped . . . and he said he was feeling a bit better every day, but I could see . . . and the doctor said . . . But he wanted to stay at home, and I said that of course he should. When his sister came and said those awful things, about me trying to trap him into marriage—'

'Dreadful woman.'

Vera nodded. 'I said I'd leave, but if I had, what would have become of him? Because he'd have had to go into the hospice. That's when he said we should get married, so that I could be his next of kin and deal with the doctors for him. So we did. He wrote it all down, what I was to do, where his little bit of money was, and how I should give Mikey all of it for his education if he couldn't get bursaries, and I said I didn't want anything, and he said I was the sort who needed to be needed and so I must go back to work sometime, not to cleaning, but to try for a better job when I felt better. Do you think it was wrong of us to get married?'

'I don't. I'm only sorry that you didn't have longer together. You made him a very happy man in his last few months, and he's given Mikey a new direction in life.'

'I wanted to see you, to ask you . . . His sister says it's immoral for me to take family money, and that I should turn everything over to her. One moment I think she's right, and the next, I don't.'

This made Ellie angry. 'His sister is a greedy harridan, who's already well provided for. Forget her. Have you been able to make any plans for the future yet?'

Vera shook her head. 'Edgar took six months' rental on this flat, and I could stay on, but it feels . . . I don't know. Mikey hates it. I've promised him we'll look for something better, but I can't seem to get moving on anything.'

True grief. Ellie compared it to what she'd seen at the Hoopers'. Which reminded her of them again. Should she try out her idea? Vera could only turn it down.

'Vera, have you been reading the papers? Did you hear about the tragedies that have hit the Hooper family? No, I don't suppose you have.' Ellie told Vera what she knew. It took some time, and when she'd finished Vera was counting on her fingers, a tinge of colour in her pale face.

'One, two, three accidents? Pull the other one.'

'Agreed. The police are beginning to think so, too.'

'Who do you think is doing it?'

'I can't think. I've talked to the three remaining Hoopers, and no one of them seems a likely candidate. Maybe I'm missing something.'

Vera took a deep breath. 'You want me to go to work for them, to sort the house out for them? But . . .'

Ellie waited. Would Vera want to play the game Ellie had in mind?

'Well, I could do, I suppose. But . . .' A swift, narrow-eyed glance. 'That's not exactly it, is it? If it were, you'd get Maria to send them someone really experienced, who . . . What is it you want me to do?'

Careful does it. 'You may not feel up to it, yet.'

Vera stood to clear away the coffee mugs. She washed them up, frowning. 'Do the police really suspect murder?'

'They're beginning to, yes. Each of the deaths, standing alone, can be written off as misadventure or accident. Three incidents can't. The police will be looking at each death, trying to work out who might have caused it, and why. They'll look at motive and opportunity.'

Vera was becoming interested. 'Who could possibly gain by killing an ex-wife, a teenager, and a toddler? Is this some kind of vendetta against Mr Hooper, do you think?'

'The police will be looking into that, searching his files, looking for someone he'd crossed in a business matter, perhaps.'

'You don't need me for that.'

'No.' Ellie waited.

Vera was coming back to life, her eyes switching to and fro. Vera was no fool.

'You think that this is being done to get back at Mr Hooper? That someone outside the family is killing them off, one by one? What would they have to gain by it? Money? I suppose each death lessens Mr Hooper's expenses, but no one would kill them just for that, would they?'

'Agreed.'

'So it must be a vendetta. In which case . . . I think I see what you're getting at. Why stop at three?'

'My thinking exactly. Who would you mark down next? The model, Angelika, who is about to leave the household to go back to her professional life? The teenager who is aiming for university? Or Mr Hooper himself?'

'Mr Hooper, I think. No, that's wrong. If it's a vendetta, and the person aimed at is Mr Hooper, then surely he'd be left till last to make him suffer more?'

'Then who would you go for next?'

Vera pulled off the band which held her hair back, and shook it out before combing it through with her fingers and fastening it again into a ponytail. 'Angelika. No, that can't be right, because Mr Hooper's going to be rid of her soon, isn't he?'

'That's what I thought at first. Then it occurred to me that if the killer really is targeting all the members of the Hooper family out of revenge, he might be anxious not to let Angelika get away. The opportunities for getting rid of her – if that is what the murderer wants – are decreasing every day. He must strike soon, or not at all. I would be very much afraid, if I were her.'

Vera was restless, cleaning around the sink. 'Have you warned her?'

Ellie shook her head.

'Oughtn't you to?'

'On what basis? "By the pricking of my thumbs, Angelika, I think you're next for the high drop"? I don't think she'd believe me. But you're right. I must try.'

'You want me to go to work there, which I suppose I could do, and act as bodyguard to Angelika?'

'I'm not quite sure what either of us can do, but I do think we ought to try. This is an opportunity for someone to get into the household and observe what's going on, see if there's anything I've missed. I can be round there some of the time, but I've got meetings to attend, other work to do. If you could be my eyes and ears . . . .? You wouldn't have to snoop around or anything, but perhaps if you could keep an eye out for Angelika, or any visitors, or anything unusual? I have an overactive imagination and I keep worrying about gas taps being left on "accidentally" or a fall down the stairs. Drowning in the bath. Overdose of sleeping tablets.'

'To arrange something like that, the killer would have to be able to get into the house.'

'I think he or she has access to the house and knows it well. How else would they know where the key to the gym was kept?'

'Also, they must be aware of the family's health problems or they wouldn't arrange for the child to eat a biscuit containing peanuts.'

'Or be familiar with the medical history of the second wife, in order to overdo it with the insulin.'

A stare. 'Who would know all that, apart from family?'

'That's what I'm trying to find out. I can ask questions but I can't be there much of the time. You could sort out the house and let me know of anything which strikes you as out of place. Have you a mobile phone? Yes, of course you have. Well, you could ring me if you spotted anything unusual.'

'Or the police?'

'I'll give you the number of a policewoman who is already suspicious of what's happening.'

Vera chewed her lip. 'I could only work there in the mornings and I'd have to leave in good time to give Mikey his lunch. I'm not going to take him into that house.'

'Agreed. There is a possibility, no more than that, of course, but I must warn you that—'

'If someone is hanging around trying to kill Angelika, then I might get in their way? Or you might?'

Ellie was silent. Why hadn't she realized that she herself might become a danger to the killer?

Vera stared out of the window at the garden. 'Mrs Quicke, I owe you a lot.'

'No, dear. You don't owe me a thing. I shouldn't have asked you—'

'I'll do it. I've the right skills for someone to help them out, and the job's come up at the right time for me, to get me moving again. It did cross my mind once or twice that I could ask if you had a suitable flat to rent which Mikey and I could move into, but . . . I couldn't bring myself to lift the phone to call you. Now you've come to me. Of course I'll do it.'

Ellie relaxed. 'Are you sure? If you do, I'll pay you and pay you well. And, yes, I'll ask my son-in-law to see what sort of accommodation he can sort out for you. In the meantime, I'll take you over to the Hoopers' and introduce you. I'll say you used to work for me and are going to help them out as a favour. Which is all true. I don't want them paying you direct because, if they do, they could order you about and perhaps make life rather unpleasant for you.'

Vera looked surprised.

Ellie felt herself go red. 'I should have said. My daughter Diana – you may or may not have come across her when you were working for me—'

Vera grinned. 'Hoity-toity madam? Sorry, but she is.'

Ellie had to smile. 'Yes, she is. She's also working for Evan Hooper and aiming to become the next Mrs Hooper.'

Vera looked as if she'd rather like to make a sour remark. Thought better of it. Frowned. Opened her mouth to say something. Closed it again.

'Yes,' said Ellie, feeling bleak. 'She is the only person I can think of who might benefit from these deaths. However, I don't think it's her style.'

Vera slanted a dark look at Ellie.

'The police will be enquiring into alibis, motives and opportunities. So yes; if you think Diana is fiddling with electrical connections, then the police must be told.'

'Only, you think it's an outsider?'

'I can't think straight. How can an outsider know how to get rid of these people? But no one on the inside looks like a murderer to me.'

Vera picked up her handbag, checked for keys. 'Let's go.'

Ellie had one of those moments when time stood still. She knew without a doubt who might have done the murders, though she didn't know why. An outsider who had inside knowledge. Of course.

Except that it was impossible. It couldn't possibly be. Could it?

TEN

Monday noon

The Hooper house wasn't far away. As they turned into the driveway, Ellie was amused to see a couple of men and a woman homing in on a man who was out walking a dog. Could they be members of the press asking a neighbour for a comment on the Hooper tragedies? Ellie and Vera slipped past them unnoticed and rang the doorbell.

The door opened so sharply that Ellie had to step back to avoid the girl who then hurtled out.

Freya, dressed in tank top, shorts and trainers. 'Who? Oh. You.' She switched her eyes to Vera. 'And . . .?'

'My cleaner. Helping you out for a couple of hours.'

Freya nodded. 'I was going crazy, cooped up inside, so I'm off for a run. Make sure the door's shut behind you. We've had the police and all sorts here today, wanting to get an exclusive interview. Some nutters on the phone.' She looked right and left, saw the members of the press still crowding around the neighbour. 'There they are again. Dad gave them an earful and now they're pestering neighbours. See you.' She loped off.

Ellie and Vera pushed the front door open and went in, shutting it firmly behind them. The hall was empty except for dust. Ellie called out, 'Hello?'

No reply.

Vera said, 'Spooky, innit?'

Quite. Ellie looked into the 'snug'. Empty. Today's papers had joined yesterday's – and probably those from the day before – on the floor. Empty coffee cups, dirty plates. A steamy fug. 'Phew!' said Vera, unlocking and pushing up a sash window to let in some fresh air.

Back in the hall, Ellie called out again. Still no reply. The grandfather clock ticked loudly in the silence. Ellie noticed that the landline phone on a side table was off the hook. She put it back on, and it rang. She jumped as if she'd been bitten, then laughed at herself. From the depths of the house someone – Evan Hooper? – shouted, 'Whoever it is, I'm not here!'

Ellie said, 'Hello?' cautiously into the phone.

'You twisted, poisonous creep! What does it feel like to kill your own child, you filthy spawn of toad? And . . .'

Ellie blinked. That wasn't a very nice thing to call someone, was it? Ugh. She put the phone down, wondering why you called it a 'torrent' of abuse. Because the person – man or woman? Probably a man – calling had dammed up the invective, only to release it in a torrent when someone answered the phone? Was this the 'nutter' Freya had referred to?

Ellie hoped the girl hadn't had to hear herself called all those names. She didn't like it herself.

Did the caller really think Evan had murdered his own child? Nasty. Ugh. The phone rang again. How could she divert the caller? Could she make him think he'd got the wrong number? She picked up the phone, listened to the same few words and said in her best adenoidal voice, 'Harrods. What department do you want?'

Silence. She replaced the phone on the hook. And waited.

It rang again. She picked it up, repeated: 'Harrods. What department do you want?'

Heavy breathing. A man? Hard to tell. 'Sorry, wrong number.'

She put the phone down. Would it ring again? Mm. Perhaps it would be best to leave it off the hook.

She beckoned to Vera. 'The kitchen's this way.' It was in a worse state even than before, because someone had dropped a container of milk on the floor and not bothered to mop it up.

'Oh my!' Vera was seldom at a loss for words, but the state of the Hoopers' kitchen managed it. Then, being Vera, she squared up to the task in hand and got to work. 'You clear out, Mrs Quicke, and let me at it.'

Ellie become conscious of a steady thrum-thrum-thrum. She tried the door at the back which let on to the gym. It opened, and she found herself in an old-fashioned, Edwardian, iron-framed conservatory. Instead of plants, there was a plethora of exercise equipment.

Angelika was on the treadmill, dressed in a cropped top, shorts and trainers. Her hair had been pulled back into a ponytail. One ear was hooked up to an MP3 player, and a mobile phone was glued to the other. She neither saw nor heard Ellie come in. She was crying, but that didn't stop her legs smoothly pounding away the miles.

Beyond the treadmill were other machines, the purpose of which Ellie did not like to think about. The thought of subjecting her own comfortable body to their horrors filled her with a strong desire to be elsewhere.

Where was the power switch? Ah. On the wall. The room hadn't been cleaned since . . . since. Dust. Fingerprint dust. Dirty footprints on the floor.

Ellie was surprised that Angelika could use the equipment so soon after her stepdaughter's death, but as her career as a model depended on keeping her splendid body in trim, she'd probably managed to override any squeamish feelings she might have about using the machine. A beautifully tuned body. Would she have done better not to have 'improved' her breasts? Perhaps she wasn't tall enough to be a catwalk model, so had had to settle for swimsuits and underwear?

Ellie's eyes roved the room. Fiona must have spun off and crashed headlong into that wall . . . there. Ugh. The stains were still on the wall and the floor beneath.

'What . . .!' Angelika realized someone was in the room. She pulled the wire from one ear and spoke into the phone. 'Call you back later. Promise.' And to Ellie, 'Who are you? Oh. I remember. What are you doing here? We've only just got rid of the police. More questions. As if we knew anything!

The press have started to buzz around, and there's some nutter on the phone, keeps ringing. As if we haven't enough to cope with, arranging the funerals and letting people know. They say we can't have the bodies yet, which is totally ridiculous, but Evan will sort it out.'

'Don't mind me,' said Ellie, extra cheerful. 'I just popped in to see if I could help out for a while. I've brought my cleaner with me and set her to work straight away.'

Angelika stopped the machine and stepped off on to the floor, swiping the backs of her hands across her eyes. 'I double-locked the front door myself. How did you get in?'

'Freya let us in.'

'Oh. We had a reporter pounding on the front door, earlier. Evan sent him off with a flea in his ear.' She'd worked up a fine film of sweat. She reached for a towel on a stool nearby and said, 'I'm going for a shower.'

'Are you all right?'

'No business of yours, but if you must know . . .' Her face creased in anguish. 'The agency has cancelled the job in Japan! They said it wouldn't look right, so soon after Abigail . . . The magazine is getting someone else.'

'I can see why you'd welcome the work, it would be a distraction, but—'

Angelika flapped the towel at Ellie. 'You don't understand anything! I can't get away soon enough. I thought . . . And now what am I going to do?' She plunged through the door back to the kitchen, drew up short on seeing Vera, said, 'Who the hell are you?' Didn't wait for a reply, but banged through the door to the hall and away.

Ellie turned the main power switch on the wall to the 'Off' position.

Now, suppose the teenaged Fiona had not been alone in the gym on the day she died. She might have known . . . whoever it was, and let them in. Or they might have thrust their way into the gym after her. In those days Fiona probably hadn't bothered to lock the door after her. Why should she?

So, let's recreate the scene.

Fiona comes in, turns on the power at the wall. Switches on the treadmill. Steps on to it and turns up the speed. The police theory was that she turned it up high in order to give herself an ultra fast workout. The speed was too much for her, she tried to jump off, which ought not to have been difficult, but instead . . . Perhaps she caught her heel, swivelled round, got stuck in some way? Then spun off and . . .

Was that realistic?

How did the speedometer work? Ellie bent over the machine. It looked as if you pressed a button and kept your finger on it, to make the track run faster.

Suppose there'd been another person there, either invited in by Fiona or uninvited.

Wait a minute. Would the girl have continued to work away on the treadmill with a stranger present? Wouldn't she have switched it off and stepped away to deal with – whoever it was?

Most likely she knew – whoever it was.

If so, he or she might have been standing by the treadmill and turned the speedometer up themselves.

What was to stop Fiona turning it back down again?

Well, suppose that another hand had been placed firmly over the button? A hand belonging to someone who was too strong to be shoved out of the way.

Then the spin off. Ms Milburn had said something about Fiona being helped on her way with a boot to her rear end. Ugh. She'd have crashed into the wall, head first. She might have lived after such an incident, but she hadn't.

The killer hadn't touched anything, except for the speedo button, which he – or she – then wiped clean of all prints, his or hers. He or she hadn't bothered to turn off the treadmill at the machine, or at the wall, before leaving.

Ellie shuddered. Man or woman?

Unknown. It might have been a school friend of Fiona's, perhaps? Mm. Wanting to have a turn on the treadmill and getting into a spat with Fiona over it? Then a pettish action, a depression on the button which turned up the speed on the treadmill, and a refusal to let it be turned down.

Possibly. But would a school friend have kicked Fiona in the rear? Not likely. No.

The conservatory was filled with light, though the day had

become dull. White muslin blinds – very expensive – were draped from rods across the ceiling, to reduce the glare on sunny days. It would be a pleasant place to sit and relax. Ellie imagined comfortable chairs, a low table or two. A rank of ferns here, a stand of geraniums there, perhaps a palm or two in big tubs?

She wondered what would happen to all the expensive gym equipment when Angelika moved out. She wondered how long it had taken Angelika to work out that she was in danger so long as she stayed in the house. Or perhaps even after she'd left it? After all, the second wife had departed years ago but had still met an early death.

Someone was pounding on the front door knocker and ringing the bell. Another telephone was ringing somewhere in the depths of the house.

Ellie went back into the kitchen, where Vera was making headway against chaos. She'd already set the dishwasher to work.

Flash!

A man's head appeared at one of the kitchen windows, and another flash half blinded Ellie. 'What the . . .!'

Vera blenched. Someone was crashing around in the garden, making their way round the kitchen . . . and there were French windows at the end, leading on to the garden.

'Vera, pull the blinds down! I'll see if the French windows are locked.'

Vera, hands slopping soapsuds, said, 'Who is it? Reporters?' She pulled the blinds down in front of her while Ellie checked the French windows. The doors were locked, so she pulled the blinds down . . . and then did the same to the last window on the other side.

They stood still, listening. Someone was still moving around outside. They could hear the crackle of footsteps on a gravel pathway.

Ellie decided not to go back into the conservatory. Anyone in there would be exposed to view.

The key to the conservatory door from the kitchen was in the lock, and she turned it.

Someone was still pounding on the front door and ringing

the bell. A telephone continued to ring. Not the one in the hall. Another one.

Vera dried her wet hands, which were shaking. 'Mrs Quicke, this isn't very nice, is it?'

'Agreed. Let's find Mr Hooper.'

Back in the hall, the pounding on the front door continued. Vera was breathing hard, but didn't lose her nerve. 'I threw up the window in the snug. I'd better attend to it.' She disappeared into that room.

Ellie hesitated. Should they go right round the house, making sure that all the doors were locked, pulling down blinds, drawing curtains? She tried to laugh. This was ridiculous. It felt as if they were under siege. She replaced the phone in the hall on its receiver, and it rang again.

She picked it up. Heavy breathing.

Feeling slightly hysterical, she said, 'Harrods. What department do you want?'

The man – she was pretty sure it was a man – put the phone down. Before it could ring again, Ellie dialled nine nine nine. Then thought it would have been more sensible to call Ms Milburn. But that number was in her handbag, and she'd put it down somewhere. The phone went on ringing in another room. *Come on, come on!*

Vera came out of the snug. Her colour had risen, but she had herself well in hand. 'I've shut the window and pulled the curtains across, but there's two of them with cameras trampling all over the garden. They saw me and must have thought I was one of the Hoopers, because they took my photo and started calling me, asking me for a quote. What do we do, Mrs Quicke?'

'Can you find my handbag? I've put it down somewhere . . .'

At last someone answered the phone. 'What service do you require? Fire, police or ambulance?'

'Police, please.' More ring tones.

A stir at the back of the hall, and Evan Hooper hove into sight. 'Who's pounding on the door! This is a disgrace!' He spluttered with fury. 'Call the police!'

'What do you think I'm doing?'

Vera tugged on Ellie's arm. 'You're wearing your handbag.'

Of course. How silly of her. Still holding on to the phone, she delved into her bag with her free hand, looking for the card with Ms Milburn's number on it.

More shouting at the front door. Camera flashes. A girl screamed.

Freya, returning from her run?

Ellie dropped the phone. 'Freya! We must let her in.'

Vera had the wits to pick up the phone Ellie had dropped. 'Yes, yes; I'm holding. Mrs Quicke, did you dial nine nine nine, or one oh one, because that's the new number for the police.'

'Heavens, is it? I can't think.'

Angelika appeared at the top of the stairs, towelling her hair dry. 'What's going on?'

'Reporters back and front,' said Ellie. 'Vera, you keep trying to get the police. Evan, help me get Freya inside.'

He gaped. 'What? Hadn't we better wait till the police get here?'

Useless man. 'Angelika, can you help?'

Angelika dropped the towel and ran down the stairs as Ellie fought to master the catch which opened the front door.

Vera attempted to help them, but the cord on the telephone wouldn't stretch far enough. 'Bother! Yes, I'm still holding . . . but hurry!'

'One, two, three . . .!' Ellie found the trick of the latch and opened the door just wide enough for Angelika to pull Freya inside. Flashbulbs went off. Freya crumpled to the floor. A turmoil of voices, all yelling for attention.

Ellie and Angelika pushed the door to. Angelika dropped the catch and, with hands that shook, manoeuvred the chain into place.

Vera's voice wobbled. 'The phone's just gone dead. Do you think someone's cut the line?'

There was a crash. A window breaking at the back of the house? In the conservatory? The door from the conservatory into the kitchen was locked, but how long would that hold them?

Surely the press wasn't supposed to break into people's houses?

Ellie said, in a voice she tried to keep steady, 'If the land-line's cut, we can use a mobile.'

Vera searched her pockets. 'I'm all fingers and thumbs.'

'Oh!' Freya was in tears, hair escaping from her plait, red marks on her upper arm.

Evan tottered around, waving a cut-glass tumbler. Drinking, at this hour of the day? 'This is preposterous! What do we pay the police for?'

Angelika was ashen, but still controlled. 'Shall I take Freya upstairs?'

Vera had her mobile out, but was looking at her watch. 'I'm going to try the one oh one number, which I'm pretty sure is just for the police. Perhaps we can get straight through.'

'I thought it was still nine nine nine for emergencies.'

'I think I'm through. Hello? Is that the police? Yes, non emergency? At least, it really is an emergency but . . . Yes, I'll hold, but . . . Mrs Quicke, I'm sorry, I know it sounds ridiculous but I'll have to go in a minute to get Mikey his lunch. Did you say you had a different number to call?'

Ellie helped Freya to her feet. 'It's in my bag. I'll find it in a minute.'

Freya was trembling, trying to brush herself down. 'What's going on? Why are they doing this to us? This man kept taking my photo, accusing me . . . yelling at me. Then another of them caught my arm . . .!'

'Come upstairs where they can't get at us,' said Angelika, helping Freya along.

Ellie detained Angelika for a moment. 'Pack a small bag. Each. Now!'

'What?' said Angelika. Her eyes widened. She nodded. 'Right.'

The pounding on the front door hadn't ceased, nor the ringing of the doorbell.

Ellie scrabbled in her handbag to find Ms Milburn's number and her own mobile. Found them both. Punched numbers.

Ring ring. Ring ring. Ring ring. *Pick up, pick up!*

Vera was still holding on to her own mobile, not yet through to anyone. 'Mrs Quicke, they're keeping me on hold!'

Ellie said, 'Hang on, Vera! Hang on!'

Evan picked up the landline phone and didn't seem to understand that the line was dead. He said, 'Hello?' into it at intervals.

Vera got through. 'Police? Thank God. We're under siege at the Hooper house. My name? Vera Pryce. Where do I live? What's that got to do with it? I'm at the Hooper house . . . What's the address? I don't know. Mrs Quicke, what's the address here?'

Ellie didn't know, either. 'Tell them the Inspector knows. He was round here this morning.'

Vera repeated that into her phone. 'Yes, there are reporters, men with cameras, all round the house, all over the garden. They tried to prevent his daughter getting in. It's quite frightening. How quickly can you get here?'

The phone quacked.

Vera looked at Ellie. 'They say that if it's an emergency, we should dial nine nine nine! Are they joking?'

Ellie took the phone off Vera. 'Ask Ms Milburn; she'll confirm that this is an emergency. Get here! Fast! Or there'll be more blood shed!' She clicked off Vera's phone and handed it back.

She killed the call she'd been trying to make on her own phone and rang another well-known number. 'Manor Cabs? Mrs Quicke here. I need a big car for four or five people and some luggage, urgently, to the Hooper house. No, I don't know the exact address but it's not far from my own place. Can you look it up? Bless you. Can you get here in ten minutes' time exactly? There are some nasty men threatening the women here, and I have to get them away to safety.'

The phone quacked. 'That is our Mrs Ellie Quicke speaking?'

'Yes; you recognize my mobile phone number, don't you? Three ladies, one man and myself. We've rung the police, but I don't know how long they're going to take. Yes, I know they can take ages. We're all rather frightened, so . . . Perhaps you could send two of your men in one of the larger cabs . . .?'

'You are in danger? I send two men, no?'

'Brilliant. Can you make sure we're not followed?'

'I will arrange. Trust me. Ten minutes.'

Ellie turned her phone off. Now, what next?

Evan was still barking into a dead phone, still waiting to get through to the police. 'Hello! Hello!'

Ellie tried to attract his attention. 'Evan, I think we should abandon ship, don't you? I've got a cab coming to take us all somewhere safe where we can think what to do next. Just till the police can get rid of the press. Right?'

'What . . .?' He put his hand over the phone to give her a moment of his attention.

'We can't stay here. The girls are frightened. I've ordered a car to fetch us. You too.'

'What! Don't be ridiculous! I'm going to speak to the Chief Constable about this.' He turned back to shout into the phone. 'Come on, come on! This is a disgrace! I've never been so . . .'

Ellie collected Vera with a glance. Together they hurried up the stairs, to find Angelika and Freya rushing around in their different bedrooms, both in tears, neither capable of packing in a sensible manner.

'Rucksack?' Vera to Freya.

'Suitcase!' Ellie to Angelika.

Vera said, 'Toilet things,' and pushed the girl into her bathroom.

Ellie swept all the toiletries off Angelika's table into a large plastic bag and thrust it into her suitcase. 'Night things. Underwear.'

Vera shouted, 'Shoes! Where do you keep . . .?'

Ellie relieved Angelika of an armful of evening clothes. 'No, you don't need those now. Sweaters, jeans . . .'

Vera unplugged Freya's laptop. 'Homework? Books . . .?'

'Address book. Mobile phone and charger . . .'

Angelika shrieked, 'My portfolio!'

'Handbag. A warm jacket?'

'Is this your favourite coat? What about some boots?'

'Your teddy bear? Yes, of course.'

'Time's up!'

'Credit cards, keys?'

Panting, Ellie and Vera took hold of the bulging suitcase and rucksack and steered the two girls, one carrying her portfolio, an evening dress and two large designer handbags and the other her teddy bear and a tote bag, down the stairs.

Evan had at last realized the landline was dead and was now on his mobile. The cords stood out on his neck. His colour was poor. 'If you don't get me the Chief Inspector immediately . . .!'

Another phone rang. Ellie's mobile phone. Best answer it. It might be the police.

Diana.

'Not now, Diana,' said Ellie, juggling luggage and the phone. 'I'll ring you as soon as we're safely away.'

'What!'

Ellie shut off the phone, dropped it into her pocket. Looking at her watch. 'When I say the word, we open the door and go straight out and into the car that will be waiting outside. Don't stop to answer questions. Just go for it.'

Angelika whimpered. She was just about holding it together.

Freya pulled on Evan's arm. 'Dad! Come with us.'

He flapped his hand at her. 'Can't you see I'm on the phone?'

Angelika was disintegrating. 'Oh God! Oh God!'

Ellie unhooked the chain on the door, opened it a crack.

No sign of the cavalry. What were they to do if the cab didn't come for them?

There was a loud bang, an explosive bang, at the back of the house.

The door from the conservatory into the kitchen? Once they got through that, there'd be nothing to stop them surging all over the house.

The shouts increased in volume as the press realized the front door was no longer fast shut.

Ellie turned on Freya. 'Is there any other way out?'

Freya gasped. 'Only at the back of the house!'

At last a large people carrier nosed its way up the drive and pulled up slowly, very slowly, outside the front door, scattering the members of the press. Two large Asian men were inside. One got out, opening the passenger door wide.

'Now!' said Ellie, opening the door to push Angelika and Freya out. One of the handbags slipped from Angelika's grasp and skittered across the floor. She was in tears, let it go.

Vera thrust Angelika's suitcase at one of the large cab drivers, who fielded it and flung it into the back of the car. Ellie followed with the rucksack, which was whisked away from her in the same way. She pulled the front door of the house to behind her.

Someone pushed a camera right into her face, but one of the drivers thrust him aside. Ellie found herself picked up and deposited into the car, breathless but unharmed.

'Fasten your seat belts, ladies!'

The door slammed. More flashes. All the women ducked, including Ellie.

Would the reporters have a car handy, to follow them? Yes, one of them was already running for the road . . .

ELEVEN

Monday noon

Everyone inside the car was shaken, breathing hard.

'Oh, my good lord!' Vera's voice wobbled. She attempted a laugh. 'Do you realize I'm supposed to pick Mikey up in ten minutes?'

Ellie tried to think. 'Can you get him on your mobile, say you're having an adventure and could he have lunch wherever he is and you'll pick him up later?'

'An adventure!' Angelika broke into hysterical laughter.

Freya managed a pale smile, clutching her teddy bear.

'Check!' The big man in the passenger seat up front was on his mobile. 'It will be taking us five minutes, no more.'

'Where are we going?' asked Vera, texting away on her mobile.

'We take you to safe place,' said the larger of the two cab drivers. 'It is being owned by my cousin. He is knowing you are coming and is preparing nice takeaway food for you. He will take you through his restaurant and out to the back, where his brother-in-law is waiting for you with another car. We ourselves will be parking at the front outside the restaurant for an hour at least, telling those pesky reporters that we are waiting there for you to finish your lunch.'

Angelika leaned back in her seat with a sob, closing her eyes. 'This is not happening.'

Freya shivered. Reaction. 'Oh. Oh.'

Vera looked out of the back window. 'They're following us. A car, and a scooter.'

The driver put his foot on the brake as they approached some lights . . . and then shot forward as they turned to red. Executing a right turn, they lost the car . . . but not the scooter.

Ellie hadn't managed to fasten her seat belt, nor had Angelika. Both fell forward off their seats and regained them with difficulty.

'Why is this happening?' said Angelika. 'Why us? Why me?'

'Why Abigail?' said Ellie.

Vera's phone beeped. A text. 'Mikey hasn't enough money to stay for lunch. What shall I do?'

'Tell him . . .' Ellie improvised. 'Tell him that when we've dropped the girls off, the driver will take you on to pick him up.'

'Where are we going?' Angelika was on the verge of tears.

The driver called out, 'Ready to go? I am double-parking outside my cousin's place, and see . . . he is waiting for you!'

'Out, out, out!' cried his co-driver. He thrust the big doors back and in one swift movement pulled Angelika out into the road. Angelika dropped her other handbag, but before she could pick it up, Freya jumped out after her, only to be fielded by the restaurant owner, who rushed her into the safety of the foyer. Angelika wailed as Vera leaped down into the road, picked up the dropped bag and followed them, but Ellie struggled to get out . . . The step was so high . . . She couldn't . . . And then she was picked up and deposited inside the door of the restaurant by . . . someone . . .

A dimly-lit restaurant, spices in the air.

'This way, this way! Come!'

Through to the back, past customers looking somewhat surprised, down a flight of stairs, and up another . . .

'Where . . .?'

Through a kitchen, shining and clean . . . and out into the open, grey sky above, a sprinkling of rain in her face, and . . .

'Hup!' Someone was pushing and lifting her into another people carrier, scented with Indian food. Ellie sprawled forward into a seat as the car door slammed behind her and the driver – a different driver – moved off down a narrow lane between the back of shops and a high wall and turned right into a quiet street. And picked up speed.

Angelika wept.

Freya barked out a laugh, eyes wide. Half frightened, half elated to have escaped.

Vera read out another text. 'Mikey wants to know how long I'm going to be. They're shutting the place up.'

'Where to, missus?' The driver.

Ellie tried to think straight. 'Freya, which hotel would you like to go to?'

Freya blinked. 'Hotel?' Freya didn't seem capable of making any decisions.

Angelika leaned back in her seat, eyes closed, cheeks wet with tears. Angelika wasn't going to be any help, either.

'Driver, drop us off at my place; you know the address? After that, we can think what's best to be done.'

Vera added, 'The driver can take me on to pick Mikey up, right?'

'Right.'

Everyone was quiet. Ellie eased her seat belt on. Vera had done hers up. The others hadn't bothered.

No one seemed to be following them.

They turned into the drive and decanted before Ellie's front door. She found her key and let them into the house. Peace and quiet. At last.

Except that there was a rumble of voices from Thomas's study.

Oh. Rethink. Ellie had assumed he'd be free and able to help her. He'd said something about a meeting, but surely it wasn't today? Was it? Which meant he *wouldn't* be able to help her sort this lot out.

Vera got the luggage inside. The driver insisted on adding some brown paper bags which contained the promised takeaway food. Ellie didn't think she could face curry at that moment, but thanked the driver profusely.

Angelika subsided on to the hall chair, still clutching an evening dress and a handbag. Her portfolio slid to the floor, and she let it go.

Freya got as far as the stairs and sat, dropping everything except her teddy bear. She lowered her head to her knees.

'Tea, I think,' said Ellie, trying to think straight. 'Then you'll want to freshen up.'

Rose. Where was Rose when she was needed?

Ellie said, 'Stay here,' to the girls and hurried down the corridor into the kitchen. No Rose. But the television was on in Rose's bed-sitting-room next door. Rose, telly on, was fast asleep in her big armchair.

Of course. Rose always had a nap after lunch. She needed it.

Ellie could have done with a nap at that moment, too. Vera appeared, looking over Ellie's shoulder. Ellie hesitated. Should she wake Rose?

No. Rose needed that time to herself and wouldn't be much use if she was woken before she'd had a good rest. Ellie closed the door on her.

Vera said, 'Do you want me to stay and help for a bit?'

'I'd love it, but what about Mikey?'

They returned to the hall, where nothing had changed, except that the cab driver was hovering. 'Is this all right, missus? Want me to take someone on elsewhere?'

Ellie straightened up with an effort. 'You drivers have been wonderful, all of you. I don't know how we'd have got away without you. I'll ring the office later and tell them how much I appreciate what you've done. I don't think we need anything more now. At least . . . Vera, you'll need to collect Mikey, so take the car on and—'

Vera was the only one who still appeared capable of making decisions. 'You can't cope on your own, Mrs Quicke. If the car could collect Mikey – I can text him the number of the car so he doesn't get into the wrong one – he'll be as good as gold if you let him have the run of the computer in your office. Then I can help you sort this lot out.'

'Bless you, my dear. Brilliant idea. Driver, can you cope? Vera will give you the details.'

'Of course.'

Vera filled the driver in while Ellie sagged, leaning against the wall. What to do next? However was she going to get this lot sorted out? If Thomas were free, he could advise her, but . . . No, she couldn't interrupt when he was working.

Freya lifted her head, tears on her cheeks. 'What about Dad?'

Angelika put both her hands to her head. 'We did ask him to come with us. Why was he so stubborn?'

Freya was bewildered. 'I don't understand. I went out for a run, and they caught me on my way back, shouting at me, wanting to know if it was me or Angelika who'd killed Abigail. How could they think that?'

Angelika shuddered. 'I was so frightened! Reporters aren't supposed to break into houses, are they?'

No, they weren't. Ellie opened the door to the downstairs cloakroom. 'I'm sure you'd like to freshen up, both of you. Angelika, would you like to go first? Freya; there's a shower and toilet next to the kitchen that you can use. Through that door there.'

Freya got to her feet and staggered. Held on to the newel post. Steadied. 'What about Dad?'

'I'll ring the police, find out what's going on,' said Ellie, guiding Freya through the door. 'When you've both finished, come into the sitting room – that's the room at the back here. We'll have a cup of tea and work out what to do next.'

'I'll make some tea as soon as I've sent this text,' said Vera, closing the front door behind the driver.

Ellie fell into the big chair in the sitting room.

Silence.

She felt her eyelids droop.

She jerked awake. She struggled to take her handbag off, and searched for Ms Milburn's telephone number. Tried it once more.

It went to voicemail. Ellie couldn't think what she wanted to say. Made an effort. 'Ellie Quicke here. I've got the Hooper girls. They're worried sick. Please, ring me.'

She snapped the phone off. Angelika was right. Surely reporters were not supposed to break into houses? They could doorstep people, even follow them, photograph them. But break in? Yet she'd heard someone break a pane of glass to get into the conservatory, hadn't she?

Which reminded her. She tried ringing Evan Hooper's home number. Foolish, really. If it worked, he would either be on the phone, or it would be off the hook. But the line was dead, still. Which meant either that there'd been a convenient fault in the line or someone had cut it.

Angelika wafted in, looking pale and willowy, carrying her remaining oversized handbag. Face freshly made up. Hair brushed out into a shining fall. She looked good enough to put in front of a camera, just as she was, but the whites of her eyes were showing. If she were a horse, she'd be about to bolt. 'Where are we? Is this your house, Mrs Quicke?'

A nod.

'Not Diana's?'

'No, Diana doesn't live here.' Ellie remembered that she'd promised to ring Diana. Well, she'd do it later.

'I don't understand why the police didn't come to protect us.'

'There was some confusion about the number we rang. I expect they got there just after we left.'

Freya came in, still clutching her teddy bear. She was clean and fairly tidy, but bruises were setting on her cheek and upper arm. 'They kept asking which of us had killed Abigail!' She shuddered. Sat down. Stared at the floor.

'I don't understand anything.' Angelika, a whine entering her voice. 'Why didn't Evan stop them?'

Vera carried in a tray of tea things. 'There's some portions of curry, if anyone would like one, but I thought we'd like some tea to start with.'

Angelika said, 'I don't eat curry.'

Freya closed her eyes and slowly slipped sideways in her chair. Stirred. Muttered something. Made as if to sit up. Subsided. Asleep, still clutching her teddy bear.

'Best thing for her,' said Vera, distributing cups of tea to the others.

Angelika rummaged in her handbag. 'I can't believe it. I can't manage without them! Someone will have to go back for them for me.'

'What's that?' asked Vera.

'My hair extensions. I can't go out on a shoot without them. They were in the bathroom.'

'Soon,' soothed Ellie, thinking Angelika had got her priorities wrong. Perhaps she always did get her priorities wrong. Career versus child. Career versus husband.

Angelika wept, loudly. 'Why did you drag me away? It's all your fault. You've made me leave my beautiful home and all my lovely clothes, and my new make-up box, and I'm sure the police would have been round in a minute and stopped those horrid men making such a racket. It's all your fault!'

Ellie took a deep breath and let it out again. Yes, put like that, she'd acted hastily.

Angelika was working herself up to a first-class tantrum. 'And my car. Why didn't you let me bring my car? I could have brought away ever so much more of my things if you'd only let me bring my car.'

Vera murmured, 'Oh dear,' and picked Ellie's cup up for a refill.

Ellie conceded, painfully, that she'd overlooked Angelika's car. It hadn't even crossed her mind to ask about a car. 'I'm sorry. Yes, you're right.'

Angelika's mouth turned ugly. 'You rushed me away without giving me time to think, when it was all quite unnecessary. I'm sure the reporters didn't mean us any harm. They'd have asked a question or two and the police would have turned them out, and . . . goodness knows what Evan will be thinking, when we left him all alone to cope!'

Ellie recognized the truth in what Angelika was saying. She couldn't think now why she had felt it was essential to get the two girls away. Angelika was right, and she should have got the girls to lock themselves into their bedrooms and wait to be rescued.

'You panicked!' said Angelika. 'And now look at the mess we're in!'

'Nonsense.' Vera wasn't having any of this. 'Behave yourself, Angelika!'

The blonde turned on her. 'How dare you! Who are you, anyway? And why are you here?'

'Stop it, both of you,' said Ellie, tiredly. 'You'll wake Freya.'

'What do I care about Freya!' Angelika took refuge in another rush of tears.

Ellie took out her mobile phone again. 'Hush, now. Let's see if we can find out what's happened. If the reporters have gone, I'll organize a car to take you back straight away.'

'I should think so, too!'

Ellie's mobile rang under her hand.

Diana. 'What's going on, Mother? Here I am, trying to hold the fort while you can't even be bothered to talk to me, when I specifically asked you to—'

'Have you been in touch with Evan?'

'What? What do you mean? Has the whole world gone mad? Of course I've been in touch with him. Or rather, I tried to reach him on his mobile, only he's not picking up.'

'Oh dear.' Sinking feeling.

'I'm wondering if he's been taken ill—'

'Diana, get off the phone. Now!'

Ellie cut her daughter off. Waited for a count of five, and was looking out Ms Milburn's phone number when her mobile rang again. This time it was the very person she most wanted to speak to. Ms Milburn herself. 'Mrs Quicke, where are you?'

'At home. My home.'

'Do you have the Hooper women with you?'

'Yes. We—'

'We're coming over, right away.'

'Yes, but what about Evan?' The phone went dead.

Slowly, Ellie dialled the Hooper landline. With the same result. Dead. 'Angelika, do you know your husband's mobile phone number?'

Angelika stared. Scrabbled in her handbag. 'It's on my mobile.'

Ellie's phone rang again.

Diana. 'Mother, what the—'

'The police are coming round here. Now. Perhaps they can tell us what's happening.'

'This is ridiculous. Where's Evan?'

'That's what we'd like to know.'

Pause for thought. 'Who is "we"?'

'Evan's wife and daughter. They're safe here with me. Evan

stayed behind, and I can't get through to him. I think the phone line has been cut.'

'What do you mean, "safe"?'

'They were being hounded by reporters, who broke into the house. We got away just in time. Evan refused to budge.'

'You're being ridiculous. Reporters don't break into houses. I'd better get over there.' She disconnected.

Angelika said, 'And . . .?' She produced her own mobile.

'Try Evan. Diana said he didn't pick up when she dialled.'

Angelika tried it. 'It's gone to voicemail.'

'The police are on their way over. Perhaps they know what's happening.'

The front doorbell rang. Steadily. A murmur of voices in the hall. Thomas, showing his visitor out. Thomas would let the police in when they arrived.

At least, Ellie hoped it was only the police and not reporters. She didn't feel up to dealing with either. She looked at Vera, who nodded and removed herself. A chatter of voices in the hall.

Vera put her head round the door. 'Mikey's just arrived and wants his lunch. He'll have curry and like it. So will I. Anyone else want some?'

Ellie shook her head and then changed her mind. 'Not curry, but there's some home-made soup in the freezer, Vera. I expect Thomas would like some, too, though he might like a curry; yes, he probably would. Anyone else fancy a curry? No? How about a ham or cheese sandwich?'

Vera disappeared, and the doorbell rang again. Ellie hauled herself to her feet and beat Thomas to the door.

'Ellie, my love?' Thomas, reading glasses high on his forehead, looking puzzled. 'What's Vera doing here? And her boy, who—'

'I'll explain in a minute. I think this may be the police.'

It was. Ms Milburn. Hurray.

Plus – oh dear! – the inspector with the sticking out ears, which turned bright red whenever he was stressed. Ellie had nicknamed him 'Ears' when he was rude to her at their first meeting, and the nickname had stuck, which hadn't endeared her to him. No.

She ushered her visitors in, telling herself that she really must find out what the inspector's real name was, as a matter of courtesy, and write it down somewhere, so she didn't forget.

His ears were already burning scarlet. Oh dear. This interview was going to be difficult, wasn't it?

'Do come in. You know my husband, don't you? Mrs Hooper and Freya are in the sitting room, both very anxious to know what's happening. Is Mr Hooper all right?'

'Don't give me that!' Ears was in fine form. 'Which one of you did it, eh?'

Ellie opened her eyes wide. 'Did what, precisely?'

Thomas moved to stand at her side. 'Would someone like to fill me in?'

'Yes, of course.' Ellie gestured to the sitting room. 'Come on in, all of you. Take a seat. But first, the girls are in great distress. Is Mr Hooper all right?'

'As if you didn't know!' Ears was really angry, a sheen of perspiration on his forehead.

'Why, what's happened?' Ellie looked to Ms Milburn, as being the more sensible of the two.

Ears strode into the sitting room and pulled up short at the sight of Angelika, prettily laid out on a chair near the window. Angelika tried on a pale smile, specially for him. It didn't hurt that she'd chosen a chair near a table with a vase of autumn flowers on it. What a pretty picture she made . . . if you didn't realize she'd moved to that chair on purpose.

Ears recovered himself, went to sit on a chair nearby, found it occupied by the sleeping Freya, and transferred himself to the settee. 'Mrs Quicke, this is not the first time you've interfered in one of my cases, but I sincerely hope it will be the last. I believe my colleague here warned you specifically to keep your nose out of it. But no, you turn up here, you shove in there, you waste police time by making alarmist phone calls, and finally, you whisk away not one but both of the witnesses to a murder case.'

'Murder!' Angelika, hand to where she, mistakenly, believed her heart to be.

'Murder?' Ellie looked at Ms Milburn. 'Not Evan, too?'

'No, no. But he is in hospital.'

Angelika shrieked and fell back, sobbing wildly. 'Evan, oh! Not Evan!' She held out her hand towards Ears, and he caught hold of it. Embarrassed, he didn't seem to know whether to throw it away, or pat it. Angelika turned tear-filled eyes towards him. 'My husband! Oh, please tell me it's not true!'

Ellie reflected that Angelika could certainly lay it on, especially where an impressionable man was concerned.

Not everyone was taken in. Ms Milburn looked down her nose. Thomas stroked his beard. Neither of them seemed amused by Angelika's histrionics.

Freya stirred in her sleep, murmuring something indistinct. She made a convulsive movement, clutched her teddy bear more tightly and gradually came back to consciousness. 'Dad?' She struggled to sit upright. 'What's happened? Who are . . . are you police? Is Dad all right?'

'Yes, yes,' said Ms Milburn, in soothing tones. 'He's in hospital. He fell, got a knock on the head.'

Angelika and Freya looked bewildered.

'How?'

'He fell?'

Ears disentangled himself from Angelika. 'So, which of you did it?'

TWELVE

Monday afternoon

'He was perfectly all right when we left,' said Ellie. 'Irate, but upright.'

The two girls nodded. 'On his mobile—'

'Trying to get the Chief Constable.'

Vera pushed open the door to bring in a tray containing mugs of soup and a small mountain of sandwiches. She took one look at the police and said, 'Shall I fetch some more plates? Or how about some curry? We've enough to feed the five thousand.'

Ellie reached for some soup and a sandwich. 'Vera was with me all morning. She can vouch for the fact that Evan Hooper was perfectly all right when we left.'

'And who is "Vera", pray?' said Ears.

'That's me.' Vera dished out plates and mugs.

Ellie warmed her hands on her mug. 'Vera used to clean for me but doesn't do that any more. She came with me today as a favour, to try to sort out the mess in the Hooper household. But when we got there—'

Thomas took the tray from Vera and set it down. 'Far be it from me to interfere, but do you think you could start from the beginning?'

'I don't know where the beginning is,' said Ellie. She sipped from her mug and almost burned her mouth. Aaargh. Just what she needed. She took a second sandwich. 'Bless you, Vera.'

Ms Milburn flourished her pad. 'Start with your involvement this morning. I called in on the Hoopers at ten fifteen to take statements relating to the death of the second Mrs Hooper.'

'Fern.' Angelika nodded. 'Silly name. Silly woman.' She took a mug of soup, too, but declined a sandwich.

Freya reddened. 'I hadn't seen Mummy in ages. I wish I'd been nicer to her. She couldn't help the way she was. That was how she was brought up, free living, and all that. She used to try to make me understand, to be more like her, but I guess there's too much of my dad in me to . . . But Fiona loved to visit her.'

'Yes, yes,' said Ms Milburn, anxious to get on. 'So what happened after I left you?'

'I suppose it wasn't long after you'd gone, maybe half an hour or so, that a man came to the door, a reporter wanting to talk to us. Dad sent him off, sharpish. Dad went to his study as he was going to work from home this morning, so when the phone in the hall started ringing again, I picked it up. First it was a reporter asking if I was the mother of the murdered child. I was so shocked, I think I laughed. Anyway, I put the phone down and it rang again and this time . . . ugh . . . I've never had an obscene phone call before.'

Vera pushed a mug of soup into Freya's hand. Freya looked at it, but made no move to drink it.

'Was it a man or a woman, and what did he or she say?'

Freya reddened. 'A man, I think. Nasty. Asking what it felt like to have killed your only child. Had I enjoyed it, that sort of thing? Going on to say what he'd like to do to me. Ugh. I went to tell Dad, and he said to take the phone off the hook and he'd report it to the police. He said perhaps we'd have to get our number made ex-directory or something. So I took the phone off the hook. Then I got ready for my morning run.'

She took a sip of the soup, then gulped it down greedily.

'Why didn't you exercise in the gym?'

'I never do. Angelika doesn't like anyone but her to use it. She made an exception for Fiona but I wasn't going to beg her for it, and anyway, I prefer to run in the open air. I was just leaving when Mrs Quicke and Vera arrived and I let them in.'

Vera pushed the sandwiches in Freya's direction again. She took two and started to wolf them down. A fraction more colour returned to her face.

'Over to you, Mrs Quicke,' said Ms Milburn, taking notes.

Ellie was on her third sandwich. 'My daughter Diana had asked me to get some domestic help to clean up at the Hoopers. I was visiting Vera this morning . . .' Should she explain about the Pryce family connection? No, probably not. 'So we went along together to see what needed to be done. We saw two men and a woman, I think it was, talking to some people in the street outside the house. I suppose they were reporters, but they didn't see us turn into the drive and didn't try to stop us getting into the house. Freya let us in as she was just on her way out. She told us they'd been bothered by a reporter earlier, but that Evan had sent him off.

'The house was in a right mess. The phone was off the hook in the hall. I put it back on and yes, there was an obscene phone call, so I left the phone off the hook. Vera started work in the kitchen. I found Angelika in the gym, and we talked a bit. She went upstairs to have a shower, and suddenly everything went haywire. Someone – a reporter? One, or maybe two – was in the garden and started taking photographs of us through the kitchen windows. It was more than a bit scary. Is there another sandwich, or a drop more soup, perhaps?'

'Actually in the garden? I don't believe it.' That was Ears.

Vera collected empty mugs. 'It's true, though. I'll get seconds.'

'Oh,' said Angelika, meltingly beautiful as she gazed at Ears. 'It was terrifying. I was so frightened!'

Ellie recollected that Angelika had been upstairs at that time, but said nothing. She continued, 'That's when Freya started to bang on the front door and to ring the bell, trying to get back in. There were reporters right round her, but we got her in somehow—'

'How many? Describe them.'

'I don't know.' Ellie looked at the others for help.

Freya said, 'They were all round me, shouting. Three or four? Terrifying. One of them grabbed my arm.' She rubbed it, where the bruise was beginning to colour up. 'Ouch! They wanted me to say, to confirm . . . I couldn't take it in. They were taking photos, snap, snap, non-stop. They seemed to think I was Abigail's mother and that I'd . . . that I'd killed her!' Her voice shook.

'Going out for a run was foolhardy in the extreme,' said Ears. 'Naturally, they thought you were making yourself available for questioning.'

There were tears in Freya's eyes. 'I didn't realize.' She brushed crumbs from herself. Looked for another sandwich.

Ears was censorious. 'You should all have stayed inside and shut the doors.'

'Until they broke in?' said Ellie. 'What ought we to have done then?'

'Dialled nine nine nine.'

'We tried that and got cut off. The line went dead. Then we tried one oh one which is the new number, and we argued about whether it was for non-emergency use only but we did get through to someone, and when you're in a difficult situation you don't always remember things like the number for the police being changed. I tried to raise Ms Milburn on my mobile but she wasn't available, and when Vera did get through to one oh one, the operator told her to try the other number.'

'There really wasn't any reason for you to call the police. Reporters don't behave the way you've described.'

Ellie nodded. 'That's what I thought, too. It's disturbing, isn't it? We heard a window smash at the back of the house and assumed someone had broken into the conservatory. I'd locked the door that leads from the conservatory into the kitchen, and after a while we could hear someone trying to break through that. I knew that once they were into the kitchen, there was no means of keeping them out of the rest of the house. We thought they were going to be on us at any minute.'

Freya nodded. 'I was so frightened.'

'I got my minicab people to send a car for us; we grabbed a few things and left. Evan was in the hall, trying to get through to the Chief Constable on his mobile. We asked him to come with us, but he wouldn't.'

'Pig obstinate. He abandoned us to our fate!' Angelika fixed large blue eyes on Ears. Blue eyes? Ellie did a double take. Her eyes had been green yesterday, hadn't they? Coloured contact lenses?

'I'm worried about Dad,' said Freya. 'We shouldn't have left him. Is he all right?'

Ears pointed at her. 'You pushed him over, perhaps, trying to get him to leave with you?'

'Don't be silly,' said Freya, exhaustion overruling the need for politeness.

Ellie said, 'We got out just in time. Some of the reporters followed us, but we managed to get away from them, and came here. So what's happened to Evan?'

Ms Milburn checked with her boss, and he nodded for her to continue. 'Two constables attended your one oh one call. They found three reporters sitting outside the front door. They said they knew someone was inside the house but that no one was answering the door. They denied threatening behaviour, said they'd not overstepped the mark in any way.

'The constables went round to the back of the house, found the glass door into the conservatory had been smashed in. The door from the conservatory into the kitchen had been broken open, too. There was no one in the house except for Mr Hooper, who was lying on the floor in the hall. He was unconscious, but beginning to come round. His foot was tangled in the handle of a large leather handbag, which someone had care-lessly left on the floor—'

'My Gucci bag!' cried Angelika. 'I wondered where I'd dropped it.'

'Indeed,' said Ears, with a sour look. 'It seems obvious that

Mr Hooper tripped over the bag and hit his head on the edge of the hall table as he fell.'

'He's all right?' A pale Freya.

Vera returned with refilled mugs of soup. Also a tin of biscuits. Ellie grabbed the soup. The first helping had hardly touched the sides as it went down.

Ms Milburn said, 'He seemed confused, not sure what was happening. The constables called an ambulance and removed Mr Hooper to hospital where they suspect concussion. They'll probably keep him in overnight.'

'A storm in a teacup,' said Ears. 'A waste of police time. You women get hysterical at the slightest opportunity. A couple of reporters exceed their brief, and you scream blue murder and run away. The only damage done is to Mr Hooper, who trips over a carelessly dropped bag and gives himself a head-ache. You ought to be thoroughly ashamed of yourselves.'

Thomas was forking curry into his mouth at speed. 'And the smashed doors?'

Ears had an answer for everything. 'There was, apparently, a young cub reporter who left the premises before we arrived. It seems she may have taken her desire to get an exclusive too far. When she started to go round the house—'

'She?' said Ellie. 'Are you sure it was a "she"?'

'Of course I'm sure.' His ears, which had been fading to pale pink, flushed to deep rose. 'When she started to go round the house, the other reporters told her to be careful, but she wouldn't listen. They didn't hear her break in—'

'No, they wouldn't, if they were at the front of the house.'

'They didn't see her leave, either. She'd disappeared before we arrived. I imagine the insurance will cover the damage. So ends the tale of the molehill which you women turned into a mountain. I should charge you all with wasting police time. Hah!'

'So,' said Ellie, 'who cut the phone line? And why?'

'What?' Ears didn't want to hear anything to disturb his neat reconstruction of events.

'We were on the landline phone, waiting to get through to the police, and the line went dead. So, who cut the phone line? The missing girl reporter?'

Ears looked as if he were going to strangle himself. 'What, what? Now you're being ridiculous, trying to make something out of nothing, in order to talk yourselves out of trouble. If there did happen to be a reporter who disappeared before we got there, then presumably she had got her scoop and left, so—'

He stopped in mid-tirade, for DC Milburn had frowned and murmured something about a back exit.

Freya clutched her teddy bear, even more tightly. 'There's a gate at the end of the back garden which leads into an alleyway. It comes out into the next road. It's rather overgrown because we don't use it any more. She could have got out that way.'

Ears turned on her. 'So you've remembered her now, have you? You can describe her in detail? Perhaps she was one of the reporters who clustered round you when you came back from your run?'

Freya blenched, hugging her bear close to her face, but didn't give ground. 'I can't say. It was all so confusing. On my way back from my run I turned into the drive, and I didn't see anyone between me and the door, and then someone shouted—'

'Man or woman?'

'Man. I think. Shouted, "There she is!" and they were all round me, yelling at me. I think one of them tried to trip me up, but . . .' She shook her head. 'I panicked, I suppose. Tried to sidestep one that got in front of me. Someone caught my arm just here . . .' She rubbed her upper arm again. 'I don't think I could tell you what any of them looked like. It was all a blur. And then I realized I'd forgotten my front door key. I usually keep it in this tiny pocket here.' She indicated a pocket in her running shorts, and flushed. 'Oh. It *is* there. I was trying to fish it out and couldn't find it, so I rang the bell, and they all crowded round me in the porch. It was frightening.'

'Well,' said Ears. 'That seems to wind it up satisfactorily. I gave the reporters a good talking to, and they'll keep their distance from now on. You ladies can return home as soon as you like.'

'Except,' said Thomas, with narrowed eyes, 'for a cut telephone line and a couple of smashed doors. Is the back of the house still open to all comers?'

Ears was anxious to get away. 'I expect you can arrange for someone to board over the door into the conservatory.'

Freya managed to get to her feet. 'I think I'd better get to the hospital first. See if Dad's all right.' She was still very pale, her hair had come loose, and her running shorts and top were stained and rumpled. She looked a mess beside the immaculate Angelika, but Ellie knew which of the girls she admired. And it wasn't Angelika.

Angelika had been trying to raise someone on her mobile phone, but realized this was a cue for faithful wifey to show willing, too. 'I'll come with you. Then we can take him back home with us. And –' with a dark look at Ellie – 'return all our belongings that we were forced to bring away with us.'

'Splendid,' said Ears, accessing his mobile. 'Now, I've rather more important matters to deal with, if you don't mind.'

He set off for the door, and Thomas followed. 'Let me show you out.'

DC Milburn lingered for a word with Ellie. 'You really think the phone line was cut? I'll have a look in the morning.'

Ellie murmured, 'I'm not sure it's safe for them to return. Will there be someone on duty outside the house tonight, particularly if we can't get the smashed door boarded over in time?'

DC Milburn clucked her tongue. 'Maybe. I'll try. But we're short-handed.'

She disappeared after her boss.

Thomas returned, looking thoughtful. 'Ladies, may I offer you a lift to the hospital?'

Angelika put her hand on his arm and lifted her face, a flower turning to the sun. 'Oh, that would be so kind of you. After all the trouble your wife has caused us.'

Thomas blinked, but nobly endured the caress. 'I was thinking we might be able to do something about the broken door, too. Ellie . . .?'

Ellie's mobile rang. 'It is just possible that it's already been attended to.' She lifted the phone to her ear. 'Yes, Diana. I was hoping it was you.'

'Mother, do you have any idea what's going on? I couldn't get any reply from Evan's landline or his mobile, so I went over there to find reporters camped out on his doorstep, who said that the police have taken him away and—'

'They found him lying unconscious in the hall and—'

'The reporters said his daughter or his wife had knocked him out and fled!'

'Absolute nonsense. I told you, they're here with me, but about to visit Evan in the hospital.'

'Which hospital?'

'Come to think of it, I don't know. I'll have to ring around and—'

'Don't disturb yourself. I'm on to it. Did you know the house had been broken into and was open to the elements? I've sent someone down to board the door over. I'm surprised the reporters haven't already been through the house taking photographs and looking into any paperwork they can find.'

'The police had words with them. They'll be on their best behaviour from now on.'

'They've got a nerve! They wanted to know what relation I am to the family. I told them to mind their own business.'

'Did you go in your own car? They can check the licence plate and soon find out who you are and what you mean to the family.'

Silence. The phone clicked off.

Ellie reported, 'Diana's getting the broken door boarded over and going to the hospital as soon as she finds out which one Evan's been taken to.'

Vera collected empty plates and mugs. 'Accident and Emergency. Around here, it'll be Ealing Hospital for sure.'

Thomas started to chivvy Angelika and Freya out into the hall, urging them to gather up their belongings. Vera hovered, sending quick glances in Ellie's direction. Why?

Ellie narrowed her eyes at Vera. 'Something's wrong. What is it? Is Rose all right?'

'Yes, but she woke up feeling a bit dizzy.'

Ellie was alarmed. 'It's her labyrinthitis. I'd better—'

Vera was soothing. 'I found her pills, and she took one. I told her to take it easy. Look, I can stay on here for a bit and sort out something for supper while you're away. You won't mind if Mikey gets on your computer, will you?'

Ellie had forgotten all about Mikey. 'That's fine, so long as he doesn't alter any of my settings. Thank you, Vera. Much appreciated.'

Thomas appeared in the doorway, holding up his car keys. 'Are you ready, Ellie?'

'Coming.'

Angelika and Freya were outside, laden with their belongings, waiting for instructions.

Thomas said, 'Luggage in the boot, ladies. Ellie goes in front with me, girls in the back.'

Angelika wasn't happy about this. 'Oh, but—'

Thomas gave her a look. She stowed her things in the boot and got in the back with Freya.

Ellie got in the front, and Thomas patted her knee as he turned the key in the ignition. 'We may have a job getting through. Rush hour. Ellie, why don't you ring the hospital while we're on our way, check that Evan is actually there?'

'I was just thinking that myself,' said Angelika, who then received a phone call on her own mobile and retreated into a mumbling silence. Ellie and Thomas exchanged fleeting glances. Angelika was on the phone to a man, by the sound of it. And his name appeared to be 'Joey-my-love'. Ellie hoped it was her agent.

The traffic on the Uxbridge road was as heavy as Thomas had predicted. The hospital confirmed that a Mr Hooper had indeed been brought in by the police, so Ellie sat back to think about cut telephone lines and back alleys and broken doors. She tried to fit pieces of the jigsaw together and failed. Some time ago she'd thought she knew the answer to the problems afflicting the Hooper family, and now she didn't.

She thought the police were taking the affair much too lightly. She didn't like the idea of the girls going back into that house. Not at all. Yet, what could she do about it?

The hospital car park was full. More than full. Overflowing. They'd been talking about building a multi-storey car park for years, but hadn't got round to it yet.

Thomas drew up outside the entrance to the Accident &
Emergency department, where he was not supposed to park.
'Out you get, girls. I'll take the car back up the hill, find a
parking space in a side road and sit there till you give me
a ring on my mobile. Allow ten minutes for me to get back
to collect you, right?'

Freya stalked into the reception area, looking more like a
battered victim than a survivor. But then, Freya *was* a survivor.
Angelika floated in, collecting admiring glances as she went.
Ellie followed, checking that she had her mobile in her right-
hand pocket and had turned it off after the last call . . . which
she hadn't. Oh dear. All this technology. Though it was useful,
she had to admit.

They found Evan on a hospital bed in one of the bays, with
a nurse taking his blood pressure.

'You lot took your time!' Resentful, slurring his words.

'We were worried,' said Freya, meaning it. Taking his hand.

'We were worried sick,' said Angelika, trying to mean it.
She leaned over to give him a kiss, which he accepted without
pleasure.

Ellie asked the nurse, 'Is he ready to go home with us?'

The nurse looked startled. 'But his wife . . .!' She looked
around. 'She's just gone to fetch a drink.'

'Ah,' said Ellie. Diana had got here already? Of course. 'It's
always a problem when a man's between marriages, so to
speak. That's his daughter there, and his current wife is the
one this side of the bed. They have the right to know what's
happening to him, don't they?'

The nurse drew herself up to her full five foot two. 'You'd
better ask at the desk.'

Ellie went to the desk and waited for someone to be free
to speak to her. A big black man was wheeled in with a cut
on his leg, bawling that he wanted something for the pain, the
big crybaby. An elderly woman on a trolley was waiting
patiently, linked up to various bottles of fluid. Now and again
she gave a little sob. No crybaby she.

A small boy wandered around, getting under people's feet.
His nappy needed changing. His mother was in one of the
cubicles, kept calling him back to her.

Ellie sent up an arrow prayer. *Dear Lord, this isn't really the seventh circle of hell, but it does seem like it. So much misery. So much pain. And now . . . whatever am I supposed to do about Evan and his women?*

Diana appeared, bearing a cardboard container of what looked like plain water. 'You here, Mother? I suppose you brought the encumbrances, knowing you.'

'Yes, dear. But which of you has the best right to be here, I do not know.'

'I got here first and have registered that I'm his wife. He's still confused. Concussion, they think. They want to give him a brain scan, and after that we'll have to wait for the results. He'll probably be kept in overnight. I shall stay with him, naturally. Or at least until he's sent up to one of the wards. So you might as well take the others home.'

'I'd much prefer to do that, dear; but I'm not sure the others would agree.'

Privately, Ellie thought the two girls wouldn't keep up their vigil for very long. They were both worn out. Indeed, after an hour of sitting and waiting, glaring at Diana – who seemed oblivious – and trying to talk to a man who kept closing his eyes and drifting off to sleep, Angelika and Freya began to realize they were fighting a losing battle.

Nurses kept coming and waking Evan up, flashing lights into his eyes. Each time, he was sick. Definitely concussion.

Finally, he was wheeled away for a brain scan.

Ellie checked the time on her watch. How long would Thomas be able to wait for them? Perhaps he could go home, and they could call him when they were ready to leave? Then there was Rose, who was not having a good day. And what about Vera? She couldn't be asked to wait for them indefinitely. And little Mikey?

'I must ring home,' said Ellie.

'I'm staying,' said Diana, who looked as fresh as when they'd first seen her. 'Why don't the rest of you go home?' An ironic smile. 'I promise to let you know when he's discharged.'

'I suppose so,' said Freya.

Angelika nodded. Ellie wondered if they'd eaten anything

at all that day, apart from the soup and sandwiches they'd had at her house. She wondered if there were any curry left . . . not that she fancied it at the moment.

Freya yawned. The skin around her eyes looked brown. Angelika drooped. They were not allowed to use their mobile phones inside the hospital, so 'Joey-my-love' couldn't contact her, or she him.

Ellie went outside to phone Thomas. 'Evan's just gone up for a brain scan. Are you all right?'

'Mm. Working on my notes for the conference.'

Ah, of course. She'd forgotten he was going away for a couple of days later in the week. 'I've no idea how long we're going to be. Vera's wonderful, saying she'd stay with Rose till we got back, but goodness knows when that'll be.'

'If you can get some indication, I could go home and relieve Vera. Then you could phone me when you need to be picked up.'

'Or I could get a cab to collect us.'

'True. But I've got all the girls' luggage in the back.'

'I'll ring you again in five minutes.'

Ellie checked back with the desk. The nurse said she had no idea whether or not Evan would be able to go home soon. A doctor chanced by, and Ellie managed to catch his attention. He nodded, talked in a low voice to the nurse behind the desk, and said it all depended on the results of the brain scan but, from what the nurse had said, it was unlikely that Mr Hooper would be discharged that night.

Ellie relayed this information to the girls. 'I'm staying,' said Diana, baring her teeth in a smile.

The two girls looked at Ellie with dull eyes, too tired to protest.

Ellie said, 'The hospital can let us know when he's ready to be discharged.'

She went outside again, to phone Thomas. Ambulances were drawing up outside, all the time, for there'd been some ruckus or other in the town centre. The department was going to be busy that evening. 'Dear Thomas; please come and collect us.'

'Get yourselves to the main entrance of the hospital. I can stop there for a minute to pick you up.'

Ellie shepherded the girls through the corridors and round to the main entrance where, thankfully, Thomas was waiting for them in his car.

Angelika and Freya lolled in the back, exhausted. Ellie used her mobile again, this time to Vera.

'We're just leaving the hospital, Vera. We'll drop the girls off at their house and come on home. How are you coping? How is Rose?'

'She says she's all right, but she's anxious, wants to know where you are and when you'll be back. If you're not going to be that long, I'll wait here till you return.'

'How about Mikey?'

'Happy as Larry. I hope you don't mind, but he's in the library, rearranging all the books.'

'Fine. No one reads those books, anyway. See you in a minute.'

The roads were still busy though the rush hour was over. It was getting dark.

Thomas turned into the Hoopers' quiet road. Quiet no longer.

The sky was alight. Red.

A roaring sound.

Mouths agape.

Fire engines. One in the road, another in the driveway of the Hooper house.

The Hooper house was on fire.

THIRTEEN

Monday evening

They got out of the car. And stared.

Angelika put her hands to her face and swayed. Was she going to faint?

Freya, eyes wide, mouthed the word, 'No!' She clutched her teddy bear even more closely.

Ellie put her arms around Freya and tried to turn her away

from the sight of her burning home. The girl resisted. She had to see what was happening.

Fire roared up into the dusk from the 'snug' at the front of the house and from the hall . . . and from the room to the left of the hall. The dining room, was it? The whole of the ground floor was ablaze. The upper floors were dark and looked all right. For the moment.

'My car! I must get my car out of the garage!' Angelika started forward, only to be caught by a reporter's camera with a flash. Three of them were lurking just inside the gate. She dodged them only to be trapped by a fireman. 'Hold on, lady!'

She struggled in his arms. 'My car!'

Freya whispered, 'This can't be happening!'

Thomas collected Angelika from the arms of the fireman. 'It's these ladies' home. Can you tell us—?'

'It's pretty bad, squire. Can you take them away? We're expecting a third engine any minute.'

There was a huge explosion from the far left of the house, where the garage was situated. Everyone felt the blast and recoiled.

'My car,' whispered Angelika and, eyelids fluttering, knees bending, hung from Thomas's arms in a faint.

Freya stated, 'This'll kill Dad. He loves his Lexus.' She wasn't weeping. Beyond it.

The fireman was agitated. 'Can you move your car; please, sir!'

Now they could hear another fire engine coming; lights pulsing, siren screaming.

Angelika moaned, returning to life. She tried to stand by herself. Thomas supported her. He said, 'Ellie?'

Ellie tried to speak and failed. She jerked her head towards their car and opened the back door to thrust Freya inside. Thomas picked Angelika up and pushed her in, too. Ellie got into the front. Thomas got into the driver's seat, and he drove off as the third engine turned into the Hooper's driveway.

'Home,' said Ellie, trying to think what was best to do.

Thomas set his teeth and concentrated on driving. Curious sightseers, neighbours, and assorted passing cars had stopped to gape and clog up the traffic.

'Not far,' he said. 'You'd better phone Rose or Vera. Tell them we're all on our way back.'

Ellie got through to Vera and relayed the information. Vera said she'd cope. Ellie shut off her phone. 'I had a teddy bear as a child. I wore out its voice and my mother had it replaced. A Merrythought? Merry-something. Not a Steiff. Not a valuable bear, but comforting. Did you have a teddy bear, Thomas?'

'A monkey. Blue. Both my children had teddy bears, though. And the grandkids.'

'We did give one to Diana, but it came to a bad end.'

'What did she do to it?'

'Put it on the bonfire. I really don't know why. Perhaps because we couldn't afford a Steiff and she rejected second-best?'

The car turned into their road.

Ellie said, 'I'm not making much sense, am I?'

'You are making perfect sense, my love. We hang on to things we love in times of stress.'

'Yes, but you don't need your monkey nowadays. You hang on to Jesus.'

'So do you.'

Ellie thought, but didn't say, that she wasn't sure her hold on Him was strong at times like this. Perhaps He was still holding on to her, though? A comforting thought.

Thomas helped her out of the car as Vera opened the front door to greet them. Thank God for Vera.

But, what about Rose? 'Is Rose all right?'

'She's resting. Don't worry about anything.' Vera helped the two girls into the house, and between them, they unloaded their belongings and put them in the hall.

Ellie said, 'Vera, I think we'll have to let the girls stay here tonight. You'll want to get back home—'

'Not till you're straight. You look as if you're about to fall down. Angelika goes in the spare room, right? That's it. Come along now, duckie. Up the stairs we go.'

Vera started up the stairs, half carrying Angelika, while toting her suitcase as if it were made of feathers.

Thomas picked up Freya's rucksack. 'In little Frank's room?'

'Thank you,' said Freya, remembering her manners. 'You're

very kind.' She was on autopilot. Her eyes were open, but she didn't seem to know how to climb the stairs when she got to them.

Ellie gave Freya a push and got her setting one foot in front of the other and so, step by step, into Frank's room. Freya was staring ahead, seeing nothing. Or seeing her home being destroyed by fire?

Ellie guided Freya to the bed and sat her down on it. The bed there was always left made up for little Frank's visits. Ellie sat beside Freya and put her arm round the girl's shoulders.

Freya was stiff, unresponsive. 'I'll be all right. You don't need to worry about me.'

'You're a little soldier. The bathroom's next door but one, along the corridor. Come down when you fancy something to eat.' Ellie left the girl there.

Vera was bustling around with an armful of sheets and towels.

Ellie said, 'I can do that.'

Vera shook her head. 'You leave it to me. I'll sort them.'

Ellie went down the stairs, slowly. She could hear the murmur of Thomas's voice, talking on the phone. She stood in the hall, not knowing what to do next. She let the quiet of the house settle around her.

Dear Lord, thank you. I can't begin to see how we get out of this tangle, but thank you. I don't know why I felt it so important to get the girls out of there this morning . . . but you must have been on my case. I probably missed some clue or other. If they'd stayed, they might have died . . .

Fire . . .

She shuddered. Fire destroys so much.

It also cleanses. Gets rid of the rubbish. *Was there something in that house that needed to be destroyed? Something nasty that's behind all this death and destruction?*

A little brown mouse of a woman crept out of the kitchen. In the poor light Ellie couldn't be sure for a moment whether it were Rose, or Ellie's long dead Aunt Drusilla. They did look rather alike, and Rose had a confusing habit of referring to Miss Quicke as if she were still alive.

'You're safe, then,' said Rose. 'I was worried.' She looked up the stairs. 'But you've brought them here, which means that trouble will follow.'

'What else could I do?'

Rose shook her head. 'As Miss Quicke says, we'd better put in an extra spot of praying tonight. And –' in a livelier tone – 'you're never going to send that girl Vera home at this time of night, are you? She hates that dark old flat that she's been stuck in and, as for that young limb, Mikey, he's building walls with the books in the library. I don't suppose he's doing any harm. No one's had any of those old books off the shelves while I've been here, and so I told him.'

Ellie nodded. 'There's nothing he can spoil.'

'I made two lasagnes with Vera's help and I said that if she would like to have the big bed in my old room upstairs tonight she could do so, and Mikey could sleep with her, or if he's the restless type, which I think he probably is, then we'd put a mattress on the floor for him out of the way, because if I know one thing about boys of that age, it's that they like to raid the larder in the small hours, and goodness knows how we're going to make the milk go round for breakfast, though the milkman does deliver early. Dearie me; what am I doing, keeping you here talking when I can see you're fit to fall down at any minute? You go into the sitting room and I'll bring you a nice cuppa.'

Rose bustled off back to the kitchen, but Ellie, instead of going into the sitting room, went down the corridor to the library. She knew why.

Edgar Pryce had been worried about Mikey. Edgar Pryce had passed the buck to her, and she'd accepted it. So now it was her turn to see what was to be done with the boy.

She told herself Mikey wasn't going to do any damage in the library, and even if he did, it wouldn't matter. The room had hardly been touched since Ellie's aunt died. True, it was furnished with some nice antiques and the built-in shelves around the walls were filled with books collected by previous generations. Some of them might possibly be valuable.

Ellie opened the door to the library and heard a quick

slithering sound as something – somebody – slid out of sight. There was no small boy to be seen, but books had been taken off the shelves and left in piles on the floor. No, not piles, exactly. They'd been built up into low walls which enclosed a small space in the far corner. An empty space.

She hesitated. What was she supposed to do next? The boy couldn't do any harm if left alone in here, could he? In the old days he'd often been unmanageable, throwing tantrums at the drop of a hat, but Vera said he was a different person since he'd discovered computers.

One dark, intelligent eye surveyed her from the darkness in the kneehole of the desk. Ellie nodded to the eye. It vanished.

She said, 'We could do with a bit of light on the situation, couldn't we?' She could put the light on, reassure him, and then leave him in peace and quiet while she had her promised cup of tea. She clicked on the overhead light and hesitated. It was as if someone had spoken in her ear.

Talk to him.

She shook her head. She was tired. This was a boy with a lot of problems.

He's fatherless. Gifted. Edgar gave him a reason for living. He's lost Edgar. Edgar asked you to look after him. His mother is loving and giving but not up to his weight mentally. Vera says he's not eating properly. Think what that's going to mean when he has to go back to school next week. If he ignores school lunches, he'll be handed over to psychiatrists and everyone will think he's crazy and they'll point at him and make nasty remarks that he can hear and bully him. It will destroy him.

Talk to him.

I see where you're going with this. You want me to take him on. Which is ridiculous. Perhaps Thomas, who is probably on his wavelength . . .

Offer him what he needs. Security. Hope.

You're off your trolley! Why, if I took him in, think how upset little Frank would be. How jealous! No, no. Find someone else.

Talk to him.

She sighed and went to sit in one of the big armchairs. 'Talk to me,' she said.

No reply. No movement. Had she dreamed she'd seen him under the desk?

She leaned back in the chair, which meant her feet didn't touch the floor. Oh well. She could rest for a while, couldn't she?

She said, 'Edgar asked me to look out for you.'

A listening silence, but he didn't emerge.

She said, 'I'm not going anywhere.'

Still no sign of him. She began to think about the other problems she had. 'Oh dear. So much violence and hatred. Oh, not from you, Mikey. Your mother's a wonder. Loving and giving. Always helping other people. You've seen how she is. Strong. Never refuses a challenge. I'm not like that. Or at least, not when I'm this tired. I'm sorry if I startled you when I came in. The light's a bit bright. Do you want me to turn it off?'

No reply.

She said, 'This room isn't used much. Thomas . . . Do you remember Thomas? Big man, looks like a sailor . . .? He thinks some of these books might be quite valuable. I've never even looked to see what we've got. I like books, of course. I've always got books on the go from the library. But these sort of books . . . Do you think there's any market for them nowadays? We could sell them on eBay, I suppose. But I'm not brilliant on computers. It takes a special kind of mind, doesn't it? Your mother said you had it. Interesting. What do you want to do with yourself in life, I wonder?'

Still no reply, but Ellie thought the boy had settled himself more comfortably in his hiding place.

Ellie yawned and stretched. 'I seem to remember that the back of one of these chairs lets down to make a bed. Do you fancy sleeping here tonight, or is it too far away from your Mum, who I thought might like to sleep over in the room above where Rose is now?' The words were out and not to be taken back.

A long silence. Not even a clock ticked in this quiet room.

Upstairs . . . Ellie turned her head to see if she could hear sounds from above, but there was nothing. The doors were well built in this house. The corridor was long.

Suddenly, the boy stood before her. Watching her. Waiting.

His father must have been of North African descent, possibly Somali. He had a fine, handsome head and an elegant body. Intelligent. His nostrils pulsed as if he were testing her scent. Or was afraid.

'No need to be afraid of me,' she said.

He nodded. No need to be afraid of her.

'Upstairs,' she said, lifting her head, 'your mother is trying to help two young women who've had their house burned over their heads. They are confused, frightened. One of them I like very much. The other . . . Well, let's just say that I don't know her very well. Three members of their family have been killed in the last few weeks, and they don't know why. I don't, either. I could send them to a hotel, but I won't.'

His eyes were intent.

'The thing is, I think they're in danger. I think someone is trying to kill the whole family, one by one. But the police won't – or don't – believe me.' She tried to laugh. 'I shouldn't be talking to you like this. It's not your problem.'

The door whispered as Midge the cat pushed it open. He stalked in, curious to see who had invaded his territory. Mikey took a half step back, his breathing lighter, faster.

Vera had told Ellie once that Mikey had never had a pet. Perhaps he was afraid of the cat? Oh dear.

Ellie said, keeping her voice soft, 'Let Midge sniff at you. You can put out your hand to him, if you like. Let him sniff your scent. If he accepts you, you can stroke him. Tickle him under his chin.'

Mikey obeyed her. Intent. As curious as the cat.

Midge rubbed his head against Mikey's hand. Midge liked Mikey. Well, hurray. The cat was supposed to be a good judge of character, which meant he could work out in two seconds which members of the human race would feed him on demand. Or provide a lap to sit on.

Mikey smiled at Midge. Mikey liked Midge. Double hurray. Was Mikey a good judge of character, too? What would he make of Freya and Angelika?

Ellie thought that she ought by rights to send Vera and Mikey back home for the night to their own place. To that quiet, dark, dull flat. Which Vera didn't like. Nor Mikey. As if it mattered what a child of his age liked.

Hm. Well, it did matter. She said, 'You like it here?'

He nodded, not looking up, continuing to rub under Midge's chin.

'It's a big house.'

He nodded again, and she wondered how far he'd explored. Had he already discovered the small door which led to the upper storey, at present housing a selection of junk and the cold water tank? She mustn't forget this boy had a high IQ. Or so it was said.

Yes, she could feel the intensity of his mind, absorbing, tabulating, processing information. Not like Vera. Not at all.

Not really a lost sheep, either . . . unless fortune played him another scurvy trick and left him, not eating properly, living in a sink estate, attending a school with teachers who didn't recognize his potential.

Ellie sighed. 'Edgar wanted so much for you . . .'

The boy stilled, eyes narrowed, looking at her.

'You can be whatever you choose to be, Mikey. You can fight your way up and out, or sink back into mindless rages. Up to you. I'll help you, if you will allow me to do so.'

He wasn't sure. And why should he be?

Thomas pushed the door open. 'Oh, there you are. I've been on to the police about the fire. I can't contact Diana because she's still at the hospital and she can't use her mobile there. Freya says she's got to go back to the hospital after supper. Angelika says she's got to go back to see what can be saved from the house. Oh, and Vera says supper's ready.' He held out his hand to help Ellie up out of the chair and extended his free hand to Mikey. 'Are you hungry?'

Mikey gave that some consideration. He avoided Thomas's hand, but took hold of Ellie's skirt. Something to hold on to while the world whirled round about him?

Thomas held the door open for them. Ellie turned off the light. Mikey followed, holding fast to her skirt. Midge scented supper and brought up the rear.

Monday evening

London's burning, London's burning.

   Look yonder, look yonder.

   Fire, fire! Fire, fire!

   O let us not pour water.

   A wide smile. The house was burning merrily.

   It had been a setback to find the old man crashed out in the hall, his foot tangled in a handbag. Probably one belonging to that cow, Angelika.

   Oh, oh! What shame is here!

   Rage, rage; rage against the storm.

   Actually, that had been a bit of a facer. The old man should by rights have been awake and able to understand exactly what was happening to him. A pity, that.

   His mobile had been on the floor, so it had been a question whether or not to dial for an ambulance. But before any decision could be taken, there were voices. A couple of policemen had arrived to tramp around the house, find their way in through the smashed door in the conservatory and discover the old man laid out in the hall.

   Fortunately, there'd been time to vanish up the stairs and into the master bedroom. If they'd searched the house . . . but they didn't. From that vantage point every word could be heard, all their phone calls, their chitter chatter, their call for an ambulance.

   Apparently, the old man had been showing signs of returning consciousness when they found him. What a pity he hadn't come round sooner.

   Look on the bright side. He wasn't dead, and the Great Plan could still go ahead.

   The upper stories had been redecorated so many times, even the room in which . . . once . . . a long time ago but still vivid . . . Take a deep breath. Don't let it affect you. You've survived so far, and there was a reason for that. There was a task to perform.

   The girls' bedrooms showed signs of a hasty flight. As if they could escape vengeance! No matter how far they fled, they would be tracked down.

Plan C presented itself, and it was a goodie. Oh yes! When the old man woke up, he was going to find his supercalifragilistic house in flames.

Check the street from the bedroom windows. All was quiet outside. Some members of the press still lurked by the entrance to the road; been told to keep off private property, no doubt. Perhaps someone would come along soon to board over the broken door into the conservatory. Not that that mattered. There were plenty of other ways for someone who knew how to get out of the house.

A few minutes' search in the kitchen turned up a large bottle of cooking oil. Someone had drawn the curtains in the snug so no one could see in. Good. There'd been plenty of newspapers left lying around. Saturate the cushions, set alight to some newspapers, and . . . woosh! Wasn't all the upholstery supposed to be flame retardant nowadays? It just went to show what a cheapskate the old man had been, getting the old chairs and settees re-covered, instead of buying new.

The door from the conservatory to the garden had still not been boarded over. Out we go. Hide in the bushes at the end of the garden. Sit still. Wait.

The back of the house remained dark for a long time. But waiting was a pleasure when you were destroying something as vile as this.

And when the old man heard about it . . .

Ah, here came a couple of men carrying sheets of ply to nail over the smashed door to the conservatory. One said he could do with a pee. Go in the garden, why don't you? But no; he went inside . . . and came back in a hurry, pulling out his mobile phone. 'Fire!' he shouted.

The waiting was over. Nee-nah. Nee-nah. Fire engines.

Too late to save the house, hopefully. Stand up. Stretch. Sigh with pleasure at a job well done.

Now to find out where those two girls had gone.

FOURTEEN

Monday evening late

'Shall I serve?' Vera set steaming dishes of lasagne on the table in the kitchen, while Rose placed bowls of cabbage and peas between them, saying there'd been some phone calls but no doubt they could wait till everyone had eaten.

Freya had black rings around her eyes and looked exhausted, but she had changed into a T-shirt and jeans and brushed out her hair. She even managed to twitch a smile as she slid into a chair. 'I can't remember when I ate last. Do you think someone can lend me some money so I can get a cab to the hospital after supper?'

Angelika came in, snapping off her mobile phone. She'd changed too, and her hair shone like spun silk. 'I really don't fancy anything to eat. Perhaps a yogurt and some fruit?'

Thomas held out a chair for her. 'Carbohydrates are recommended for shock. You'll feel better when you've had something hot to eat.'

She seated herself. 'Do you always eat in the kitchen?'

'Unless we have company,' said Ellie, collapsing on to a chair. 'The dining room's out of commission at the moment.'

Freya seemed to have forgotten that she was a vegetarian and ate well.

Mikey took a stool at her side, his eyes on the food and his bottom lip jutting. Was he going to refuse to eat? Midge the cat managed to squeeze on to his chair, too.

Thomas brought them up to date. 'Freya, we'll ring the hospital after supper and find out how your father is doing. I don't think he needs to know about the fire yet, do you? Perhaps it wouldn't be a bad thing if they keep him in overnight, or he'd have to go to a hotel. We'll ask if you're allowed to visit tonight, all right?'

Ellie remembered that Diana had announced her intention of staying at the hospital. For the first time – and with a feeling that she'd missed a step – Ellie remembered that Diana was pregnant, and that this possibly wasn't the best time for her to be looking after Evan. Ought she not to be resting? Mm.

Mikey was hoovering up his food. There was no other word for it. One moment his plate was full, and the next it was empty. Oh, good. Midge was licking his chops, too, so Mikey might have shared his food with the cat. Ellie had hardly started on her plateful. Vera ladled some more on to her son's plate without comment. Yes, it was best not to praise Mikey for eating up his plateful. Treat it as if his behaviour was normal.

Angelika was pushing her food around her plate, her fabulously blue – or were they green this evening? – eyes filling with tears. 'How can I eat while . . .!'

Thomas patted her arm. 'Do you good. Get as much down you as you can.'

She treated him to a soulful look. 'I should never have left.'

Her husband, or the house? Ellie had a bet with herself which it would be.

Thomas nodded. 'I'll take you round there in the car after supper and we'll see if they've got the fire under control.'

Really, it was a no-brainer to work out which was uppermost on Angelika's mind, was it?

Rose was picking at her food. 'You'll all be wanting hot baths, I expect. Miss Quicke says they're more relaxing than gin.'

Freya suspended operations with her fork, eyes rolling at Ellie for information.

Ellie tried to smile. 'My dear great aunt – she died a while ago – was a fount of useful information. Vera, do you have to go back to your flat tonight? Perhaps I can order a cab to take you back there so that you can collect some overnight things? Then you can have the bedroom at the top of the stairs here, the one that used to be Rose's. It has a bathroom next door.' A hand pressed Ellie's side. 'We can make up a bed for Mikey there, too.'

The pressure eased off. Mikey's plate was empty again. He

disappeared. One moment he and Midge were there, and the next they were gone.

'I'll get his sleeping bag,' said Vera, clearing plates. 'Then he can doss down where he likes. Only ice cream for afters, I'm afraid. Tomorrow we'll do better.'

'Tomorrow,' said Angelika, weeping. 'Oh, what's to become of me?'

'Well,' said Ellie, 'I think the best thing would be for me to find you a furnished flat somewhere nearby that you can move into for the time being. I'm sure the fire damage will have been covered by insurance, though the house probably won't be habitable for a bit. There'll be lots of stuff that you can rescue and put into store for the time being. That will give you time to sort out what you want to do.'

'It will have to be a big flat,' said Freya, perking up. 'So that Daddy can have his own bedroom and study. I can make do with any old space, but—'

'Who's going to housekeep for us?' demanded Angelika. 'We need a four bedroom house, with room for live-in staff.'

Vera and Rose turned away, stashing plates in the dishwasher. They were keeping out of this.

Thomas said, 'I expect the thing to do will be to look for a service flat somewhere for, perhaps, a week. By that time your father will be able to decide what he'd like to do.'

'Or a hotel,' said Angelika. 'I knew we shouldn't have left the house. If we'd still been there, there wouldn't have been a fire and we'd be perfectly all right now.' She looked at Ellie as if to say, 'It's all your fault.'

Ellie tried not to wince because it was true. In a way. On the other hand, the girls might have died in that awful fire.

Thomas came to her defence. 'We're between the devil and the deep blue sea here, aren't we? Let's hope the police catch whoever it was who broke into the house and frightened you all to death.'

Freya tried to smile. 'We're all still alive. Thanks to Ellie.'

Angelika shrugged. 'I suppose.'

Vera took off her apron – actually, it was one of Rose's aprons – and said, 'The sooner we're off, the sooner we get back.'

Rose said, 'Take my front door keys. You can get some more cut tomorrow.'

Mikey appeared. He nudged Ellie and handed her her handbag. Ellie smiled at him, and he grinned back. She took out her mobile phone, called the cab company and gave them their instructions.

Meanwhile Thomas had used his own mobile to get on to the hospital. 'I'm enquiring about Mr Evan Hooper who was brought into the Accident and Emergency department this afternoon. His daughter . . . Yes . . . Yes, I understand . . . Thank you.' He ended the call. 'Sorry, Freya. No visitors. He's being kept in overnight, and we're to ring again tomorrow morning.'

Ellie remembered that she'd promised to ring Diana. If she were still at the hospital she wouldn't be able to answer, but she tried her number anyway. Ring ring. To voicemail. Diana was still at the hospital. Oh dear. Something else to worry about.

Angelika stood up. 'I need someone to take me back to the house. Evan will be furious that we've just walked away and left it without making any effort to retrieve any of his things.'

Thomas pushed back his chair. 'I'll take you round there. Freya . . .?'

'Yes, I'll come; though I don't know what I can do to help.'

For some time Ellie had been conscious of a bell ringing. Someone's mobile?

Thomas exclaimed, 'The hall phone.' That broke up the supper party, but by the time Ellie reached the phone it had stopped ringing. There were messages left on the answerphone, but Ellie decided they could wait.

Vera and Mikey collected jackets while Rose found them a roll of black plastic bags to collect any belongings they needed to bring away that night. Freya hauled herself up by the banisters, saying she'd better collect a heavy sweater from her bedroom. Angelika remained at the bottom of the stairs and called after Freya to bring hers down as well. The hall phone rang again, and this time Thomas picked it up.

Ellie dithered. Should she go or stay?

The front doorbell rang, and she let in . . . Ears. Oh dear.

Thomas was still on the phone, but Ears didn't stand on ceremony.

'Well! All here, I see. Which of you did it?'

'Huh?'

'Set the fire. I suppose you thought the insurance would cover it.'

'What?' Ellie groped inside her head for an answer. 'You mean, the fire was set deliberately? Ah, of course.'

'What do you mean, "of course"?'

'It's all of a piece, isn't it? This vendetta against the Hoopers. Is the fire out?'

'How should I know?'

'Then why . . .?'

'You think you're so clever, whipping the only two witnesses away, but—'

Thomas said, 'Thank you,' into the phone and put it down. 'Now,' he said, folding his arms at Ears, 'to what do we owe the pleasure?'

Ears gaped but thought better of being rude to Thomas, who was bigger than him, often wore a dog collar under his beard and knew a lot of influential people. In a reasonably quiet tone, he managed, 'I am trying to get at the truth, and your wife doesn't make it any easier. Everywhere I turn, she's been there before—'

'It was the girl reporter, wasn't it?' said Ellie. 'Did you catch her?'

'Doing what?' A stare from Ears, impatient at being interrupted in his conversation with a rational being such as Thomas.

'She set the fire. Must have. It's the only thing that makes sense. It was she who broke into the house from the back—'

'Now, you don't know that.'

'Who else? You said yourself that normally reporters don't break into houses, but that there was this one cub reporter . . . Although I really don't understand about her, because I thought it was a man who was targeting the—'

'What man?'

Ellie blushed. 'I'm not sure. Just a guess. Better not say. Anyway, it looks now as if it were a woman, doesn't it?'

Ears turned away from her, cutting her out of the conversation, but Angelika fastened on to his arm. 'Please? You will help us, won't you?' Tears welled up in her beautiful eyes.

Ears softened. Ellie flicked a glance at Thomas, who flicked one back.

Thomas blew his nose. Was his cold getting worse? 'Inspector, it's getting late, and I'm sure you should have gone off duty hours ago. I'm just about to take the ladies over to the house, to see what the position is.' He spoke with authority, and Ears – like any other bully – backed down. 'You can come to take statements tomorrow morning, can't you?'

'Oh, very well,' said Ears. 'We can continue this in the morning. You will all make yourselves available for questioning, won't you?'

Nods. Smiles for the inspector from Angelika, who released his arm with reluctance. Freya pulled a strand of hair across her mouth and bit it. A childhood habit, perhaps? Where had she left her teddy bear?

The inspector departed. Angelika and Freya got into the back of Thomas's car; Ellie sat in the front.

Thomas said, 'That phone call was from my son. I missed my Skype date with him, so he rang to see if anything was wrong. I told him it was a temporary hiccup and we were looking forward to their arrival.'

Mm. Yes. Of course. Ellie's brain skittered between the availability of beds – or rather the non-availability of beds – and Betsey's promise to ring her that morning – had she done so? Was that one of the unanswered calls that Rose had spoken about? Then there was Diana's pregnancy; surely she ought not to be sitting up all night at the hospital? But what to do about it? And then . . . and then . . .

'It looks as if the fire's out,' said Angelika, peering at what could be seen of the Hooper house over the garden wall. Certainly, the night sky was dark. No flames leaped from windows, and only one fire engine was still in the driveway. Various shadowy figures lurked in the road; curious neighbours and, possibly, some members of the press?

Thomas parked the car on the opposite side of the road to the house and took the two girls across and into the drive, to talk to the firemen.

Ellie wandered along the road, not really thinking anything coherent except that she'd be underfoot if she tried to go with them. She clutched her arms, thinking it was going to be a chilly night. She came upon a group of four people: a man with a dog who was waiting patiently for him to resume their walk, two teenagers messing around on skateboards, and a man leaning against a motorbike. Ah, would the man with the motorbike be a member of the press, the one who chased after them when they'd fled the house in a cab earlier that day?

She stopped nearby, saying, 'What's happening, then?' And shivered. 'Chilly, isn't it?'

They turned to look at her. Harmless little old lady, out for a walk, good for a gossip. 'Do you know them?' asked Motorbike, indicating the Hooper house. The upper windows had blown out.

'Oh my. A fire engine,' said Ellie, knowing there'd been three at one time. 'What started it, do you know? An electrical fault, perhaps?'

'Gas explosion, I expect,' said the man with the dog. 'Usually is.'

'Nah,' said one of the teenagers. 'You'd see a wall blown out, if it were gas. Happened to my mum's neighbour, over beyond the Avenue. Whole front of the house, nothing left.'

'Neighbour, are you?' Motorbike to Ellie.

'Not far. Saw the sky all lit up earlier. Whose house is it?'

'Don't you know?' The motorbike lost interest in her.

The man with the dog pontificated. 'It's the super rich that's responsible for everything that's wrong with society today. Like him.' He gesticulated towards the Hooper house with the dog's lead. The dog, Ellie noticed, was sitting patiently on his foot. An elderly dog. Happy to rest when he could. Ellie had a fellow feeling.

The man with the dog continued, 'Filthy-rich folk attract nutters. It's a well-known fact.'

'This man was filthy rich?' said Ellie, wondering if she were overdoing the innocent bit. 'You knew him? Or her?'

'Not to say, exactly, "know". We bought our house from him, ten or fifteen years back. Estate agents.' He didn't spit, but looked as if he'd like to.

'Got a bad reputation?' asked Motorbike, interested.

'Not to say, exactly, "bad",' said the man with the dog, 'but there've been rumours.' He actually tapped the side of his nose.

'About . . .?' Motorbike.

The man with the dog said, 'She's a rich bitch, see?'

Motorbike nodded. 'Yeah, I could do with a word from her.'

One of the teenagers tipped his skateboard this way and that. 'The girl runs in the park, like, every day. Dedi-whatsit.'

'Dedicated?' said Ellie. 'And you?' To Motorbike.

'Press,' he said.

Which is what she'd surmised. 'There's a story here?'

He had sharp eyes. 'Could be. You know the family? Or where they might have gone?'

Ellie shrugged.

He lost interest in her as Skateboard said, 'That's one of the girls now, innit, gone in with a man with a beard. Who's he, when he's at home?'

The reporter paid attention, fast. 'I'll get them on the way out. There's one thing for sure, no one's going to sleep in that house tonight. Brrr.' He stamped his feet to keep the circulation going. 'I'll have a word with the firemen before I leave. They'll likely be here all night, watching to see there's no flare up.'

The man with the dog said, 'Envy leads to action, ten times out of ten. It'll be arson, mark my words.'

Ellie tried to seem bored. 'There's not much to see now, is there?'

Skateboard said, 'You shoulda seen it earlier. Reporters. Police. It was a riot.'

The other said, 'I wouldn't mind being a reporter when I leave school.'

'They've got women reporters too, now,' said Skateboard. 'Din't you see her? She was a cracker.'

Ellie blessed the boys. All she had to do was keep looking interested, and the information should pour out.

Motorbike's eyes sharpened again. 'I wouldn't mind knowing a bit more about her. You didn't happen to take a photo of her on your mobile, maybe?'

'Didn't think.' Feet shuffled. Skateboard slipped. He asked his friend, 'You?'

Motorbike said, 'I could maybe spring to a fiver.'

'Wish I had.'

'Why, what's she done?' Skateboard.

'A girl reporter, you say?' Ellie was wide-eyed. 'Whatever next!'

Motorbike was miffed. 'Plenty of them around, lady. Professional, I mean. But maybe this girl wasn't.'

'Go on,' said one of the lads. 'I heard she was really cool. Big and plenty up front, too, if you know what I mean.'

Motorbike nodded. 'If you can ask around, find me a photo, I might be interested.'

'Didn't you snap her?'

Motorbike looked embarrassed. 'She was going off half cock, yelling and screaming that she knew a way into the house. Someone followed her around, but not me. I know better than to be caught trespassing. We have to obey the law, you know.'

'What was she dressed like?' said Ellie, hoping she wasn't pushing too hard.

'Oh. You know. The usual. Jacket with pockets, jeans. Long hair, glasses. Lots of red lipstick. A voice to frighten the pigeons.'

'That'd turn me right off,' said Skateboard. The other nodded.

Ellie melted away into the darkness between the street lights. When she was far enough away, she took out her mobile and got through to Thomas.

He picked up straight away. 'Ellie, where are you?'

'Down the road a little way, back towards our house. Have you nearly finished?'

'About. The fire's out. The ground floor at the front is gutted. They had to pour water into the rest to stop the fire spreading, so they're wrecked, too. The firemen won't let anyone into the house, not even at the back, until they've checked that the building is safe, and that won't be done till tomorrow some-time. The firemen will stick around in case the fire breaks out again.'

'Are the girls all right?'

'Shocked. In tears. They need putting to bed with hot milk. I'll pick you up at the corner, shall I?'

'There's a reporter still hanging around, out front. With a motorbike. See if you can get one of the firemen to go out and talk to him, so that you can get away without him following you.'

Trust Thomas. In a little while he drew up in the car with the girls in the back, both drooping.

Ellie slid into the front seat and said, 'Can you drop the girls off at home and take me on to the hospital? I must have a quick word with Diana before I can relax.'

Neither of the girls spoke on the way home, or when they were extracted from the car and let into the house. Vera was there, welcoming them in, so Ellie felt they were in safe hands.

Thomas took Ellie on to the A & E entrance at the hospital, saying he'd drive round the block and be back to pick her up in ten minutes. Ellie waited her turn till someone on the reception desk was free to speak to her. Being a Monday night, not too many drunken accidents had been taking place and the place was comparatively quiet.

When it was her turn, Ellie asked the nurse if it were possible to speak with Diana. 'She's my daughter, you see, engaged to Evan Hooper, who was brought in earlier suffering from concussion. He's being kept in overnight. I don't suppose she'll complain, but she's pregnant and I'm worried about her maybe having to sit up in a chair overnight.'

A sympathetic nurse produced Diana, who was indeed looking tired.

'Mother? Why . . .?'

'Quickly, dear. Lots happening. Thomas and I have taken the girls back to sleep at our place, because . . .' Was Diana up to getting more bad news? 'The thing is that there were reporters all round the house today—'

'I know that.'

'One of them, a girl, they say . . . although . . . Anyway, a fire broke out after we all left—'

'Fire!'

Ellie guided Diana to a chair. 'Yes. It's quite bad. The

ground floor is gutted and the rest badly affected. They're keeping one of the fire engines there overnight, to make sure. It was probably arson.'

Diana slumped. Closed her eyes. 'What *is* going on?'

'The police would like to know that, too. It does look as if someone has got it in for the family, doesn't it?'

Diana kept her eyes closed for a moment longer. Then straightened up. 'Evan's very poorly. I don't think he needs to hear about this for a while.'

'Agreed. Freya wanted to come and sit with him, but she's exhausted.'

A flicker of a smile. 'I suppose she's the best of the bunch.' Diana hauled herself to her feet. 'I must get back to him. He frets if I don't hold his hand all the time.' Her head held high, she returned to her vigil.

The sympathetic nurse hovered. 'I'll make sure your daughter gets some rest once Mr Hooper is settled for the night. There's a bed we use for relatives.'

'Thank you.' Ellie went outside to wait for Thomas, who turned up within the minute.

'Home, now?'

'Home.'

FIFTEEN

Tuesday morning

T homas was an early riser. Ellie was not. She'd not slept well, worrying about her guests, and the series of deaths in the Hooper family, and Diana and . . . well, everything.

The alarm went off at the end of the seven o'clock news. Ellie heard Thomas groan and mutter as he got out of bed. By this time of the day he was usually up, dressed and in his quiet room, saying his morning prayers. But not today.

Ellie hunched herself under the duvet. The central heating

ticked. Oh? Was it really that cold outside? It had been a blustery, rainy night.

She sighed and struggled to sit up.

'Are you awake?' asked Thomas, which wasn't as silly a question as it sounded, for Ellie was on autopilot for the first hour in the morning. Her eyes would be open and she'd be dressed and preparing breakfast, but her brain wouldn't be engaged, so to speak.

'Urrgh.' A qualified 'yes'.

Thomas had showered and dressed. He smelt sweetly of good soap. He sat on the bed beside her and gave her a gentle kiss.

'Urrrm.' She loved his bearded kisses. She prised her eyes open. 'Urrgh?'

'Three-day seminar in Oxford, remember? I overslept. I won't bother with breakfast but I'll grab my notes and be off. I thought of cancelling, but . . .'

She shook her head. No, he mustn't cancel. The Hoopers should all be safe for at least one more day. No one except the police knew where the girls were, and a man had to do what a man had to do.

'I'll ring you twice a day. I'm booked to stay at a hotel; I'll leave the details in my study. If there's the slightest hint of trouble, I'll come back. Right?'

Brace up, Ellie! You'll manage.

He said, 'We can't throw them out.'

She shook her head.

He stroked her cheek. 'I see you as an angel with a flaming sword, protecting them from harm.'

The thought of her sixtyish self, rather more than plump and not particularly tall, brandishing a sword and, possibly, clad in shining armour, reduced her to giggles.

He laughed, too. 'Freya might be able to stay with a school friend.'

She shook her head. Her tongue was stiff. 'Half-term.'

'My family must go to a hotel when they arrive. I'll confirm today.'

She shook her head again. 'Betsey's going to work out something. Give it another day.'

He was dubious, but nodded. 'You'll ask Vera to move in?'

'If only we'd got the planning permission for a flat upstairs in time! I can't really ask her to bunk up with Mikey in that one small bedroom.'

'You'll think of something. I like Mikey. It will be an education having him around.'

She pulled herself up on the pillows. 'Yes, but they need their own place, and Vera ought to be going back to college or training for something.'

'You'll sort it.' Another kiss, this time on her forehead. 'Don't ring me, unless there's a disaster.' He dragged on his dog collar – formal wear, today – and reached for a jacket. 'Oh. One other thing. Would it help if I moved my study into the library? Give me more space. Then I could have my quiet room in the study, and that would give you another bedroom upstairs.'

She shot upright. 'That's your own special space. I told Betsey on no account was that room of yours to be disturbed.'

A grin. 'It doesn't take long for a room to be imprinted with prayers. Can you arrange it?'

She swung her legs out of bed. And groaned. 'What was the weather forecast? Is it going to rain again?'

He drew back the curtains. 'I wasn't paying attention. It looks all right. Wear your best, official, going-to-chair-a-meeting dress and your diamond rings. Throw your weight around.'

'Anything else?'

'Who do you think is responsible for what's been happening to the Hoopers?'

She reached for her dressing gown. 'I did have an idea about that; I thought it might be the unsatisfactory son, Philip. But it was a woman journalist who set all the alarm bells going yesterday, so now I haven't a clue.'

'Trust your judgement. Then test it.' With one more quick kiss, he left the room to start on his busy day – away from her.

Was it a good idea to ask searching questions at breakfast? Perhaps, because people were still muzzy from sleep at that time and might reply without thinking.

Angelika looked her usual immaculate self, but every now and then she frowned . . . and then massaged her forehead to smooth out any possible wrinkles.

Freya looked as if she'd lost weight.

Mikey had taken up his position at Ellie's side once more. His bright eyes observed everything.

Ellie and Vera cooked and served between them, while Rose fluttered around trying to find some herbal tea for Angelika who said she never drank tea or coffee.

Ellie threw the question out in a quiet, unthreatening voice. 'What about Philip?'

'Who?' Angelika looked blank. 'Oh, you mean *Philip*? Evan's eldest? Yes, of course. We ought to let him know what's happened.'

Freya shook her head. 'I suppose we ought, though I don't know what he can do. Dad has refused even to have him in the house recently, though he said he'd continue to pay Philip's bills.'

Angelika sipped herbal tea. 'I suppose he could drive us around. Evan says Philip's got a driving licence and some sort of van or car.'

'What precisely is wrong with him?' said Ellie.

'Dunno, exactly,' said Freya. 'He's a lot older than us. When Fiona and I were growing up we just accepted that he was a bit odd. He had his own nanny. She was supposed to be our nanny, too, but she always paid him far more attention than us. Then one day there was the most terrible row. We could hear Philip shouting and screaming from our bedrooms. Fiona and I wanted to see what was happening, but when Dad saw us hanging over the banisters, he sent us back to our rooms. After that Philip went away to boarding school and we had a different nanny. She was much nicer to us.'

'What was the row about?'

Freya shrugged. 'Dad said Philip had a problem with his nerves and that he'd be happier in a structured environment with people to look after him who would see that he took his medication. He did come back for the odd weekends in the holidays, but mostly he went off to camps and on study trips. Fiona thinks – thought – he was cool, and he is good-looking in a way. He drops in now and then to see us when Dad's not around, and occasionally he meets us in town for a snack.

Fiona fancies him, but I can't seem to get on his wavelength.
He says I'm too serious, and I suppose I am.'

'He wasn't much at home when you were growing up, then?'

'Not after the great row, no.'

Angelika said, 'Evan introduced me to Freya and Fiona early
on, but I didn't realize that there was a boy as well till later. I
first met him when I was out shopping with Fiona one day, and
we all had a meal together. He kept staring at me, but not in
the usual way. Men often stare at me, but not like *that*.'

She wriggled her shoulders. 'I thought he was a bit creepy.
I told Evan, and he explained that Philip wasn't well. He said
he paid for Philip to be properly looked after in a quiet environment, and that I didn't have to bother about him in any
way. I knew he came round to the house sometimes to see
Fiona, but I kept out of his way when he did.'

Freya was thoughtful. 'You're right, Philip ought to be told
what's happened. I mean, suppose he took it into his head to
go the house and found it . . .?' She shuddered.

'He has keys to the house, then?' asked Ellie.

'Of course. If he saw the mess the house was in, he wouldn't
know that Dad was all right. Well, in the hospital, anyway.
We ought to let him know.'

Angelika shrugged. 'Have you got his address? I haven't.'

'Uh, no. The last I heard he was at some kind of horticultural college, down in Surrey. I remember Dad complaining
about the fees, because I think it was the third or fourth time
that Philip had started to train for something and left without
finishing the course. He's never been able to support himself.
Such a shame. I suppose I could look in Fiona's room to see
if . . .' Her voice trailed away, remembering what had happened
to Fiona's room.

'Wait a minute,' said Angelika. 'Wasn't he working for some
charity or other after that? I'm pretty sure Evan said something
about it. Gardening?'

'Which one?'

Neither of them knew. 'What does he look like?' Ellie tried
to make the question sound offhand.

Angelika said, 'Oh, tall and thin. Skinny, really. Deep-set
eyes.'

'Red hair but not auburn,' said Freya. 'More ginger. He's the only one of us who's got the red-haired gene. Takes after his mother, I suppose. When I was little, I used to think he was like a stick insect, all hands and feet.'

Ginger hair. Didn't someone say the clown who'd given Abigail a peanut butter biscuit had ginger hair? No, no. It had been a wig, hadn't it? If only she'd taken better care of that photograph!

She said, 'Did Monique have ginger hair?'

Angelika looked surprised. 'Mm? No idea. Never met her.'

Freya screwed up her eyes. 'She used to send us – Fiona and me – wonderful Christmas and birthday presents when we were little. Expensive. We had to write thank-you letters back. I can't remember ever meeting her. She could be a redhead, I suppose.'

'Why do you want to know?' asked Angelika.

'Because,' said Ellie, choosing her words with care, 'I wondered if it would be easier for Philip if his mother broke the news to him, rather than people he doesn't know very well.'

'That's not a bad idea,' said Angelika. 'Let her break the news.'

Freya said, 'Did Dad say she'd moved to the south somewhere? Brighton? Hove? Dad will have the address on his computer or iPad or address book or something. In his study . . . ouch! Change of subject; when can we ring the hospital?'

'Yes, we must ring them,' said Angelika. 'When do you think we might see if anything is left of the house? Mrs Quicke, can you drive us round there soon?'

'Sorry, I don't drive.'

Both girls looked amazed. Angelika said, 'Well, I could take your car and—'

'Thomas has taken the car to Oxford for a conference.'

'You mean, he's not here to help us today? He's not retired?'

'Not exactly, no. I'll ring the hospital in a minute, and then we can decide who does what. For a start, is there anyone you'd both prefer to go and stay with for a few days? A school friend, Freya?'

'My two best friends have gone away for half-term. I was supposed to be going with them until Fiona died, and then obviously Dad said I couldn't.'

Angelika shook her head. 'I can't go anywhere till . . . My parents are both . . . They're not exactly . . . And my sister's got three kids. My agent says I can't just up sticks and . . . and there's the funeral.'

Silence. Angelika sat like a statue.

Vera said, 'More tea or coffee, anyone?'

Heads were shaken. Vera began to take the boxes of cereal off the table.

Angelika made a sound like a hiccup, but nothing moved on her face.

Freya turned towards Angelika as if to throw her arm around the girl, but stopped short of doing so when Angelika said, 'No, don't touch me.'

Freya bit her lip. Hard. Then turned away. In an uneven voice she said, 'That's the cereal Abigail always used to have. Fiona liked it with apple juice. I thought it was good riddance when Fiona died, but things get to you . . .'

Silence while everyone readjusted their ideas about Angelika and Freya – and grief.

Rose was sitting in the big chair at the side, nursing a mug of tea. 'I had an older brother once, tormented the life out of me. Killed himself in a motorbike crash. I was that pleased, couldn't understand why my mother kept crying for him. It was ages before I began to miss him. Now I think to myself, maybe he'd have straightened out, been a blessing instead of a curse. It takes all sorts.'

'Yes,' said Angelika, face like a stone. 'Abigail was a millstone round my neck. When she was born she looked up at me and I could see I wasn't what she wanted. I never did work out what it was that she wanted, except her own way. She always wanted that. She made me feel . . . inadequate. But sometimes, when she was asleep, I could look at her and love her.' Angelika gulped. She stood up, crashed back her chair and fled from the room, banging the door on her way out.

Freya stood up, moving with care, as if her legs might break under her. And went after her.

Ellie followed the two girls out into the hall and watched them make their way up the stairs and disappear into their rooms. Vera came to stand beside her. And Mikey. With Midge bringing up the rear.

Before Ellie could say anything, Vera jumped in. 'You're never going to cope with that lot by yourself. How would it be if we moved—?'

'I'd love it if you—'

'Rose says I can store anything on the top floor that we might want to keep—'

'I was going to offer you a proper flat upstairs, but the planning permission hasn't—'

'I've only got to give a fortnight's notice, and the rent's paid up till—'

'It's a bit cramped and we'll have to find another bed for—'

A big grin from Vera. 'He likes his sleeping bag on the floor. No problem. That's settled then.'

Ellie flapped her hands. 'No, no. We have to ask Mikey what he thinks.'

Mikey grinned. Nodded.

Vera looked at her watch. 'We'd better get busy, get over there, pack up and move back. Tuesday morning. You still have a cleaning team come in on Tuesday mornings?'

Rose appeared behind them. 'That funny blondie woman called round twice yesterday and rang I dunnamany times to speak to you, and that so-called secretary of yours, Pat, will be here in a minute, wanting you to go off with her and look at paperwork—'

'I don't know any blondie woman,' said Ellie. 'And bother the paperwork. Vera, I'll ask the cab company to pick you and Mikey up and take you back to the flat. I'll get Maria to send someone in to clean up after you. Oh dear, it's half-term and I know she's short-handed.'

'I can manage. If I can't get us out of there and clean up—'

'If you get stuck, I could ask Stewart if he can find someone to help you. I'll tell the cab people that you'll give them a ring when you're ready to come back. Tell them I'll pay both ways. Of course, you'll get a proper wage for helping Rose to keep this house going from now on, but it's to be understood that at some point you may want to go off to college or train for something, you hear me?'

'Oh, no. I—'

'Non-negotiable,' said Ellie. 'Edgar's instructions. For the time being, consider yourself part of the family.' She bent to give Mikey a hug. 'You, too.'

'Sorry to interrupt.' An acid tone in Angelika's voice as she appeared at the top of the stairs. 'Have you got the phone number for the hospital?'

'Yes, of course.' Ellie wondered where she might find it. Thomas had made the calls yesterday, hadn't he? Where would he have left the number? Perhaps on the top of his desk? If not, it would be in the phone book.

Which reminded her that she was supposed to be organizing the removal of his study to the library at the end of the corridor . . . and Mikey had taken a lot of the books off the shelves . . . and was that hailstones striking the glass of the conservatory? What horrible weather.

The doorbell rang.

Ellie recognized the Voice of Doom, even if no one else did. Rose was nearest the door and opened it. Diana.

An exhausted Diana with sunken eyes, pulling a carry-on bag after her. Rain had slicked her hair to her head. Her car was parked near the front door, but she'd got drenched in the few steps she'd taken to get into the house.

Diana was wearing a plain gold band on her fourth finger. Well, well. Jumping the gun, wasn't she? But a sensible precaution to wear a ring at the hospital if you wanted to claim you were Evan Hooper's current inamorata.

On Diana's heels came Ellie's secretary, Pat, umbrella blown inside out. Abominably cheerful. 'Woohoo! What weather! It's blowing a gale out there.'

Rose banged the front door shut and stumped off back to the kitchen, where she could be heard crashing plates into the dishwasher.

Ellie told herself to count ten. Or maybe eleven.

Mikey picked up Midge, who mewed once but allowed himself to be cuddled. Midge didn't like Diana. The feeling seemed to be mutual. Mikey took off with the cat in his arms, up the stairs, round the landing and through the unobtrusive door which led up to the top, currently uninhabited storey.

Pat cleared her throat. Loudly. By this time of the morning she expected Ellie to be at her desk, ready to tackle her correspondence, dictate replies, and work hard during the hours Pat was in attendance. Pat ignored the visitors to say, falsely cheerful, 'Well, shall we be getting on, Ellie? You've got that appointment with the landscape gardener at ten, remember.'

'Have I? Oh dear. In this weather?' Ellie was worried about Diana, who had eased herself down on to a hall chair and was shivering.

Ellie dithered. Too many people wanted her to help them, and she hadn't a clue which to look after first – or even if she ought to bother. Almost, she wrung her hands. An arrow prayer seemed to be in order.

Dear Lord, help!

Then she remembered Thomas saying she was like an angel with a flaming sword, defending those who had come to her for sanctuary. Which made her smile.

She also remembered Thomas reminding her that she should put on the bling and throw her weight about. He hadn't meant that literally, of course. She'd pulled on the first warm clothing that had come to hand. But he'd reminded her that God had given her the wherewithal to get things done; i.e, money.

She said, in her briskest tone, 'Well, Pat; I'm not going round the Pryce garden with anyone in this weather. Give him a ring, cancel it. Make another appointment.'

'Can't do that,' said Pat, amused. 'He's coming in from Kent specially.'

'See if you can get him on his mobile. Divert him.' Ellie helped Diana off with her jacket, which was soaked. Diana didn't wear perfume, but Ellie recognized a faint, sickly smell on the jacket. Diana had recently been sick. Oh. How far was she on with her pregnancy? Wouldn't all this excitement be bad for the baby?

Meanwhile, the others were waiting for her to do something, anything, to sort them out. 'Pat; ring for a cab to take Vera back to her flat. She's going to collect some of her belongings and bring them back here. Tell the cab people that she'll want the largest of their cars to put her stuff in on the return journey; or a small van if they can lay hands on one. She'll contact them when she's ready to leave. Make it clear that I'm paying, both ways.'

With an ill grace, Pat disappeared.

Freya and Angelika walked down the stairs, staring at Diana. Resenting her, but not prepared to make a scene.

Diana looked back, just as steadily. Not resenting them, either. Diana was too sure of her ground for that. 'Evan's being kept in for more tests. He didn't want me to leave him, but I need a shower, a couple of hours' kip and a change of clothes.'

Angelika drew closer to Freya. Or perhaps it was vice versa?

Ellie asked, 'Diana, why don't you go back to your flat?'

A shrug. 'The heating's on the blink. I rang the engineer. They said they couldn't come till Friday.' She put her hand over her mouth and half closed her eyes. Gulped. 'I didn't think you'd turn me away.' For once Diana was not demanding, but asking for help.

Ellie wished she hadn't had to get out of bed that morning. She wished Thomas hadn't had to go away. She wished she had the brains to work out what to do. There wasn't a spare bed to be had, except possibly . . . But she couldn't ask Diana to doss down in the library on an adjustable chair. Could she? No, she couldn't, even if the room had not been earmarked for another purpose, because Diana was clearly being sick at frequent intervals and needed to be near a bathroom.

Freya spoke first. 'I'll go and sit with Dad. I've got a bus pass. I can get a bus to the Broadway and then another from there to the hospital, can't I?'

Angelika said, 'I'll go round to the house, then. See what can be saved.'

They were looking at Ellie for approval – or for help with the arrangements? For both.

Ellie said, 'Freya; you've got the right idea. I'll order a cab to take you there. Have you enough money for food and something to drink? You have? Good. Is your mobile fully charged? Yes? Ring me when there's any news about your father and when you're ready to come back. Angelika; I'll ring my son-in-law who runs a property company and ask if he can spare someone to take you to the house. He'll know what arrangements you'll have to make to salvage what's left, and to have the house made secure. I suggest you concentrate on Evan's study, find all the documents relating to insurance, the builders he uses, that sort of thing. The insurance people will need to inspect the damage before you can get any repairs done.'

Let's hope there's no structural damage, because if there were, it would take months to rebuild such a big old house.

'That stupid Mr Abel,' said Diana, closing her eyes. 'I told him to go round to the house to board up the conservatory door and, wouldn't you know, it was him that reported the fire. I told the police, I wouldn't have put it past him to have started it.'

Ellie was horrified. 'Now, Diana; you know he wouldn't do a thing like that.'

'Why not? He was against me from the start. I ought to have given him the sack the first time he refused to do as I asked, but he's leaving at the end of this week, thank heavens. Now, if you can find me a bed I think I'd better crash out for a while.'

Ellie said, 'You told the police Mr Abel might have set the fire? Oh, Diana!'

Pat reappeared, looking smug. 'I phoned the cab company and they're sending a cab round for Vera. The landscape gardener's well on his way and will be at the Pryce place in twenty minutes. He says he doesn't mind the weather.'

Ellie tried not to grind her teeth. Was Pat being deliberately obstructive? 'Would you order a second cab, please? For Freya, to take her to the hospital. Put it on my tab. And would you please get Stewart on the phone, now!'

Diana slid down in her chair. Put her hand over her mouth. Her colour was bad. 'I rather think I . . .'

Ellie helped her daughter to the cloakroom and tidied her up once she'd been sick. 'Up to bed. Use my bathroom and my bed. I'll bring your bag up. What would you like to eat or drink? Nothing? Well, perhaps for the moment, but later . . . I'll have a word with Rose. She'll know what to get you.

'Listen to me, Diana; I want something in exchange. I want you to ring Hoopers before you do anything else. I imagine Mr Abel will be in charge there – at least till he leaves at the end of the week. I want you to tell him that I'll be ringing him shortly, and that he should have some addresses and phone numbers ready to pass on to me. In particular those of Evan's son Philip, and his first wife, Monique.'

Diana dragged herself up the stairs. This pregnancy was taking it out of her. 'What on earth would you want those for? Evan's not going to die.' But when she tottered into Ellie's bedroom, she got out her mobile and made the phone call as requested.

A small miracle. Ellie couldn't think when Diana had last done something her mother wanted; at least, not without an argument.

Ellie helped Diana to undress and made sure there were some clean towels in the bathroom. 'Shower first.'

Diana drew back. Perhaps she was remembering the last time she entered that bathroom, when there'd been an altercation with her mother which had almost ended in tragedy. Since then the bathroom had been completely revamped. Nothing was in the same place. Even the tiling was different.

Ellie switched on the shower and gave Diana a little push towards it. 'Get on with it. Then bed. I'll draw the curtains and leave you in peace. It seems I have an appointment in the next road.'

As she drew the curtains, she realized that the rain was driving almost horizontally at the house. She spared a thought for Thomas, praying that his journey had been made in easier weather conditions.

SIXTEEN

Ellie went downstairs, thinking that an umbrella wouldn't be much use in that stormy weather. It would be a good idea to change into her wellington boots, which she'd used for the football match the previous weekend and would surely have dried out by now. She rummaged for them in the cupboard under the stairs.

Pat emerged from the corridor, phone in hand. 'Stewart's out for the day, and the garden designer has arrived at Pryce House. He's not amused at being kept waiting.'

Vera had her jacket on, ready to go. She called up the stairs. 'Mikey? Where are you? The cab's come to take us back to the flat.'

Angelika was on her own mobile phone, walking backwards and forwards, concentrating. 'But Terry-my-love—'

Ellie did a double take. Hadn't Angelika been on sweetheart terms with someone called 'Joey' a little while back?

Freya opened the front door. 'My cab's here, too. Mrs Quicke, it's tipping it down. Why don't you come in the cab with me? It's not much out of the way to the hospital—'

'Mikey!' A despairing cry from Vera.

Ellie shed her shoes and started to force her feet into the wellington boots. 'Anyone else want to borrow some wet-weather gear? Help yourselves. Vera, leave Mikey behind. You'll manage quicker without him. Pack up everything you need for the next few days, and go back for the rest later. Pat!'

Pat wiped the smile off her face. Ellie didn't often use that authoritative tone of voice.

Angelika shut off her phone and wailed, 'My manager says he's got a big deal on and can't come over here to help me. Whatever am I to do?'

Ellie stamped, to get her foot all the way down into the wellington boot, and reached for her heavy-duty mackintosh. 'Pat; I don't care where he is or what client Stewart's seeing. Get him on his mobile. Now!'

Midge the cat made his stately way down the stairs and across the hall to the kitchen . . . from which emerged, with a burst of cheerful pop music, Ellie's two cleaners, armed with Hoovers and a box of cleaning materials. They stopped short, round-eyed, when they saw strangers. 'Is it all right to go ahead as usual, Mrs Quicke?'

'Definitely. Oh, except don't bother with my bedroom. Vera; off with you.'

Vera disappeared, with one last pleading look up the stairs. Ellie suspected that Mikey was sitting just out of sight, waiting for them all to leave. Wasn't he supposed to be at some computer class or other this week? Well, never mind that now.

The cleaners went slowly, oh so slowly, up the stairs, taking it all in, enchanted to have such an interesting interruption to their usual routine.

Freya said, 'Shall I tell my cab to wait?'

'Yes, please do.' Ellie took the phone out of Pat's hand. 'Stewart? Emergency. Evan Hooper's in hospital with concussion, and his house went up in flames last night. Mrs Hooper is staying with me for the time being. I need someone to collect her from here, take her over to the house, assess the damage, contact the insurance people, arrange to have windows boarded over or whatever . . . and oh, have anything salvageable put into store. I realize you're working out of the office today. Yes, Pat did say. Can you get someone to take over from you?'

'Ellie, I can't just abandon this job.' Exasperated.

'Could Nirav do it? Yes, I know he's not really experienced enough to take over from you, but this takes priority.'

'You're barking mad to get mixed up with that lot; you know that?'

'You'll do it, then? What a relief. You know Mrs Hooper by sight, don't you? She hasn't many clothes with her. I'll see if I can find her a mac and some boots or something. Oh, and by the way, it would be best if you didn't tell anyone where Mrs Hooper is staying. There's some nutter going around knocking off the Hooper women—'

'What! Ellie, what on earth—'

'Oh, and Diana's been up at the hospital all night with Evan and she's sleeping it off in my bed at present. Don't spread that around, either. Understood?'

'Ellie, you can't mean—!'

Ellie killed the call. Angelika was standing there: fragile, helpless, beautiful – and dressed in the most unsuitable fashion for contending with the elements. Ellie said, 'Oh, come on, Angelika! Shift your stumps! Take this mackintosh; it'll drown you, but will give you some protection. Then get a notebook and pad or something to write on from my office. What is it now, Pat?'

'The garden designer is—'

'I dare say. Now, I'll be back . . . whenever. Hold all calls.' She grinned. 'I've always wanted to say "hold all calls". It sounds as if I know what I'm doing.'

Freya was pushing her arms into an old anorak – one of Thomas's by the look of it. At least it had a hood. 'Shall I take a couple of umbrellas?'

A giant umbrella, red and white striped, walked across the hall towards the front door. It was carried by Mikey, wearing a hooded cape which dragged on the floor behind him. Apparently, Mikey wanted to come, too. Ellie didn't want him, but couldn't think what words to use in order to stop him.

Freya held the front door for the three of them to dash round Diana's car and into the waiting cab.

Once belted up, Ellie fumbled for her mobile phone and didn't find it. Where had she left it? Well, never mind that now. 'Freya, have you a mobile on you? I'd better ring Rose and tell her to warn the cleaners not to talk about you staying with me.'

Freya handed hers over. 'You aren't serious, are you? You really think someone's out to get us?'

'Diana, too. Probably. Any idea who it might be?'

Pryce House. There were several cars tucked under the overgrown hedge at the end of the drive, but not much evidence of men actually at work. There was, however, a super-splashy Range Rover parked before the front door, the sort of car that always looked immaculate because its owner never subjected it to anything but good roads. Ellie seemed to remember that such high status vehicles were called Chelsea tractors because they never left town.

Mikey struggled to unfurl the huge umbrella but had difficulty holding it above them as they left the shelter of the cab and scurried to the front door . . . which was standing ajar, thank goodness.

The garden designer was already in the hall. Handsome if you liked your men a trifle fleshy. Mid forties but trying to look younger, blow-dried hair, perfectly fitted jeans, designer full-length army style coat and stubble. Incredibly clean fingernails.

To Ellie's mind, real gardeners could never quite get their fingernails clean, their pockets sagged from carrying secateurs around in them, and they wore clogs or heavy boots rather than polished dress shoes.

She disliked him on sight, then told herself not to jump to conclusions. Perhaps he'd dressed up to meet a high maintenance client, someone who wore Gucci and Prada. She could see he didn't think much of a middle-aged woman arriving in a mack much too big for her, muddy wellington boots, and with a small boy in tow . . . who had apparently disappeared, leaving the red and white umbrella dripping on the floor.

Mikey did like to explore new places, didn't he? She wondered if he knew that Edgar Pryce had been brought up in this house.

The hall was dark and seemed cavernous on that rain-soaked morning. Ellie shivered. It was a good thing the place was being made over, banishing the memory of those who'd lived and died here . . .

'Mrs Quicke?' A tone full of doubt.

She nodded, smiled and tried to disentangle herself from her ancient mack.

He held out his hand to her and winced as she took it. 'I was afraid you'd stood me up, har har!'

Ellie apologized. 'Sorry. Cold hands. I'm afraid I've kept you waiting. Domestic dramas. I hope there was someone here to let you in?' Stupid, Ellie. Of course there was someone to let him in, or he'd still be sitting in his car outside.

A wave of a hand. 'Some underling. Acting foreman, rather officious, I thought. Now, shall we go through to the back of the house, so that you can get a better idea of the design I have created for you?'

Even on that wet, grey day, the back garden lifted the spirits. Some of the rambling roses had come adrift from their moorings at the back of the house and hung in loops to the patio below. The surface of the pond was ruffled by wind and pitted with rain drops, and the lawn was a sodden meadow, with spikes of dying weeds poking up through matted grass. The greenhouses looked romantically dilapidated, and ivy had taken hold of the boundary brick walls here and there.

But even in October the roses, which had been the pride

and joy of the last owner, were a delight. Great splodgy splashes of pink and white. Showers of red.

Moreover, the fruit trees, which separated the vegetable garden from what had once been a fine lawn, were bending low under the weight of luscious fruit. It made her fingers itch to get out there and bring order into this neglected garden of Eden. Were those really grapes ripening in the far greenhouse? Dilapidated though they were, the greenhouses were still producing fruit.

The designer unfurled a roll of thick paper. 'I have devised a spectacular garden for you, something to marvel at, something to amuse and intrigue the guests at our hotel.' He shot her a glance full of doubt. 'I don't know whether you can make any sense of my drawings . . .' His pursed-up mouth indicated that he didn't think she'd know how to read the instructions to turn on a kettle, never mind make sense of anything as complicated and professionally produced as his plans.

Ellie wished she'd taken Thomas's advice literally and dressed in her best bib and tucker, with diamond rings large enough to impress even this nasty little snob.

'All shades of green,' he fluted. 'Not the usual box or privet, of course, but a variety of plants from all over the globe. Nothing obvious. Serenity is the keynote. Close-clipped low hedges to enclose, rounded bushes to outline, granite blocks to lead the eye to this obelisk here which, as you can see, is made of spirals of wire, extremely unusual, created by a much sought-after artist of my acquaintance.'

She put her finger on a strange contraption occupying most of the middle ground. 'What is this?'

'My Japanese-style pavilion. Cool, coolest, baby. Bamboo, tied in traditional fashion, no nails to be used.'

'No roof, either?'

A condescending smile. 'This is a work of art, to be admired and appreciated.'

'Not for sitting in, then. All this space around it—'

'Water surrounds us, from the moment of conception. So here we are embraced by an expanse of water which mirrors the changing role of the skies.'

'Taking up almost half of the garden. Is that right? And stepping stones for people to cross the water. Wouldn't they be a mite tricky for elderly people to negotiate?'

'Like you, you mean?' Another condescending smile.

'Or children?'

'Oh, we won't allow children to play in our very sophisticated garden, will we?'

She thought the design completely out of character. 'Won't it be very expensive to create such a very large body of water, and how is it to be maintained free of weeds? Will there be fish in it?'

Another condescending smile. He *was* deeply in love with his design, wasn't he? '"No pain without gain," as they say. The plan is to excavate the whole area, line it with concrete, and then build in piles to support the stepping stones. It will cost something to build and to maintain, but it will be the marvel of the neighbourhood, be photographed for every important magazine, perhaps even appear on television. This –' and he beamed with pride – 'is the future!'

'The hotel people want to make a point of retaining all the late Victorian features. I had imagined the garden would reflect that.'

'I suppose you thought we'd keep the roses! Har, har.'

'Correct,' said Ellie, deciding that this man would get the job over her dead body.

'My dear Mrs Quicke, what might have been considered suitable in the past . . .' He frowned, tugging at his coat. 'What the . . .?' His coat was jigging around, developing a life of its own. He looked down, frowned, his mouth mean. 'Let go of my coat, you . . .!' He lifted his hand to swipe at Mikey, who'd been trying to attract his attention.

'Don't!' Ellie was too late.

The garden designer caught Mikey around the ear, spinning him sideways. 'That'll learn you!' Catching the boy up with his free hand, the man drew back his fist to punch him again.

Mikey twisted round and bit the man's wrist.

'Yow! My wrist! You little horror! You'll pay for that!'

Ellie made a dive for the boy and captured him in her arms. 'Let go, Mikey!' She pulled the boy away, while his victim danced around, screeching blue murder.

'What the . . .!' A middle-aged, grey-haired, competent-looking man stood in the doorway. Hard hat. Business suit, not overalls. Grey eyes with crow's feet around them. Eyes that usually smiled, but were hard as they addressed the garden designer. 'Didn't you get my message, sir? I asked the boy to tell you the lorry carrying the scaffolding had arrived but can't get into the drive with your car in the way.'

'He *bit* me!'

Mikey clung around Ellie's neck.

'You hit him,' said Ellie.

'Is he yours? I'll sue the pants off you! Yow! I'll have to have a tetanus shot!'

'Don't let me hold you up!'

Snarling, the designer picked up his roll of plans and staggered out. Were those tears in his eyes? Diddums, then.

'All right, missus?' The newcomer was sizing her up, but apparently liked what he saw. 'Mrs Quicke, I presume? I've heard a lot about you. I'm the project manager here. Hugh's the name. Glad to meet you. I saw him hit the boy, and I'll say so, if necessary.'

'Would you put that in writing? Knowing his kind, he'll make as much trouble as he can, and I don't want to give him the job, anyway.'

Hugh grinned. 'I'll put it in writing the moment I've seen him off the premises. We can't start to put up the scaffolding in this weather, but we'll unload and send the lorry back. They should have been here earlier, but got delayed. This weather . . .'

He left. Mikey had attached himself to her like a limpet. There were no chairs in this empty house. She half carried and half dragged him to the stairs in the hall and lowered herself on to them, with Mikey in her arms.

She rocked him gently to and fro.

It occurred to her that she'd never yet heard him speak.

Ah. Perhaps Vera hadn't given her the full story? Perhaps the boy was not off his food, as Vera had intimated, but had become mute after Edgar's death? Would Vera have lied about that if she'd thought it would make Mikey more acceptable as a house guest? Had Vera really been thinking that far ahead? Mm. Yes. Perhaps.

Vera had said the doctors thought the problem – whatever
it was – would resolve itself naturally. Ah, well . . . How about
some counselling? Possibly not on the National Health? Oh
dear, oh dear.

Was Mikey crying? Possibly. What should she do now?

She would tell him a story. That's what you did to calm
children who were upset . . . And no, he ought not to have
bitten the man, but whacking him for it wasn't the answer.

'Once upon a time,' she began, 'there was a man living in
this house who worked hard and made a lot of money. He and
his wife had two children, who were given everything in the
world that they could wish for.'

Mikey's head moved against her neck. He was definitely
listening.

She said, 'Sometimes, if everything comes too easily, if
children are given everything they ask for the moment they
ask for it – or even before they've asked for it – they don't
value what they're given. What's another electronic toy, if
you've got three already?'

Mikey nodded. He understood.

'Children like that,' said Ellie, 'can get very spoilt. They
think it's their right to have everything they want, without
their having to work for it. That happened here. The two Pryce
children—'

Mikey started.

'Yes,' said Ellie, holding him even closer. 'Edgar, your
stepfather, was one of them. I don't know which of the rooms
upstairs was his. Perhaps we can find out one day. Sadly, his
mother – who could have given him a more balanced upbringing
– went away to make a new life for herself, and there was no
one then to stop him or his sister from playing ducks and
drakes with their father's money. Then one day Mr Pryce met
a business lady who liked him as much as he liked her, and
they got married.

'Mr Pryce was worried about the way his children had
grown up and decided to make them stand on their own two
feet. He didn't turn them off without a penny; oh, no. He
bought each of them a nice place to live and set them up in
business for themselves, but he said there would be No More

Handouts, no more paying off their debts. Do you think he was wise?'

Mikey nodded.

She said, 'It was almost too late for the children to change. Edgar made a lot of mistakes and so did his sister before their father died. Instead of leaving his money to the children, as they'd expected, he left it all to his second wife, Mrs Pryce, asking her not to shower money on his children, but to make sure they never suffered want.

'That's when Edgar finally began to grow up. He found a job he liked, working in a school. He came to appreciate his stepmother, and she him. Then two bad things happened; he got cancer, and his stepmother died. Do you know who she left all the money to?'

Mike lifted his head from her neck to give her a long stare.

She nodded. 'Yes, she left it all to me, including this house . . . which is far too big for a family now. Edgar suggested that it be made into a hotel, a place where people can come and have a rest and go back into the world refreshed. In return for giving me this house and her money, Mrs Pryce wanted me to keep on looking after what's left of her family.

'At that very point in time Edgar met you and your mother, and fell in love with you. He left me a letter, asking me to look after you both. Maybe not with money. Money can be a blessing, and it can be a curse.

'So now it's up to me to see what can be done to help you and your mother. I think that you, Mikey, are capable of making your own way in life. If you put your mind to it, you could get scholarships and go to university under your own steam, and not cost your mother a penny. You're a survivor. Of course, it would help if you could keep your temper under control and not bite people.'

He hid his face against her neck again.

She smiled. So he was ashamed of himself already? 'Now as it happens, over the past year or so I've been wondering how to do something for your mother. She's had some rotten luck. Oh, not you, Mikey. You are the light of her life and her main reason for living. But she missed out on her chance of further education because she had to go out to earn a living for you both. It might be that I could arrange for you and her to have some better living accommodation, and perhaps for her to have some sort of part-time job so that she could continue to provide a home for you, while picking up her studies again. I'm not sure about that. Edgar wasn't sure about it, either. Some day soon we'll have to have a meeting – you, me and your mother – to discuss it. Understood?'

He did seem to.

She went on sitting on the stairs, listening with half an ear to the clash and crash of scaffolding poles being unloaded and stacked outside . . . thinking of this and that . . . hardly aware when Mikey slipped out of her arms and disappeared.

She thought of the parallels between Evan Hooper's methods of bringing up his children and those of the Pryce family. There was the missing wife element in both cases; how much blame should be attached to them? Were the wives more sinned against than sinning? Surely they had contributed to their children's problems by leaving?

Ellie shrugged. She couldn't tell. Perhaps their disappearances had mattered a lot, perhaps not much.

There'd been too much money thrown around, in both cases. The money had attracted Angelika because it meant . . . what? Security, or help with her career? Both.

Diana was attracted to money like a bee to honey, and for much the same reason.

Had anyone ever truly loved Edgar Pryce? Yes, Vera had. Lucky man.

Did anyone really love Evan? Freya did, but no one else around seemed to care what happened to the living or the dead.

Did Diana love Evan? Ellie sighed. She hoped very much that Diana did, but couldn't be sure.

It was said that having money brings happiness, but it didn't. Too little money, on the other hand, equals unhappiness. See Mr Micawber on the subject. Income one pound and sixpence, expenditure one pound: equals happiness. Income nineteen shillings, expenditure one pound: misery.

Compare the two families' record on discipline. They used to say "spare the rod and spoil the child". It sounded as if both Fiona and Abigail Hooper had been spoilt brats. No restraints had been applied there.

In the case of the Pryce children, the rod had been applied too late for the girl, who had still not learned to live within her means and whose selfishness was a byword . . . See the way she'd tried to get Vera to hand over the little Edgar had left her. Edgar, however, had learned from adversity and come through.

Lastly, Ellie considered the matter of rejection. Freya had been rejected but was still in there, fighting for recognition from her father. Maybe she'd make it. Maybe not. It would be a pity if her craving for her father's love warped her life.

Philip, now. First spoilt and then rejected? It sounded like it.

Ellie shook herself back to the present moment.

What was next on the agenda?

The project manager, Hugh, appeared in the doorway. 'Finished here, Mrs Quicke? I've set up my office in the old garage. The boy's in with the scaffolders, cadging a sandwich and a cuppa from them. Bright as a button, isn't he? I understand you're the major shareholder in this project. Would you like to go round with me now, and I'll show you what's planned?'

It wasn't a question, but a command. Ellie looked at her watch, held back a grimace, and said she'd be delighted. She could see, as well as he, that if the two of them established a good working relationship now, any snags in the future could be ironed out without too much trouble. Conversely, if she got on her high horse and walked out, he wouldn't be so ready to listen to the way she'd like things to be done.

She tested her theory. 'It's a grand old house this. Do you like it?'

'Very much.'

'What do you think should be done with the garden?'

'It's going to be a very special kind of hotel, making a feature of all the period detail.'

'Mrs Pryce was a period piece herself. She loved her roses. I was thinking we could have roses and climbing plants all around the walls and a smooth lawn to rest the eye. There could be pergolas, and lots of places to sit out, and benches, and a fine herbaceous border and a children's play area in one corner. But I suppose I'm hopelessly out of date.'

He inclined his head. 'I would rather say you are "dateless". As is the house.'

So, they were in agreement. 'Thank you, Hugh. I'd be delighted to go round the house with you.'

SEVENTEEN

Tuesday noon

F inally, Ellie was free to leave Pryce House. She called Mikey down from where he was exploring the attic rooms and asked Hugh to summon a cab for her. It wasn't raining quite as hard as before, but it was still drizzling in a nasty, insidious way. The wind had developed a horrid habit of dropping away, and then coming round a corner to lift your skirts and lash at your legs.

'Hungry?' she asked the boy as they got into the cab.

He shook his head. He'd probably been given more food from the workmen than he'd get at home, though it might not have been as organic or healthy.

Ellie asked the cab driver to take them to the Hooper Estate Agency on the Broadway. She would pop in, check that Mr Abel was coping, pick up some addresses, and then go on home. Perhaps there might be sardines on toast for lunch?

She would have liked to raise Thomas on the phone, but oh dear! What had she done with her mobile? Anyway, he was really too busy to bother with their domestic problems at the moment, and he had said he'd ring her twice a day. Did that mean she'd missed one of his calls already?

There was a police car outside Hoopers.

Why? Ellie remembered, with a chill going down her back, that Diana had pointed the finger at Mr Abel as a possible arsonist. Surely the police wouldn't take that seriously, would they? Granted, a case could be made out for Mr Abel being so furious at being forced to resign that he might want to harm the agency, but anyone who knew him would think that highly unlikely. As for wanting to kill a teenager, a toddler, and a slightly potty old woman – forget it!

On the other hand, Ears would be under considerable pressure to make an arrest in a case involving Evan Hooper, and he might twist the facts to suit himself. He might even want to brush off the deaths as misadventure in order to concentrate on the arson, just because he had a likely suspect to hand. Mr Abel had certainly been at the house at the right time.

Motive and opportunity. Oh dear.

Ellie walked into the main office, which was crowded with people suffering from different degrees of excitement and distress. There were rows of desks manned by men and women all looking towards the back office, while their phones rang unregarded.

Ears, looking pleased with himself, emerged into the main office holding on to Mr Abel's arm. Behind them came Ms Milburn, boot-faced.

Ears had got hold of the wrong end of the stick, as usual.

Mr Abel, whom Ellie knew as a capable, practical person, thoroughly trustworthy though perhaps not quite top management material, was red of face and looked ready to explode with fury.

He spotted Ellie and tried to hang back in order to speak to her. 'Mrs Quicke; you won't believe this, but the police seem to think that I—'

'Come along now,' said Ears, pleased with himself. 'We don't want to bother Mrs Quicke with this, do we?'

Mr Abel looked wildly around. 'But the office! I can't leave! Mrs Quicke, could you contact Diana and—'

'This way!' Ears propelled Mr Abel out of the door, still talking.

Ellie called after him, 'Have you a solicitor?'

He disappeared into the police car.

Silence, except for the ringing of the office phones. Uneasy glances. Someone laughed.

Nerves.

One of the men cleared his throat. 'Well, there's a turn-up for the books. What do we do now?'

An older women turned to Ellie. 'You're Mrs Quicke, Diana's mother, aren't you? Do you know where she is? We expected her this morning but she hasn't appeared. Someone said Mr Hooper had been taken ill and was in hospital, and then they said his house had burned down, and now it seems that Mr Abel did it!'

'Nonsense,' said Ellie.

One of the men said, 'We should close the office.'

His neighbour was against it. 'We can't do that! He'd have our guts for garters!'

Ellie thought that this contretemps was no business of hers and she could walk away from it with a clear conscience. Evan Hooper had brought all his troubles on himself. Neither Evan Hooper nor Diana would thank her for interfering.

But Mr Abel was a good man and hadn't deserved to be hauled off to the police station for questioning or even – heaven forbid! – arrested for something he hadn't done.

So Ellie said, 'Who is the most senior among you?'

An older woman, greying hair, business suit. 'I suppose I am.'

'Your name?'

The woman primped her over-lipsticked mouth. 'Mrs Lavery.'

'Then, Mrs Lavery, you must take over till Mr Abel or Diana return. Everyone else should get back to work. Now, shall we go into the back office and see what we can do to sort this out? First off we must get Mr Abel a solicitor.'

'Who'd have thought Mr Abel was capable of setting fire to a house?' The most senior member of the staff might be very good at her job, but she didn't seem to have any loyalty to Mr Abel. 'Of course we could all see he wasn't going to fit in easily with the new regime, Diana running a tight ship as they say, but . . . to go and burn the boss's house down!'

Ellie wanted to say, 'Don't be ridiculous!' Or alternatively, 'Try not to be so stupid!' She held her tongue because neither comment would be helpful. Mrs Lavery might not be the brightest blade in the box but she probably suited Diana very well. Diana would not want to be outshone by a sharper business mind nor have a member of the staff question any of her decisions . . . which was one of the reasons why she'd forced out Mr Abel, who might be dogged but was also a man of integrity who didn't believe in cutting corners.

Mrs Lavery led the way into the back office and seated herself behind the big desk, trying out the chair and relishing the authority it gave her. 'Me, acting manager!' She reached her hand to the landline phone. 'I must tell my husband.'

'One moment,' said Ellie, conscious of time marching on, things to do, people to see – and a small boy holding on to a giant umbrella with one hand and clinging to her coat with the other. 'Do you happen to know who Mr Hooper is insured with?'

Round eyes. Hand to mouth. 'Oh my! His house burning down. Yes, of course. Everything here is with the Britannia. I'd better ring them, I suppose. It will be up to me to make the arrangements if he's kept in hospital.'

Ellie didn't think that a good idea. 'May I suggest that I contact my daughter first? She can confirm your temporary status and tell you what she would like you to do.'

'Oh. Yes. I suppose.' Reluctantly.

Ellie smiled sweetly, chucked off her heavy mack and dialled her home phone number. Rose answered.

'Rose, dear; is my daughter downstairs yet?'

'Not she, the little madam.'

'Well, do you think you might take a cup of tea up to her in a minute and ask her to phone me at her office? There's a problem here that only she can solve. Is Vera back yet?'

'No, but she rang to say she'd be here in a while. Am I supposed to wait on Diana? Pat says there's been people calling for you. That blondie for one. Most insistent. Thomas rang, wanting to know if you were all right, and I said probably but one of the cleaners found your mobile in the sitting room, so that's why he couldn't get through to you, which got him worrying, and he wanted to know if he ought to come back tonight, but I said no, he ought to see to his own business. As it is, we've got such a houseful I don't know whether I'm coming or going. How many should I expect for supper, do you think?'

'Think big, and we'll freeze any leftovers. No news from Stewart or the hospital?'

'No, though the phone was ringing a while ago when I was out in the garden fetching in some roses, which are a bit rain-spotted but still got some colour in them, and I didn't get to it in time. I expect they've left a message.'

'Right. I'll be back soon.' She put down the phone but held on to it. The temporary manageress made a couple of passes towards the phone, but Ellie wasn't about to let go. 'Now, Mrs Lavery, the most important thing to do is to find Mr Abel a solicitor. I haven't my own mobile with me, so I'll have to look a number up in the directory. Mikey, would you be so kind? I can see the phone directories on that shelf over there.'

Mikey brought over the directory, Ellie picked out her own solicitor's name and got through to him. 'Dear Gunnar, another small problem . . .'

As she talked to Gunnar, she could hear that the phones were ringing in the outer office, but they were now being answered. Good.

Mrs Lavery kept casting uneasy glances in Ellie's direction. Under normal circumstances Ellie would have agreed she was being high-handed, but not today. She finished the call to Gunnar and smiled at the woman. 'Now, Mrs Lavery, as Mr Hooper is still in hospital we need to contact his first wife, Monique, and his son Philip. Diana asked Mr Abel to look up the information for me, but unfortunately he was prevented from passing it on. Do you think you could help me find their details?'

Mrs Lavery tossed her head. 'I really don't think I can give out any personal information. Perhaps you can ask your daughter when she sees fit to oblige us with her presence.'

Ellie pretended to acquiesce. There must be another way round this woman's officiousness. Ellie's stomach rumbled, reminding her that it was lunchtime. 'Oh, Mrs Lavery, I'm dying for a cuppa. While we're waiting for my daughter to ring, do you think you could ask someone to make some tea for me and perhaps find me a couple of biscuits, too?'

For one moment Ellie thought the woman would refuse, but she did acquiesce, if with a bad grace. And left the office.

'Quick, Mikey. We need those telephone numbers. Mr Abel may have run them off for me from the computer, or he may have accessed a Rolodex or address book. Let's see if we can find them.'

Mikey homed in on Mr Abel's desk, while Ellie rather distractedly looked in his drawers. She was always happier with paper than with a computer.

Mikey plucked a piece of paper from the top of the in tray and held it high in the air before handing it over to Ellie. *Yes! Thank you, Mr Abel.* It had the details she'd asked for. 'Bravo, Mikey! Now, as soon as I've had a cuppa, let's get out of here.'

Tuesday afternoon

Back home all was quiet. No guests. No cleaners. Rose bustled out to meet them and take their wet macks and the outsize umbrella, talking the while.

'The phone's been ringing off and on, but I left it for you to listen to the messages. Pat stayed for a while, because she said there was a pile of mail to deal with, and that blondie came by and seemed very upset not to see you—'

'What blondie?'

'Dunno. Pat didn't know, either. Pat said that if you wanted her, she'd come back this afternoon, which it already is, though I don't know how she thinks you're going to be able to concentrate on business with so much else going on. Before you ask, yes; I took some tea up to her Royal Highness, and she didn't thank me for it, oh no. But there; I didn't expect thanks, her being what she is. So I gave her your message and she asked me to hand her her Blackberry, which I didn't know what it was but it turns out to be some kind of phone but not the usual sort, she says. She had a sharp word or two to someone at her office and off she went in her car as if the devil was after her, which he probably is, leaving her things all over your bedroom, which I told her was a disgrace but she took no notice, as you'd expect.'

'Oh, good. At least she can pick up the pieces at Hoopers. Is Vera back yet?'

'That she is, and some of her things are in my room down-stairs and some upstairs and she said Mikey would help her when he got back . . . which it looks like he's already gone off to do, the little tyke. Oh, and here's your mobile, take it and put it away safely before you forget it again.'

Ellie listened to her messages.

Short and sharp from Freya. 'I'm still at the hospital. More tests have been ordered. Dad doesn't seem to know where he is half the time, but he does like having me hold his hand. I'll ring again when I can get some sense out of the doctors.'

Nothing from Angelika.

One from Stewart. 'Ellie, I'm in Nightmare Alley. The whole of the downstairs is just a shell of blackened rooms. The garage likewise, with the remains of two cars in it. The back of the house is intact, but everything there's been spoiled either by smoke or water. Evan's study is at the back, but the firemen say it's not safe for anyone to go in, so I can't rescue his computer or his papers. I've told Angelika the insurers will want everything left as is till they've had a chance to inspect the damage. I suggest you get on to his office to see if they know who the insurers may be, because Angelika hasn't a clue. In the meantime I'll get all the downstairs doors and windows boarded up.'

Good old Stewart. She got him on her phone. 'Stewart? Ellie here. I've been to the Hooper office and they think he's insured with Britannia. Diana's gone over there now and I expect she'll deal with it. Are the reporters still hanging around? We don't want anyone to know where the girls are staying.'

'One did come by, took some photos, wanted information about the members of the family – which I didn't give, inci-dentally – and left. The firemen say it was definitely arson, started in the big room to the right of the front door. Angelika is pretty calm, on the whole. She assumes she's staying with you for the time being. Hope that's all right. I'll ring again when I know more, shall I?' And he shut off.

Stewart was a man in a million.

The next message was from Thomas, worried about her, wanting to make sure she'd ring him if he was needed, saying that if so, he'd come straight back.

She'd manage, wouldn't she? Somehow. She'd ring him back in a little while. It was no good ringing when he was in one of his important meetings, or lectures or whatever they were.

The next message was from a woman whose voice Ellie didn't recognize. Ah, Betsey, from Harmony in the Home; Ellie had forgotten all about her. She must be the 'blondie' who Rose said had been calling round. Well, it looked as if Betsey would have another big project on, when the Hooper house was renovated. But what about the job Ellie had asked her to do, of reorganizing their own house to accommodate Thomas's family?

'Mrs Quicke, I've called round a couple of times with some suggestions and estimates, but I gather you're in the thick of a domestic drama at the moment. I'll leave the material with you, and perhaps you'll get back to me when you've a minute.'

Nice woman. Understanding. Put that on one side for the moment. Thomas was right; his family would have to go to a hotel.

Ellie riffled through the pile of mail which Pat had left for her, but couldn't concentrate on any of it.

Vera appeared, flushed and laughing, with a cup of tea and some sandwiches on a tray. 'Mikey thinks you're hungry. Do you have time to wait till we can cook you something?'

'I wish I did, but I haven't. Bless you, and welcome home. I know it's chaotic at the moment, but—'

'It's just fine, and Mikey's loving it. Sit down, and eat up.'

Ellie relaxed, smiling; and obeyed.

'Now,' said Vera, 'Rose and I have made out a shopping list, and I'm going to show Rose how to order online, if you don't object. I'll use the laptop Edgar gave me and set it up in the kitchen for the moment, though no doubt I can find a better place later on.'

Ellie grinned and flapped her hand at Vera as she bit into an enormous ham and tomato sandwich. 'Mmflm. Soon . . . be able . . . top floor?'

'Yes, Mikey's up there now with his scooter. I hope you don't mind. He needs to burn off some energy. It's so light and airy I'm sure we'll be very happy to live up there when it's got running water and some heating. I've told him he's got to put those books back in the library where's he set up his laptop, but he just stared at me, so I dare say we'll have a spot of bother about that. Is there something else you'd like me to do?'

'Mm.' Ellie swallowed. She was so hungry she was eating far too fast and was going to get indigestion. 'Thomas wants to move his office into the library, which will give him more room and be more convenient in every way. Do you think you could start on that? If Mikey doesn't object?'

'He'd better not. Now, shall I get you another cuppa?'

Ellie shook her head, reaching for the sheet of information Mr Abel had got for her. Poor man; she did hope he'd be cleared of wrongdoing soon. But there, her solicitor could be trusted to get him out.

Evan's son. Well, a Philip Hooper appeared to be living at an address up Greenford way. There was a landline phone number, but no mobile. She dialled. Nobody picked up, and there was no answerphone so she couldn't leave a message.

Next, Ellie braced herself to ring the first Mrs Hooper. The code number was not for anywhere south of London like Brighton in Sussex, as Freya had thought, but for an Inner London area. This was borne out by the Knightsbridge address, which was within spitting distance of Harrods. Upmarket, or what?

'Mrs Hooper? Mrs Monique Hooper? You don't know me, but . . .' Ellie tried to explain without giving too much away, or causing panic. Best to say only that Evan had been taken ill and Ellie was trying to sort out the resultant confusion. 'Would it be possible to see Mrs Hooper?'

A cool alto voice. 'Very well. I'm at home this afternoon but will be going out this evening. Would you care to drop by within the hour?'

Mrs Quicke would. But first Mrs Quicke had to take her husband's advice and – not before time – dress up a bit. A fine cashmere and wool sweater over a heather tweed skirt. Her best ankle boots, the ones that were a bit difficult to get into, and a jacket. A gold bracelet. A pity, but she seemed to have mislaid her pearls. Oh dear. Well, no time to look for them now. Ring for a cab. Her bill with the cab company this month was going to be something horrendous.

She could hear Vera shouting, 'No, Mikey!' as she went down the stairs. He was probably objecting to Thomas moving into the library. Well, tough. Ellie bit her lip. Should she interfere? Er, no. She hadn't time. The cab was at the door. It was still raining. Up with the umbrella, and out goes she.

Fiends take them. Where are they? It's as if they've dropped off the face of the earth, but however far they go, wherever it is they've taken shelter, they can't get away from me.

The den of iniquity is uninhabitable. Good.

Our progenitor has been whipped off to hospital and is being kept in for tests, no visitors allowed, or so the woman on the switchboard at the hospital says. Could the wicked stepmother have removed him from there and hidden him in a hotel?

They've taught me to be logical. If there's a puzzle, find a way to solve it. This one's called Hunt the Angel. I don't hate her, particularly. She's pretty enough, if you like that kind of thing. Pretty stupid, too. If she hadn't been contaminated by him, I might have let her live.

Now Fern and Fiona are dead, there's only one place I can be sure of getting some information, and that's at the house. There'll be insurance people and reporters hanging around. Someone there is bound to know something.

No more disguises, though I've enjoyed using them from time to time. It's a wonder what you can buy on the Internet these days. Wigs, masks . . . even the ingredients to make the Big Bang, though I'm saving that till I can get Daddy together with the last of his women.

But for now, I need to take something to calm my nerves. This is all taking longer than I'd hoped it would. Concentrate on the next step; it would be only natural for me to have heard about the fire and so turn up to see what's going on. Yes, that's what I'll do.

That's how I'll find the Fallen Angel.

* * *

The first Mrs Hooper lived on the first floor of an exclusive block of flats round the corner from Harrods. Very quiet. Very expensive.

As was Mrs Hooper.

Taller than Ellie. Bulkier. No fool. Mid sixties? A massive head with features that reminded Ellie of a Roman emperor. Handle with care.

Mrs Hooper was wearing something from a designer's boutique in filmy black georgette over silk, with a socking great diamond brooch on her lapel. And pearls.

Ellie felt underdressed.

Mrs Hooper's hair was short and beautifully cut. She might have been a redhead once, but now she was silver grey. She was discreetly made up. There were five rings on her fingers, all of them heavy with gemstones, and her shoes were crease-less, impeccable. No glasses. Contact lenses?

The flat had been furnished with lots of money, and Ellie felt that Betsey, of Harmony in the Home, would have approved. There were some good modern drawings on the walls.

The surprise was that Mrs Hooper was a smoker. 'You don't mind?' Taking a cigarette from a box on the table and lighting up. A gold lighter, of course.

Ellie did mind, but wasn't going to say so. She reminded herself, Handle with Care, and shook her head. 'Thank you for seeing me at short notice.'

Mrs Hooper inclined her head. Interested, but not curious. 'You say my ex-husband's been taken ill?'

Ellie took a deep breath. 'I don't know how much you keep in touch?'

'What is this about?' A narrowing of the eyes.

'Perhaps he's told you that the police are looking into several recent deaths in the Hooper family?'

'No. Really?' A stare as hard as the diamonds on her breast.

Ellie stumbled on. 'I'm afraid so. They would very much like to write them off as misadventures or accidents, but three deaths are two too many.'

'*Three*? What! Who?'

Ellie explained, adding, 'Mr Hooper is currently under

observation in hospital following a fall, and last night an arsonist set a fire which destroyed the front of his house.'

'What? I don't believe it!' The woman got to her feet, reddening beneath her make-up.

'Which?' Ellie was confused.

'About the house! It's *my* house. My father's house. I was brought up in it, and I still own it.'

'But—'

'I didn't want to sell it to Evan. I thought that some day I might want to live there again, though as it turns out I prefer Knightsbridge. Evan rents it from me.'

Monique ground out her cigarette and took a short turn around the room. Giving herself time to assimilate the news?

Ellie could hear Monique's breathing. Hard and quick and shallow. Asthma? Ought she to be smoking?

It was growing dark already. Monique switched on a couple of side lamps. 'Evan's all right, I suppose? Nothing serious, or you'd have said. I'll have to contact the insurers because I'm responsible for the building. What a bore. Is it still structurally sound?' She had herself well under control again.

'It's too early to say. I think, probably, yes.'

Monique had managed to control her distress. Reseated herself. Lit another cigarette. 'Arson, you said. Did they catch him?'

'The police are questioning a man from Mr Hooper's office about it, a man who's under notice to quit. I don't think he was responsible.'

The woman blinked, cigarette suspended in mid-air. 'You said Evan's in hospital. What's the prognosis?'

Ellie told her what she knew. 'It sounds like concussion. He's in the best place, being well looked after.'

'Thank you for letting me know. Now, if that's all?'

Ellie nerved herself. 'I think the police may wish to question your son Philip about what's been happening.'

'Really? How absurd!' Yet her eyelids flickered, indicating unease.

'I can't think of anyone else who has the opportunity and the knowledge to commit these crimes.'

'How ridiculous.' Monique had excellent control. She lit

another cigarette from the butt of the first. 'I don't know whether I am more amused or horrified. You think my son is killing off members of his own family? What nonsense! You should be careful what you say. The laws of slander are rigorous.'

'It's a possibility, only, but one that I feel should be explored. I wanted to speak to you about it before I took my theory to the police.'

EIGHTEEN

Monique gave herself time to think by walking over to the windows to draw the curtains, which were floor length, double width, heavy damask, interlined. With her back to Ellie, she said, 'By what right . . . ? How have you come to be involved with the Hoopers?'

'I've given sanctuary to Evan's current wife and his surviving daughter, and my own daughter is at this moment sitting beside Evan in hospital.'

'You intend to go to the police with this ridiculous theory of yours?'

Ellie chose her words with care. 'I have no evidence that your son is responsible for what's happening, but I believe that he is. Don't you?' A shot in the dark.

'No, of course not. There is nothing to indicate that . . .' Her voice trailed away. She returned to her chair. 'He does get the odd bee in his bonnet, but I take no notice.' Was Monique trying to convince herself that there was no reason to suspect Philip? Who could blame her for that?

Ellie said, 'Have you any idea why he might be doing this?'

The smallest of hesitations. 'No, of course not.' A lie?

'You are not in contact with him?'

'Yes, of course. Birthdays, Christmases. A night at the theatre, a meal at the Ivy, that sort of thing.'

'His decision or yours to restrict contact?'

Monique fingered another cigarette. 'Three deaths, you say?

That's shocking, but nothing to do with Philip. What an imagination you have!'

'Yet I think you know, or suspect, something?'

Monique seemed to make up her mind to be frank. 'I was forty-three when my father took Evan Hooper into the firm and one night – somewhat to my surprise – I ended up in bed with him. Yes, it turned out that I was pregnant. I wasn't particularly pleased but we got married, my father retired and Evan was made a director. Everything went wrong when the baby was born. I was in a coma for sixteen days. They didn't think I'd live, but I did. Only, there would be no more children, and I was paralysed from the waist down.

'Evan found a nanny, moved me to a specialist hospital. I hardly saw the baby. His nanny became his mummy. It was almost a year before I went home, walking with a frame. The boy didn't want to know me. Such a poor, pale little thing. He started at every sound. I tried to be a good mother.' A hard laugh. 'I read books, I talked to professionals, but there was no bonding between us. Maybe I was just too old, more like his granny than his mother.

'Evan and I tried to paper over the cracks for a couple of years though my health was still not good and we slept in different bedrooms. I wasn't particularly surprised when he found himself a playmate. He was highly sexed, and I wasn't. I pretended I knew nothing about it. When Philip was seven Evan came to me with the news that his little bit on the side, Fern – yes, the woman who became the second Mrs Hooper – was pregnant. He asked me for a divorce. He was prepared to buy me out of the business, but wanted to keep the boy and the house. I agreed, and we parted on good terms. I started up a new estate agency in South Kensington . . .'

Not South coast, but South Kensington.

'. . . and my health gradually improved. I had other chances at marriage, but once was enough for me. Philip visited me at weekends and for odd days in the holidays, but I fear both he and I regarded these visits as a duty, rather than a pleasure. As time went on, he seemed to become more, not less, nervous. I wondered if he were being bullied at school. Evan enquired, but it seemed not. His teachers said he was a loner. I wondered if he felt neglected by Fern and his little sisters, but again, it seemed not, as his nanny had stayed on to give him some continuity in his life.

'When he was eleven, I suggested that I took him abroad for the summer holidays, but he wanted his nanny to come, too. Ridiculous! Luckily, Evan agreed with me that it was time to cut the apron strings. There was the most almighty row, Nanny got the sack and Philip . . . Well, I'm not absolutely sure how serious about it he was, but apparently he went for Evan with a knife, tried to stab him.

'We talked it over, Evan and I, and it was agreed the boy should go, privately, to a doctor, who recommended this and that, tranquillizers, of course, a boarding school for children who need special attention, various camps in the holiday times, all in the name of building up his confidence, developing personal skills . . . you know the sort of thing? Costs an arm and a leg and probably doesn't work.

'Philip declared we'd ruined his life by parting us from his nanny and that he'd never forgive either of us. I don't think he ever did. He refused to see me, or communicate with me in any way, for a while, but eventually we resumed our formal outings, though I never again asked him to go away with me. I don't turn up to family functions, but I meet up with Evan every couple of months and we talk on the phone, so I've been kept updated with what Philip was doing: the college courses, the horticultural course, the voluntary work for charity. We share all the costs for our son, including the very expensive cognitive therapy treatments. We thought Philip might react badly when Evan took a third wife and they produced another little girl, but luckily he didn't seem to care.'

'Evan has told you all about his marital ups and downs?'

A nod. 'Including his plans to marry again. Your daughter Diana is his latest, right? As for Philip, I didn't know whether to laugh or cry when he told me a while ago that he'd traced his old nanny and gone to live with her.'

'Ah, the Greenford address. What's she like?'

A frown. Another cigarette. 'A little waif of a thing. Wispy. Not Evan's type at all. He was never interested in her physically, which I did wonder about, if that's what you're thinking.

She used to hover on the edge of sight. Annoying. But there's no doubt she was devoted to Philip, and he to her. I haven't seen her for years, not since the Big Row. I wonder how she's turned out.' She pleated her skirt with beringed fingers. Undecided what to say next.

Ellie prompted her. 'You've seen Philip recently, and he said or hinted at something which you found disturbing?'

Would Monique admit it, or would she continue to protect Philip?

Ellie pressed her point home. 'Three deaths. Who's next, do you think?'

Monique threw up her hands. 'I can't think that he'd ever go so far as to . . . No. Unthinkable. But he did say he'd found a new "therapist" who'd uncovered a memory he'd repressed . . . Oh, such nonsense! Have you heard about these people? Charlatans with no professional background, who latch on to vulnerable people with money and tell them all their problems in life are due to their having been abused by their fathers in early childhood?'

Ellie drew in a long breath. 'Philip swallowed that?'

Monique flushed with anger. 'What's more, he thinks I knew about it and covered up for Evan. I told him, absolute twaddle, no truth in it whatever. As if Evan . . .! I mean, Evan, of all people! Philip said he *remembered* it. That's how they work, these people. They put the idea into your mind that you've deliberately forgotten this dreadful thing, and that that's why you've grown up with neuroses and nightmares. Even if you refuse to believe it at first, they go on and on, saying you're in denial because it hurt so much. Finally, you begin to think it might be true, because it explains why you've never got on with your family or whatever.

'In Philip's case, the therapist has latched on to someone who was easily persuaded that he'd been the victim of child-hood abuse. He wanted me to admit that I'd helped Evan to abuse him. I laughed, which made him angry. He said that if I wasn't going to help him uncover the abuse he'd have to take steps to punish Evan himself, and everyone else whom he'd contaminated. That's the word he used, "contaminated".

'I said it was absolute nonsense and forbade him to mention

it again. It was stupid of me, but I really thought the idea was so implausible that he'd forget it. I can make excuses: my back is playing up, I'm due an operation, I've got a lot on my plate. I suppose I ought to have phoned Evan to warn him, but I didn't. Tell me again; how many in the family have died?'

Ellie counted on her fingers. 'Evan's second wife, Fern. His second daughter, Fiona. His third daughter, Abigail. Then there's the fall which has landed Evan in hospital. And the fire at his – your – house.'

Mrs Hooper ground out one cigarette and lit another. This time her fingers trembled though her voice remained steady. 'You really think he's punishing . . .? By killing them? I can hardly believe it. Three deaths! You think I'm next on the list?'

Ellie shook her head. 'If this is Philip's vendetta against Evan, then he would want to keep him alive so that he can suffer more and more each time one of his family is killed. I think Angelika, wife number three, is next.'

'By which reasoning, Freya would follow. Do you think your daughter ought to be included on the list? And where would I come in?'

'Possibly second to last?'

'Why Angelika next, rather than Freya?'

'Because Angelika was thinking of leaving him, anyway. That marriage is dead and cold, and Angelika has no intention of trying to revive it. She wants out, and I'm sure she'll go as soon as she can come to some sort of financial agreement with him for a quick divorce. Freya, on the other hand, intends to stick around in the vain hope that her father will eventually come to love her and allow her to go into his business.'

'A vain hope, indeed. He's only interested in sons.'

'Yet Freya would make a worthy successor to him. Then there's my daughter Diana, who is pregnant with a baby boy and aims to be the next Mrs Hooper.'

Monique pulled a face. 'A boy? Lucky old her. Does she realize the risk she's running?'

'She's probably up to his weight, even as you were. I'm worried by his use of the word "contaminated". Does he hate his father so much that he wants to destroy anyone Evan has ever loved?'

'You're overestimating Evan's capacity for love. Shall we substitute the words "cared for"? Or would it be more accurate to say "anyone Evan has ever owned"?'

'He never owned you.'

'That's true. It was a one-night stand for me, entered into out of curiosity and the fact that he was something of a stallion in those days. It's turned into a nightmare for everyone.' A glance at the clock. 'I'm due to meet friends at Covent Garden in an hour's time, though how much I'll be able to concentrate on the opera, I don't know.'

Ellie took the hint and rose to go. 'You'll take some precautions? Not accept chocolates sent to you through the post, not get into the first taxi that passes by?'

'I will. And you'll keep in touch?'

Ellie nodded, agreeably surprised to find that she liked Monique and wished her well. 'I'll give you my address and phone number, just in case. May I make a suggestion? When all this is over, and provided we are all still in the land of the living . . . would you consider taking Freya into your business?'

Monique's rather hard expression melted, and she laughed, full-throated. 'That would indeed be a suitable revenge on Evan. Thank you for the suggestion. I will certainly take it into consideration.'

Tuesday early evening

It was completely dark by the time Ellie left Monique's flat. She took the underground back to Ealing Broadway, caught a bus to the Avenue and walked back home from there. It gave her time to think.

She didn't much like her thoughts.

Angelika. Freya. Monique. Evan. Which was next?

Or was it Diana?

Diana was no fool, and had probably understood the threat to the Hooper family quicker than most, which meant she knew she was on the target list.

Ellie didn't want to suspect her daughter of duplicity on this occasion, but it did occur to her to wonder whether the heating in Diana's flat was really on the blink or not. Had she taken refuge at her mother's house because she felt she'd be better protected there?

Home at last. But no rest for Ellie.

Midge greeted her at the front door, rubbing around her legs, indicating that he hadn't been fed for ever. A lie, of course, but Ellie picked him up and took him into the kitchen to give him a few mouthfuls of cat food.

Rose and Vera greeted her with the busy, absorbed expressions of chefs in the midst of preparing a feast for a hundred. Do Not Disturb.

There was no sign of Mikey but a rumble rumble rumble from above indicated that he'd taken himself off to the top floor and was expressing his displeasure at something by making a lot of noise. Vera had said something about him and his scooter, hadn't she? Well, as Vera didn't seem worried, Ellie decided to forget about Mikey for the moment.

There was a message on the answerphone from Angelika, asking if Ellie could collect her from the Hooper house. Nothing from Stewart or from Freya. Another pile of mail.

Ellie riffled through the letters and messages. There was a fat package from Betsey, of Harmony in the Home, containing folders with samples of fabrics and pictures of furniture for different rooms . . . Ellie shoved them aside.

One piece of paper floated to the floor.

Ellie stared at it. A somewhat dog-eared photocopy of a clown handing out biscuits and balloons. The missing picture!

But how . . .? She turned it over and saw that she'd written notes for Betsey on the back of the photograph of the clown. Ah. So that's where it had gone?

Her hand went to the phone. Should she ring Ms Milburn to say the picture had turned up? Of course, it was getting late, and the girl had probably gone home by now and in any case would be more interested in the fire and questioning poor Mr Abel . . . which reminded Ellie that she'd set her own solicitor on to the case and . . .

She wanted to chuck all her papers into the air and let them fall where they would.

Only, she knew that she would then have to get down on

her hands and knees and pick them all up again. Oh, her knees!

She sighed, picked up the phone and left a message for Ms Milburn. 'I've found the missing photo of the clown, and I've got a possible address for him.' She wondered if she should voice her suspicions about the identity of the clown. But no – she didn't have enough evidence. Feelings and suspicions are not legal tender.

She put her phone down, and it rang under her hand.

Diana. 'Mother, where have you been?'

'Out. I had to—'

'Well, never mind that now. I'm ringing to say that I'll be going back to the hospital in a little while, and I won't leave till I've seen Evan asleep. So—'

'Have the police released Mr Abel?'

'I can't think why, but yes, they have. I shot him straight out again, of course, stood over him while he collected his stuff and saw him off the premises.'

'He's innocent, you know.'

'You know more than I do. I'm glad to be rid of him.'

'Mrs Lavery is no substitute.'

'She'll do. Did you tell her to contact the insurance people for Evan's house? There's nothing here about it.'

'No, there wouldn't be. I've discovered that the house is still owned by the first Mrs Hooper, Monique, and that Evan merely rents it from her. Monique will contact the insurers about the fire.'

'What? I don't believe it! He never said anything to me about that.' Unwelcome news. Evan obviously hadn't broadcast the fact that he didn't actually own the house. Diana recovered quickly enough. 'Well, be that as it may, I'm just ringing to put you in the picture. Someone will have to wait up for me tonight, as I forget to get a front door key from Rose before I left.'

'I think you'd better go to a hotel. You'll be safe enough there.'

'Are you refusing me a bed for the night?'

'Yes,' said Ellie, wondering how she dared. 'I've got a full house. There's no beds to spare. I'll have your things packed up and leave them at the hospital for you when I collect

Freya, who's been sitting with Evan all day and must be exhausted.'

'You can't—'

'Watch me.' Ellie put down the phone with care, feeling guilty, triumphant and ashamed all at once. Had she really dared to throw her daughter out of the house?

Was she going to regret it? Well, probably. But she really did not have a bed to spare, and Diana was perfectly capable of finding herself a hotel.

Ellie ordered a cab to collect her in twenty minutes and went upstairs to put Diana's things back into her carry-on bag. Checking the time on her watch, she darted into the kitchen to touch base with Vera and Rose before she left. The whirring, banging, and bumping continued above. Ellie looked a question.

'Leave him be,' said Vera. 'He threw a tantrum because you didn't take him with you this afternoon, so now he's got his scooter up there and is trying to make a point by running it round and round on the top floor. He refused to eat any tea, but I suppose he'll come down when he's hungry.'

Ellie knew she was being a coward, but fled. Bringing Mikey into the household was not going to prove an unmixed blessing.

The cab driver dropped Ellie off at the main entrance to the hospital. She said she wouldn't be long and arranged for him to circle the block till she came out again.

Evan had been moved into a side ward on one of the top floors. Nice and clean. Ellie was afraid she might have been refused admission to see him until visiting time but, when she explained the position to the nurse in charge, she was let in a few minutes early. Evan was hooked up to all sorts of machinery and seemed to be asleep. Freya was sitting beside him, holding one of his hands.

Ellie beckoned the girl to come out into the main ward to speak to her. Freya looked exhausted, moved like a sleepwalker. It was a trying situation for an adult, and the girl was only fifteen – or was it sixteen?

'How is he?'

'They're keeping an eye on him because he seems very

confused still. They said they might have to have an operation to relieve the pressure on his brain. They keep waking him up and testing his reflexes. He's mostly asleep, and when he's awake he vomits and complains of a terrible headache. One of his eyes looks funny.'

Concussion.

'He's in good hands and you've done a sterling job, keeping him calm today. Now, Diana's on her way here. Can you put this tote bag of hers in Evan's cupboard and then come home with me? There's a good meal waiting, and after that you must go straight to bed.'

'I'll leave when she comes.'

'You'll leave now, with me.' Ellie wondered at herself, giving orders left, right and centre, but it seemed to work, probably because Freya was too tired to object.

Ellie continued to be on edge. Worrying at the problem of the Hooper family. Thinking over what she'd learned, what she'd been told. Some lies, here and there? Mm. Not many. A picture was emerging, but would the police take Philip's strange ideas seriously?

Perhaps most parents had been through times when they'd wanted to beat the living daylights out of their children, but nearly all managed to restrain themselves. Ditto the other way round. However angry you might be with a parent or a sibling, it was unusual to go to the lengths of murdering them.

Another thought: had Philip been responsible for knocking his father out before he started the fire at the house? Or after? Or, had Evan's fall been an accident?

Ellie dropped Freya off at home and took the cab on to the Hooper house, in order to rescue Angelika and see for herself what was happening there. She asked the cab driver to park a little way down the road and to wait for her . . . just in case a reporter or two might still be hanging around.

Thankfully, the rain had died away, though clouds still obscured the moon.

She couldn't see any reporters, either outside the house or lurking in the garden. She stopped by the entrance to the drive to survey the desolation of the burned house, illumined by the street lights in the road. And gagged. The stink was appalling.

Everything in sight was black and wet, saturated with the water used to dowse the flames.

Would the whole house have to be pulled down and rebuilt, or was it still solid enough to be restored to what it had once been? All the windows facing the road had been boarded over, as had the front door. The roof seemed intact, so maybe the fire hadn't taken that much of a hold before the fire engines got there.

A large white van sporting the logo of Ellie's trust was parked in the driveway, together with Stewart's car and two others which she didn't recognize, probably belonging to workmen.

Angelika was sitting in the back of Stewart's car, but got out when she saw Ellie. 'Can we go now?'

'In a minute. I must have a word with Stewart first.' Ellie made her way round the house, taking care not to trip over anything as she skirted the kitchen, the windows of which had also been boarded over. Stewart had run some electricity cables around the house from his van, to power floodlights at the back of the house. It wasn't as bright as day, but it enabled the workmen to see well enough to do their job.

The conservatory was intact. The broken door had been boarded over.

A couple of Stewart's maintenance men appeared in front of her, wearing hard hats and carrying tools. 'Hey, there, Mrs Quicke. Nearly done. You're after the old man?'

She nodded. 'You've managed to make all safe?'

'One more to go. Himself's round the back.'

She found Stewart checking over a back door which was hanging open. The upstairs windows here looked all right, but there was a familiar wash of muddy water around her feet. And that smell!

Stewart looked tired. 'Nearly done. The front of the house isn't safe to enter so the firemen broke in from the back to fight the flames from this side, too. This is the last door we'll have to board over. The windows downstairs are just cracked, and it may be safe to leave them as is. Then home and a shower before supper.'

'Can the house be saved?'

He shrugged. 'Hard to say. I spoke to the firemen before

they left. One lot had stayed overnight to make sure no more fires broke out. He said no one should try to go in to the front until they'd worked out if it were arson or not – though he thinks it was – and a surveyor has given the all clear. There's a risk of ceilings falling in there, and the staircase has almost burned through.

'The electricity's out, of course. Fortunately, the fire didn't reach the gas boiler or the whole lot would have gone up. The house was solidly built, and from what I've seen, the main structure is sound enough. My guess is that everything in the rooms at the front is a write-off while at the back the damage is from nearly all from smoke and water. Mrs Hooper was dying to get into the house to rescue some of her belongings, but her bedroom was at the front so I couldn't let her.'

Ellie picked her words with care. 'Was Angelika very distressed?'

A tired grin. 'You mean, did she come on to me? Well, she tried, poor little thing. I felt like putting her over my knee. Then I wished I could take her home to Maria to look after. She's had a rough few days, hasn't she? She needed a shoulder to cry on.

'It sounds as if you saved her life, whipping her away from the house as you did. What a carry on! At first I thought she was exaggerating what she'd been through, especially about the phone line being cut, but when I'd had a look around at the back here, I saw where someone *has* severed the phone line into the house. It's over here . . .' He showed her the cut line, shaking his head. 'I don't think reporters would have done that, do you?'

'There's no reporters around now?'

'There were a couple when I arrived. I sent them off sharpish, said I was the builder, carrying out orders to make the house secure. Angelika kept close to my side, said she was afraid they'd return to bother her again, but there's been no sign of them for some time. I suppose they've got their story and gone on to the next one. To do her justice, Angelika did her best to help. Some neighbour or other came to keep her company for a while, she went to the shops to buy some sandwiches and hot drinks for us all at lunchtime, and after that I got her making detailed notes of everything we've done to secure the house.'

One of his men called out, 'We're short of a board for the door. What do you think?'

Stewart turned back to Ellie. 'I have to get this sorted. Can't leave that door hanging off its hinges. Do you want to wait for me?'

Ellie nodded. 'I've got a cab outside, but I'll send it on home.'

Ellie went back to Stewart's car and explained to Angelika that she was going to have to stay on till Stewart finished. 'Now, I collected Freya from the hospital and dropped her off at my place before I came on here. The cab's in the road, waiting for me. Would you like to go back in that, to be with her? She's been sitting at her father's bedside all day. She's dead on her feet.'

'How is Evan? I kept trying to ring the hospital, but they said they'd only give information out to family, as if I wasn't! It's just as if I don't exist.'

Ellie avoided comment. Had Diana brainwashed the nurses to believe that only she and Freya had the right to news of Evan? 'He's in a side ward now. Diana's going in to sit with him this evening.'

A resigned nod. 'I'll wait for you.' She got into the back seat, pushing aside some takeaway sandwiches and coffee cups. She helped herself to some bottled water. 'Want something to eat or drink? Philip got these in for me, but I don't eat mayonnaise on tuna, or drink coffee.'

NINETEEN

A larm bells rang in Ellie's head. 'Philip . . .? You mean *Philip*?'

'Mm. He'd heard about the fire so came round to see if he could do anything. He went and got some food and drink for me without asking what I'd like. I didn't want to hurt his feelings by saying I couldn't eat what he'd bought, so I waited till he'd gone before I went and got a salad for myself.'

Ellie felt a trickle of fear down her back. 'Did you tell him where you were living?'

'Might have. Why?'

'You didn't touch any of the stuff he brought you?'

'I said, didn't I? What's bothering you?'

'I think, though I may be wrong, that your being a picky eater might have saved your life.' Ellie rummaged around for a plastic bag in her handbag – always useful to carry the odd purchase in nowadays when shops were trying to cut down on providing carrier bags – and popped the sandwich and the coffee into it. 'I think we should let the police have these.'

'What?' Angelika turned round in her seat to face Ellie. 'You think Philip was trying to poison me? That's silly. I know he's a bit odd, but he's not stupid. You're just trying to frighten me.'

'About time, too. Surely you understand that these deaths are connected, that someone is trying to kill off all Evan's family?'

What little colour there was drained from Angelika's face. 'You really think he was . . .? But why? I mean, he is a bit creepy, but I've always been perfectly nice to him.'

'I think it's a question of his wanting Evan to suffer, so he's killing off everyone around him.'

Angelika flushed. 'You mean that he killed Abigail just because Evan was her father? That's . . . that's monstrous! No, I can't believe it.'

'We'll give the police the food and drink he brought for you. They'll soon tell us if it's got anything harmful in it.'

'You're quite wrong! He was ever so nice to me this time, asked me how I was feeling and how was Evan doing, and I assumed . . .' She broke off with a sob. 'You know, it's like a dream, my life with Evan and Abigail, living in that house. You must think me a total cow, but I can't seem to feel anything, about anything or anybody.'

'Shock,' said Ellie, almost able to sympathize with the girl.

Angelika stared out of the window at the blackened shell

of the house. 'As soon as Abigail died, I knew it was over
with Evan. I could see it in his eyes. Then there was your
daughter ready to take over, and I knew she'd flatten me. I
thought there'd be a reasonable financial settlement, enough
to get me a nice flat somewhere. I've always had plenty of
work till now, so . . . I'll take jolly good care not to get pregnant again, I can tell you.'

'Did you get pregnant with Evan by accident?'

A twist of her shoulders. 'Not really. I don't know. He was
so . . . I thought he was going to transform my life. He wanted
a son so badly, and he said it wouldn't make any difference
to my career because he could afford a nanny, so why not?
The scans weren't really clear, and then there was Abigail and
she was definitely not a boy but totally Evan, if you know
what I mean. I thought we could muddle through, though after
a while I could see . . . And then Diana . . . I will not go back
to filling shelves in the supermarket!'

Ah, so that was Angelika's background, was it? It explained
a lot. 'Surely Evan will make you a generous settlement?'

'Not if he dies. I have a horrible feeling that he will and
I'll have to go through the courts to get anything at all because
I signed something called a prenup which means I don't get
anything if we divorce and I'm sure Diana will fight me for
the business, and I wouldn't be any good at running that
anyway. My guess is that Diana will scoop the lot.'

'Now, come on! You are Mrs Hooper, Evan's legal wife.
Surely it's up to you to . . .' Ellie's voice faded away. Angelika
was not the baddie she'd been made out to be, but she wasn't
a strong personality who could take control of this situation.
Diana probably *would* trample all over her.

Ellie struggled with an idea. It wasn't at all the sort of thing
which she ought to suggest. It was sneaky and it would do
Diana no good at all. On the other hand, Ellie felt some
sympathy for Angelika. 'You are signed up with a modelling
agency?'

'They're not being frantically helpful. They don't think I
can take any more jobs till after Abigail's funeral, and goodness knows when that will be; poor little tyke, she didn't
deserve this.'

'The agency hasn't suggested that you might be able to cash in on your moment of fame, sell your story to the newspapers? "How My Life was Wrecked", sort of thing?'

Angelika's eyes narrowed in calculation. 'It had crossed my mind, but then I thought it was all too difficult to arrange and Evan would hate it, though goodness knows I needn't worry about that now, need I?'

'Perhaps you might talk to your agency about it, discuss what could be done? Why don't you take my cab on back home and think about it?'

'I might as well. But you're wrong about Philip, you know.'

Ellie saw Angelika into the cab, then went back round the house to see if Stewart had finished. Which he had. Wearily, seeing the last of his men off. 'The house is as safe as I can make it. Shall I take you home now?'

'One last thing. Mr Abel was taken in for questioning by the police this afternoon, because Diana wanted him out. They think he had motive and opportunity for setting the fire.'

'You're joking.'

'I wish I were. I set my solicitor to work, and he got Mr Abel out, but Diana has cleared his desk and won't allow him back. I wondered –' with an angelic-seeming smile – 'whether you or I ought to phone Mr Abel this evening? We had thought there was plenty of time to let him know we have a job waiting for him, but now . . .?'

Stewart smoothed out a grin. 'Diana will be furious when she finds out we've given him a job.'

'Mm. So, would you like to ring him, or shall I?'

'I will. Definitely.' Stewart laughed out loud. 'Bless you, Mrs Quicke.'

She was wistful. 'Can't you bring yourself to call me "Ellie", after all we've been through together?'

'I've talked this through with Maria. I feel more comfortable this way.'

Oh well. Perhaps, one day . . .

Now, what else must she do before she went to bed? Phone the police. Tell them what Monique had said, give them an address where Philip might be contacted. Ask them to collect the picture of the clown and the food and drink Philip had given Angelika. Ears would probably be sarcastic about Ellie losing the picture, but that couldn't be helped. She wasn't superwoman, was she?

Oh dear, she did so hate having to talk to Ears . . . but perhaps he'd be out, and she could just leave a message.

Her luck was out, and he was in. She tried not to sound unsure of herself, but could hear her voice lacking assurance as she reminded him that no one had yet collected the photograph of the clown from her. 'Also, there's been another development. You know Evan has a rather unsatisfactory son? Well, he may well have gone off his rocker . . . I mean, he's been seeing a quack "therapist" who has put some very odd ideas into his head . . . What I mean is, he may well think he has a reason to harm Evan and the rest of the family.'

Ears barked at her, 'Now what red herring are you trying to drag in?'

She quailed, but persisted. 'Philip found Angelika at their house and gave her some sandwiches and some coffee which luckily she didn't touch, and I've kept them so that you can check if they contain poison—'

'Stop right there! You really cannot expect me to take your suspicions seriously. All the deaths in that family have been accidental. Or misadventure. The only crime so far has been arson, and we have a suspect for that. Do you understand?'

'Yes, but—'

'Don't waste my time.' The phone crashed down.

Ellie noticed her hand was trembling as she replaced the receiver. Oh dear, oh dear. Yet she was sure she was right. At least, she was pretty sure she was right. She took a deep breath. There was one thing she could do to make herself feel better, and that was to ring Thomas and have a good old gossip. And put in a spot of prayer afterwards.

Wednesday morning

Breakfast was a difficult, mostly silent affair. Ellie was worrying about how to get rid of her guests and reorganize the house in time to receive Thomas's family.

Thomas had been concerned about her when she'd rung him the previous evening. He'd said he'd better miss the last few sessions and return early. Naturally, she'd told him that she was perfectly all right, that he was not to worry about her and absolutely not to think of leaving early.

She knew he'd continue to worry and to pray for her, which she found most helpful, rather like being buoyed up in the sea with water wings. The waves might become choppy, but she wouldn't drown while he was her lifebelt. And Jesus. Whatever. She really must put in some praying time about, well, everything.

The two girls had their own preoccupations at breakfast. Every few minutes Freya would look at the clock and wonder aloud how soon she could ring the hospital. Angelika toyed with her breakfast cereal, keeping her eyes down.

Vera and Rose were united in an attempt to make Mikey attend to his table manners. The boy was sullen and uncooperative. He slid out of the kitchen as soon as he could in order to run round the garden on his scooter, even though it was raining. Vera ordered him back in, saying he wasn't to go into the garden without permission. At which he put out his tongue at her and hauled his scooter up the stairs to the top storey to resume his endless running around there.

'Sorry about that,' said Vera, flushed and uncomfortable.

Ellie said, 'It's I who am sorry. We've always planned to fence part of the garden off for use by whoever moves into the top storey, and we'll get round to it as soon as we can. Young things need a bit of space.'

'Young things,' said Rose, 'need to know their place. Now you've forbidden him the garden, Vera, he'll be back there in no time at all.'

This word of truth caused a certain amount of coolness between Vera and Rose, although, if she'd been asked, Vera would probably have agreed with the sentiment.

Diana's phone call broke up the tension around the breakfast table. She was as crisp and to the point as always. 'Evan is to be operated on this morning. I shall sit with him till he goes down to theatre. The office is closed for the day, and the phones switched to the answer machine. I spent last night at a hotel and will call round shortly to get an update from you about the Hooper house.'

'But . . .!' said Ellie as the phone was cut off. To the dead phone she said, 'Oh well. You can sort that out with Monique.' She put the receiver down, worrying about how soon the police would be able to take Philip off the streets.

Freya hovered. 'What can I do to help?'

Ellie bit back some sharp words. Would the girl help with the housework, make her own bed, clean her shower and toilet? Shop and cook for everyone? Er, no; she wouldn't.

But Freya wanted — no, needed — to be of use. Ellie led the way to the dining room and laid out all the materials which Betsey from Harmony in the Home had sent her. There were sheets of suggestions for this and that. Swatches of fabric. Photographs of furniture available for hire.

'What's all this?' Angelika, following them. 'Looks like Betsey's work to me. Oh, look at this gorgeous fabric. What are you planning to do with it, Mrs Quicke?'

Ellie explained about the projected visit of Thomas's relations and how they needed to reorganize the house. For one thing, she didn't think the torn dining-room curtain could be mended in time, so they were going to need a complete new set of curtains. Then they needed to shift Thomas's office into the library and turn his old office into his new quiet room. This would in theory make another bedroom available upstairs, for which they needed furniture and furnishings. And . . . and . . .

'But,' said Ellie, in despair, 'I've only one pair of hands and young Mikey's laid claim to a corner of the library and Thomas is away for another day, and I really don't see how we can be ready in time.'

'We can sort this for you,' said Angelika, running an experienced eye over the swatches of material. 'I don't think much of the flowered chintz for this room, but . . . what do you think of this cream and gold brocade, Freya? Too old-fashioned?'

'Mikey's only trying it on, being in a new place,' said Freya, drawing up a chair beside Angelika. 'Vera was telling me all about him last night . . .'

The front doorbell rang, and Ellie left them to it.

A stranger. No, the first Mrs Hooper in a superbly-cut black overcoat, carrying a handbag the size of a suitcase. A sleek black car stood outside, matching her elegance.

'Monique?'

'If I may come in? It's stopped raining but the wind's getting up. I couldn't get any sense out of the hospital about Evan's condition—'

'Too many Mrs Hoopers, I fear,' said Ellie, closing the door behind her visitor. 'Diana's sitting with him at the moment, but he's going down to the theatre this morning for an operation.'

'Serious?'

'I don't know. Something to do with the concussion. Releasing pressure on the brain? I'll ring and see if we can get some news about when he's likely to be back in the ward.'

Monique looked about her. Nodded approval of the wide hall, polished staircase and conservatory. 'I tried ringing my son's place last night and again this morning. The nanny said he wasn't with her any more. I didn't believe her.'

'I've rung the police, given them what information I have. I hope they'll pick him up before he can do any more damage.'

The doorbell rang again. Ellie opened it to admit another gust of wind and a wispy female in layers of grey clothing. She, also, was clutching a handbag, though it was neither imposing nor very new. Who . . .?

'Ah,' said Monique. 'I know you, don't I? So, where's Philip?'

The newcomer ran her tongue over her lips. 'Philip left me a note to say he was coming round here today to . . . Well, he said he was going to finish what he'd started. I'm not sure what he means, but I thought I'd better warn you, though really he's not responsible for his actions. He's suffered so much. It's you who've driven him to do—'

'Nonsense, woman!' said Monique. And to Ellie, 'Odds on he's not far behind.'

Ellie drew the newcomer in. 'I'm afraid I don't know your name.'

'I'm Jeanette. Mrs Jeanette Hooper.'

Monique rolled her eyes. 'If you believe that!'

A querulous tone. 'As the only person who's ever cared about Philip, my adopted son, I can call myself that if I like.'

Ellie blinked. Was the woman for real?

Angelika and Freya were standing in the doorway to the dining room with their mouths open.

Ellie said, 'Angelika, Freya: may I introduce some more Mrs Hoopers? This one's called Jeanette and I believe she used to be Philip's nanny. The other one is Monique.'

'The first, so to speak,' said Monique. 'Evan is getting to sound more and more like Henry the Eighth with his half a dozen wives, isn't he? I seem to remember only a couple of them managed to survive him. Henry, I mean. Let's hope we have better luck.' She ignored Angelika to advance on Freya. 'You are Fern's daughter, the one who wants to follow your father into the business? Yes, I can see him in you. What subjects are you studying, my dear?'

The doorbell rang, and the knocker rapped. Impatiently. It must be Diana.

It was. Clad in dark blue with white trimmings today. She seemed to have abandoned her usual black for the duration. Her bulge was just beginning to show, and the band on her ring finger had grown larger and more prominent since Ellie last saw her.

As Diana stepped inside, Ellie said, 'And this is the next Mrs Hooper. Diana; may I introduce you to your predecessors? This is Monique, the first. The second is unfortunately deceased—'

'*I'm* the second,' said the wispy female. 'I'm Jeannette.'

'Born Jean Marks,' said Monique. 'Now calling herself Hooper. I always called her Jean. She was good with Philip, I'll give her that.'

Diana shot a frowning question at Ellie. 'Is she legal?'

'Of course not,' said Monique, impatient as ever. 'Evan wouldn't. Evan didn't. Not his type. Now, can we all go and sit down somewhere? My back's killing me.'

Ellie said, 'In here.' She led the way into the sitting room, collecting her handbag on the way, thinking she might need to use her mobile phone in a minute to get it touch with the hospital . . . if, that is, she had replaced it in her bag, which was something she couldn't be sure about.

The others filed in after her and found themselves seats.

Monique, predictably, took the high-backed chair by the fireplace.

Where were the police? And – as the song would have it – where, oh where, has my little boy gone? Where, oh where, can he be?

If she was any judge of the matter, Philip was lurking in the shrubbery. Or round the corner. With intent to kill more of the family off?

No, he wouldn't want to hurt his nanny. Or would he?

Diana, baulked of the most commanding chair, took up a position in front of the fireplace. Freya and Angelika seemed to have formed some sort of alliance in adversity and subsided, side by side, on to the settee.

The wispy Jeannette dithered, unsure of herself. Ellie remembered Monique had described Jeannette as a hoverer.

Monique shrugged off her coat, revealing a fine wool-and-silk black trouser suit with a diamond brooch on the narrow lapel. The rings on her fingers glittered as she extracted a cigarette from her bag. 'You don't mind?'

Ellie said, 'I'm afraid I do.'

Angelika looked horrified. 'Oh, please don't. I get asthma.'

Monique shrugged, put the cigarette away. 'Oh, do sit down, Jean. You make the place look untidy.'

Jeannette flushed, but sat on the edge of Thomas's reclining chair. 'You have no right to speak to me like that.'

Diana was not accustomed to being relegated to second place. 'I don't understand why you're all here. I'm due back at the hospital soon and have only dropped in to check the details of the insurance company and decide who's to board up the house—'

'I've contacted the insurance people,' said Monique. 'I don't suppose you realized it, but Evan merely rents the place from me.'

'Actually, I did know, but I find it's best to double-check.'

Angelika eyed Diana with dislike. 'The delicious Stewart – who I gather is one of your ex-husbands – has had the house boarded up for me most beautifully.'

'What?' Diana didn't like any of this. She looked to Ellie for information. 'You got Stewart involved? Why?'

'Angelika very sensibly asked Stewart to board up the house to repel looters and stop people going in and getting hurt. The staircase has almost burned through and might come down at any minute.'

'But Evan wouldn't want—'

'Hah!' said Monique, smoothly taking over again. 'As I see it, Angelika's the only one who has a legal right to speak for him at the moment. So here we are, all Evan's women, past and present, gathered together in one place. Waiting.'

'For what?' said Diana, though she almost certainly knew.

'For Philip,' said Ellie. 'I rather hope the police will make it before he does, but it's going to be a close run thing.'

Someone rapped on the French windows that led into the back garden, and everyone looked that way. Predictably, it was the wispy Jeannette who went to let Philip in.

There was a sharp intake of breath from Angelika. Everyone else froze.

Philip – if it was Philip, because the figure was wearing a balaclava, jeans and an ominously bulging anorak – was carrying a mobile phone. Or what looked like one. 'Anyone moves, and I blow us all up!'

TWENTY

B low them all up?

Did he mean that he'd packed explosives around his body and could trigger an explosion by using his mobile phone? Oh. That was the way terrorists had worked on public transport, wasn't it? Could Philip be copying them?

Angelika was on her feet. 'Philip? Why? I don't understand!'

'You! Why aren't you dead? There was enough weedkiller in the sandwiches I got you to kill a dozen people.'

'Yes, but I don't like tuna!'

'Sit!'

Angelika sat.

Freya, sitting beside her, stared at Philip, refusing to cringe.

Monique said, 'Oh, really, Philip!' in an exasperated tone.

Diana was no coward, either. She turned away from the fireplace and took a seat on an upright chair. 'So this is Philip, the black sheep of the family?'

Philip sang in a rough tenor, '"Baa, baa, black sheep, have you any wool? Yes, sir. No, sir. Three bags full." It was always, "Yes, sir. No, sir," wasn't it? But now it's my turn to call the tune. Get my father back here, now!'

Jeannette was wringing her hands. 'Oh, Philip; no!'

Monique said, in a voice which refused to tremble, 'I'm afraid he's unable to join us for the time being. He's having an operation this morning.'

'Concussion,' Diana explained. 'They have to relieve the pressure on his brain.'

'I don't believe you! He was coming round when the ambulance people got to him, so he can't be seriously hurt. You're hiding him from me, that's what you're doing. Get him back here, now! Or I'll blow up the lot of you.'

Monique blinked, fingered her cigarettes. 'Philip, dear. You can't blow us up without blowing yourself up, too. And if you blow yourself up, then you'll never get to confront your father – if that's what's on your mind.'

Silence while Philip thought about what his mother had said.

Ellie was more intrigued than afraid. This wasn't either tragedy or comedy; it was farce. She didn't think they were in any danger . . . or were they? Um, well; perhaps they were. Philip was so unstable that a wrong word might easily set him off. But wasn't he overdoing the amateur dramatics? Why, for instance, was he bothering to wear a balaclava, when everyone knew who he was?

Did he think its presence made him into a menacing figure? Well, yes. Probably. He liked disguises, didn't he? First he'd dressed as a clown, then as a woman reporter. Maybe there'd been other disguises at different times. Disguises gave you confidence, if you weren't naturally a confident person.

Yes, looking at it that way, the balaclava made sense. He aimed to frighten, but Ellie doubted that the odd bulge in his anorak contained dynamite, or whatever it was terrorists used nowadays. After all, where could he have got dynamite from? Ah, but the terrorists had made up their own bombs hadn't they? Not dynamite, but just as effective.

Oh, but he really wouldn't want to blow everybody up yet, would he? In the first place, Evan – who must be considered the chief target – was unavoidably absent, and in the second place, Philip was surely enjoying the situation too much to let it end quickly.

Ellie took a step back and let herself down on to a chair, opening her handbag and placing it on her lap. Monique had hers on her lap, as did Jeannette. And Diana. Ellie fingered through the contents of her bag till she found – eureka – her mobile and switched it on. And pressed buttons to put a call through to the police. Nine nine nine for emergencies. She hoped she'd got the right number this time.

She had thought of trying to contact Thomas but he'd have his phone turned off while he was in the conference auditorium, so that was no good.

Philip unzipped his anorak with his free hand, revealing that he had a bulky rucksack strapped to his chest. Filled with enough ingredients to blow them all up? It did look as if he'd taken some trouble to copy the terrorist's favourite weapon of destruction.

Angelika certainly thought so. Eyes wide, she made herself small on the settee, huddling closer to Freya . . . who watched, wide-eyed, breathing faster, but not allowing herself to show fear.

Monique's eyes switched from Philip to Freya and back. Monique had written Philip off years ago. Perhaps she was now assessing Freya as a possible substitute?

'Excuse me if I light up.' She extracted her cigarettes from her handbag and lit one. This time no one objected.

Ellie wondered if Monique had also managed to switch her mobile phone on while fumbling in her bag for her cigarettes. And if so, who had she called?

Ellie could hear her own call going through. She could hear a woman's voice saying, 'What service do you want?'

Somehow she had to alert the woman as to what was happening. 'What a pity the police couldn't make it in time to join the Hoopers at play. Coffee, anyone? Monique? Or any of the other ladies? I can easily get my housekeeper to brew some up. And for you, Philip? What would you like?' She hoped she sounded sufficiently silly. She didn't want him to take her seriously. He probably wouldn't because she wasn't a Hooper and therefore not in the first line of fire. And perhaps the woman on the other end of the phone might be sharp enough to put two and two together.

'Shut up, you! Let me think!' He held his mobile phone high. 'One touch on this and I blow you to blazes, because you deserve it, all of you!'

Jeannette was weeping. 'Oh, Philip! No! My darling boy!'

'Yes; you, too! You covered up for my father when he abused me. You're as bad as my mother!' He was working himself up into a rage.

Jeannette made the mistake of reaching out for him with both arms. 'Come to Mummy!'

He hit her, backhanded, catching her under her chin. She stumbled backwards and fell. Her eyelids flittered, and then she was still.

Everyone else's eyes switched back to Philip.

'Ow!' he said, nursing his hand under his arm, but still holding the device in his left hand, steady. Very steady.

If he dropped it . . . If he inadvertently pressed the button . . .

The message was clear. Don't mess with me. Or else.

Heavy breathing all round.

Monique said, 'For God's sake, Philip!' She sounded more amused than alarmed, but her voice grated and the fingers holding the cigarette shook.

'You shut up! You sold your soul to him, didn't you! You let him mistreat me night after night in my own bedroom. You never interfered or told him to stop or even came in to comfort me when he'd finished.'

'What absolute nonsense!'

'You won't think it's nonsense when you wake up to find yourself in hell! All of you! All contaminated material should be burnt. You, too,' he said, turning on Diana. 'I didn't realize

I could get so many of you all at once, but now I have you're all going to die with me.'

Jeannette moaned. Was she coming round?

He spurned her with his foot. 'As for you, you said you loved me more than Monique, but you betrayed me, too.'

Dear Lord above! He means it! He's capable of anything because his mind has been twisted out of the true by the lies told him by his so-called therapist. I never thought he'd turn on Jeannette, who did love him more than his birth mother.

Time for me to interfere? And draw his wrath upon myself? Help, Lord! Tell me what to say . . . or do.

Angelika was visibly trembling. 'Philip? You don't mean it. You can't!'

'You stupid bitch! Do you really think I care about blue eyes and blonde hair when I know what a stinking, maggot-ridden little soul you've got? You're going to die, like everyone else he's touched.'

'What about your father?' said Ellie. It seemed he'd momentarily forgotten her presence for he turned on her, taken off balance for a fraction of a second . . . during which Ellie glimpsed something, someone, looking into the room from the garden. A small figure, not an adult. A child. Mikey? Who'd been forbidden to play in the garden and so had gone out to do so the moment his mother's back was turned?

No; there was no one there. The phone in her handbag was ringing. The police ringing her back? No, it couldn't be, because she hadn't ended the call she'd made to them earlier. But . . .

'I'd better answer it, hadn't I?' she said in a bright tone, reaching into her handbag.

'Give it here!' He snatched the phone from her hand and threw it across the room. It shattered against a bookcase. Oh. Would the police realize something was amiss? If they did, would they act upon it or think it a prank call?

A phone was still ringing. Ah, but it wasn't hers.

'Mine, I think,' said Monique. 'If I don't answer it, they'll be coming in search of me here, as I said I'd be in to work by ten. I'll tell them I'll call back later, shall I?'

Philip bit his lip, undecided.

Monique took out her phone and with a perfectly level voice said, 'Bit of a crisis here. Can't talk now.' She put it back in her bag. Had she switched it off? Now that Ellie's phone had been destroyed, Monique's might be a lifeline for them all, relaying what was said to the outside world . . . or the police, if Monique had been clever enough to dial their number.

Monique said, 'Which reminds me; Diana, what time are we supposed to get news about Evan?'

Diana, pale but composed, also made an effort. 'I was told to ring about noon. He was asking for Philip last night. I don't know if you feel up to visiting him, Philip?'

'What!' With his free hand he tore off his balaclava, revealing a hot, red face and redder hair. 'If you don't all do as I say, I'll—'

'I know,' said Monique, in the soothing tone of mother to toddler. 'You'll blow us all up. We understand. We really do.' She looked around. 'Is there an ashtray anywhere?'

'Do you mind?' said Diana, 'I'm still throwing up at the slightest thing.'

'Sorry,' said Monique, taking what looked like a snuff box from her bag and stubbing out her cigarette in it.

Philip lifted the mobile phone into the air. 'Are you all sitting comfortably? Then I'll—'

'I don't understand.' Freya, resolute, despite a quaver in her voice. 'Philip, you are my half-brother. I've never heard anything about you being abused. Are you sure?'

'Don't pull the innocent. Of course you know. He abused me, over and over.'

Freya shook her head. Her mouth tried to smile. 'You're joking! No, Philip. He couldn't. He didn't.'

'All these years I tried to forget, and I did forget. I told myself that he didn't love me because I wasn't as clever as him, and because my mother didn't love me at all. And that's true!' He shot the words at Monique. 'You never loved me. You only pretended to be ill, so that you wouldn't have to have me with you. And when he, my father, started to do that to me, you covered up for him.'

'That's not how it was.' Monique had another cigarette out.

'Please,' said Diana, hand to mouth.

'Sorry, dear.' Monique put the cigarette away. 'Have you some peppermints you could take?'

Diana scrabbled in her handbag, produced a tube of mints, and took one.

Philip cried, 'You never loved me!'

Monique took that on the chin. 'I tried. By the time I could hold you in my arms you already had a mother, and you made it quite clear that you didn't want me.'

'You got rid of my real mother.'

'Make up your mind; is Jean your biological mother, or am I?'

Through his teeth. 'You got rid of her when I needed her most. I was being bullied at school—'

'Evan enquired. The teachers said you weren't.'

'I was! I should know, shouldn't I? It was all your fault. Then Dad said I wasn't suitable to go into the business and had to learn carpentry or gardening or something, anything to get me out of his sight for good. That was fine by me!' He stood up, menacing, phone lifted high. 'So . . .!'

'Ooops!' said Ellie. 'I think Jeannette's coming round. You pack a wicked punch, don't you, Philip? Do you think we could get her up off the floor? She looks so uncomfortable. Freya, can you help me get her on to the settee, poor thing? I don't think she hit her head on anything as she went down, but perhaps we ought to get her checked over.'

'Leave her be,' said Philip, but he made no move to interfere when Ellie and Freya lifted Jeannette on to the settee, displacing Angelika as they did so.

'There, now. That's better,' said Ellie, disposing of Jeannette comfortably. 'Now, Philip, we're all going to sit here quietly and listen to you until we get hungry or thirsty and could do with a cuppa. Did you have any breakfast today?'

'What . . .?' He didn't appear to know. But Ellie had broken his concentration.

Freya had lost her place on the settee to Jeannette, so now took one nearer Philip. 'Tell me; why did you kill Fiona? She always looked up to you.'

'All the evil seed must be exterminated.'

'You killed Fiona just because she was our father's daughter?'

'Of course. And the toddler. That was fun.'

Angelika gulped, hand over mouth. Was she going to be sick? 'Why now?'

He pointed to Jeannette, who moaned. 'She found a new therapist for me, someone who helped me understand why my father disowned me. It took me a while to remember what he'd done. Then Fern told me that Dad was going to get married again and have another son whom he'd also get to abuse. She didn't see how wrong that was. I told my mother, and she refused to believe me, too. What else could I do? I had to take things into my own hands and destroy everyone he'd contaminated. Fiona was the easiest. I took her by surprise when she was on the treadmill. I had to be more careful with Abigail, disguising myself as a clown. If she hadn't been so greedy, she wouldn't have died, would she?'

'You killed Fern, too?'

'Of course. She talked about going to the police. She laughed at me and called me a silly boy. So I killed her.' A sob. '*No one* laughs at me.'

'No, indeed,' said Ellie. 'We all take you very seriously indeed; don't we, girls?'

Everyone nodded.

Angelika took a step forward, slowly, arms akimbo. 'Yesterday you said you understood how awful I must be feeling. I trusted you.'

'More fool you, Little Miss Blue Eyes! Goldilocks!'

'How dare you!' She advanced on him, narrowing her eyes. 'Evan was the kindest, most understanding of men, and he would never, ever have . . .' She took a deep breath. 'You killed my baby! You are out of your tiny, warped little mind! You hopeless, brain-dead piece of shit! You turd!'

'Don't you dare speak to me like that!' He lifted the phone high in the air. 'Prepare to die, all of you!'

Angelika was not to be stopped. She yelled, 'I spit on you!' And did.

Philip recoiled.

The door to the hall was flung open.

There was a rush of movement, and a small boy on a scooter whooshed past Ellie, aiming for Philip . . .

Who screamed.

Impact! Boy and scooter caught Philip amidships.

The phone, jolted out of his hand, flew high in the air.

Lazily, turning over and over . . .

Freya, athlete that she was, leaped into the air, and caught it in one hand.

Everyone froze.

One . . . two . . . three . . .

Everyone made themselves small.

Ellie put her hands over her ears.

Four . . . five . . . six.

Dear God in heaven . . .!

Seven . . . eight . . . nine . . . ten.

Nothing.

A long sigh of relief. Everyone straightened up.

'I don't think it's going to set anything off,' said Freya, breathing hard. 'I think it's just an ordinary mobile phone. I'll switch it off, shall I?'

'It's not, it's not!' yelled Philip, disentangling himself from Mikey and scooter. 'It's going to send you all to hell and beyond. Give it here!' He lunged for Freya.

'Ha!' Angelika put out her foot and tripped him up. He fell headlong, but in falling turned sideways so that his rucksack and its contents didn't hit the floor.

Again, everyone held their breath.

One . . . two . . . three . . . four . . . five.

Nothing.

They were not going to be blown up.

Mikey abandoned his scooter to rush into Ellie's arms. He snuffled into her shoulder. Clung to her.

Ellie murmured into his ear, 'You are a hero.'

Philip began to sob. He drew his knees up to his chest and wrapped his arms around his head.

'Anyone know what we do now?' enquired Diana, white of face, but still composed.

Monique withdrew her mobile phone from her handbag. 'The police should have been here by now. Really, it's a poor service we get nowadays. I shall complain to my MP.'

Jeannette inched herself down off the settee to crawl to

Philip's side, covering him with her body, crooning soft words.

Ellie looked up to see Vera standing in the doorway, looking anxious. 'Mikey?'

Ellie said, 'He's all right. He's a brave boy.'

'Has someone sent for the police?' said Vera. 'Because they've just arrived.'

'About time, too,' said Monique, extracting another cigarette from her bag.

In came Ears, with DC Milburn at his back. 'What's all this, then? I'm called to the scene of a riot and find you having a mother's meeting.'

'How true,' said Ellie, feeling limp. 'A mother's meeting is exactly what it is. That's Philip Hooper on the floor. He is responsible for the three deaths in the Hooper family, though goodness knows if he's fit to plead. Probably not. Will you please take him away and get him seen to by some doctors? Oh, and find the charlatan who filled his mind with thoughts of revenge and who needs to be certified, or struck off or something, as well.'

'What,' said Ears, 'is going on?'

No one replied. No one was up to it for the moment.

Ellie closed her eyes. *Thank you, Lord. Oh, thank you. Praise be.*

Monique lit her cigarette.

Diana went to open a window on to the garden to do some deep breathing exercises. It had stopped raining, for a wonder.

Angelika, the avenging angel, stared into the past, not liking what she saw.

'You'll need this.' Freya held Philip's mobile phone out to Ears, who took it without realizing its significance. Freya put her arms around Angelika and led her out of the room.

Ears finally summoned reinforcements, but Philip made no demur when asked to accompany him down to the station. Jeannette, in tears, told the police that she'd given her life to Philip and that he didn't really mean it, any of it. It was all the fault of the therapist he'd been seeing.

Which, thought Ellie, to a large extent it was. She thought about asking her solicitor to represent Philip and decided against it. It didn't seem likely to her that he'd ever be fit to stand trial.

Everyone gave statements. Tiredly. Without emotion. One by one, going into the dining room, where Ears had set up his headquarters.

They drank coffee, tea, bottled water. Gin for Monique.

Ellie handed over the food and drink Philip had prepared for Angelika, and the picture of the clown.

Monique and Diana went into a huddle.

Angelika came out of her interview in tears and was led into the garden by Freya, to walk round and round. Now and then they paused to embrace. Sisters in distress. Both weeping for their losses.

Ellie watched Monique taking note of how well Freya was behaving.

Vera and Rose served up hot soup and ham sandwiches. Angelika said she was on a diet and asked for fruit. Diana ate, went to the cloakroom to throw up and, pale-faced but resolute, phoned the hospital for news of Evan, who had come through the operation 'as well as could be expected' . . . whatever that might mean.

Stewart, summoned by Ellie, conferred with Monique and left to deal with the insurance people.

Ellie phoned the hospital to ask when Evan might receive visitors. She was told he'd be in intensive care for a while.

'I'll go to sit with him,' said Diana, 'and organize some accommodation for when he comes out.'

Monique nodded. 'We can take our time, sort things out between us: the insurance, rebuilding the house, everything.'

Ellie could see that these two strong women could easily form an alliance; the past and the future, leaving Angelika out of it. She said, 'I would like your assurance that Angelika will be fairly treated.'

'Of course.'

'Naturally.'

They didn't mean it. Well, Monique might. Diana didn't.

'Otherwise,' said Ellie, 'Angelika might well have to sell her story to the tabloids. That's right, isn't it, Angelika?'

For once Angelika was quick on the uptake. Her voice might

be croaky from crying, but there was no doubting her firmness of purpose. 'I've been in touch with my agency and they're looking into it, though I'm not sure I want to go down that road. But if I have to start out all over again, without a husband or a home, or a car, or anything, then I might have to.'

Monique produced a grim little smile. 'Very well, my dear. We understand. I can fix you up with a furnished studio flat in Knightsbridge, rent free, till your solicitor can sort something out with Evan. Diana, you can arrange some sort of allowance for Angelika from Hoopers, can't you? Just till the divorce is through and alimony can be arranged.'

'Agreed.' Diana also tried to smile. 'I'm sure my mother can put Angelika in touch with a good solicitor to represent her interests.'

Ellie smiled, too. It served her right for interfering. She could guess who was going to have to pay the solicitor's bills, and it wouldn't be Angelika. Well, well. The child deserved some good fortune, after all.

What about Freya? 'Don't worry about me. I expect I can stay with a school friend for a little while, just till Dad says what he'd like me to do.'

Monique looked as if she'd like to offer Freya a home there and then but decided against doing so. Really, Ellie reflected, Monique was too old and too busy to look after a teenager, though she might well keep an eye on her for the future.

TWENTY-ONE

The police left.

It began to rain again.

Diana and Monique departed, the tyres of their cars swishing in the rain.

Ellie waved them off and returned to find Angelika and Freya with their heads together.

Freya said, 'We've been thinking. Mrs Quicke, you've been marvellous. We know you've got people coming to stay and

will need our rooms, but you've got ever so much to do before
they come and we'd like to help, if we may. If you could put
up with us living here for a couple of days more, we could
help you get the house ready for your guests. We promise to
move out in good time.'

'I can always go to a hotel.' Angelika wasn't going to accept
Monique's offer of a flat? Mm. Well, perhaps not. Angelika
would have to housekeep in a flat, and she'd be lonely, all by
herself. She'd be lonely in a hotel, too, wouldn't she? Well,
that wasn't Ellie's problem, was it?

Ellie said, 'Bless you, my children. I accept with thanks.
We've got till Saturday to get ready. If you're game to try it,
then so am I.'

It struck Ellie that she might offer them both a home for a
while. Angelika would probably get back into work soon
enough, and she would have a reasonable income from Hoopers.
Sooner or later she'd be bound to attract another sugar daddy.

Freya? Although she was growing up fast, she needed a
stable background till her schooldays were over. Diana would
probably want to send Freya off to a boarding school, which
might or might not be a good idea. Freya would definitely not
want to live with Diana, who was no one's idea of a cuddly
stepmother.

Plenty to think about. She would talk to Thomas about it
when he got home. Meantime, she would go into the quiet
room and spend some time thanking God for all his goodness
. . . for Angelika's courage, Freya's quick thinking, for their
new-found respect for one another . . . for Mikey's interven-
tion . . . for so many things. *Thank you, Lord. Oh, thank you.
Praise be. Etcetera.*

And, what were they going to have for lunch?

D-Day: Saturday, noon

D-Day was arrival day for Thomas's family. It was not D
for Diana day, and yet, when Ellie was interrupted laying the
table for lunch, it was Diana who rang the doorbell and stepped
into the hall before Ellie could stop her. Diana was dressed
in cream and blue. She looked tired. Was she beginning to
lose her looks?

Diana looked around the hall. 'No changes here, I see. The builders are starting on Evan's house on Monday, so I thought I'd better get an idea of what this Betsey woman can do before I get her started on the redecoration.'

She brushed past Ellie into the dining room, where the table shone with polish and new floor to ceiling curtains lightened the heavy Victorian decor. 'Pleasant enough. What else has Betsey done downstairs? Your study? The library?'

Diana started off down the corridor, so Ellie put down the cutlery she'd been holding and followed. Before she could stop her, Diana opened the door to what had been Thomas's study. 'What's this?'

'This is our quiet room now. Thomas uses it all the time.'

'What's a sleeping bag doing there?'

'Mikey likes it in here, and Thomas doesn't mind.'

A twist of shoulders. 'I knew there'd be trouble with that boy, the moment I laid eyes on him.'

Ellie didn't reply. Yes, Mikey could be trouble with a capital T, but he was also adorable, loving, hyper-clever and a blessing. Rose alternately hugged him and scolded him, which Thomas said was exactly what grannies were supposed to do. Mikey could often be found sitting on Thomas's knee while he was praying.

Mikey had begun to talk again. His first word, predictably, had been 'no'.

Diana moved along to Ellie's study. Nothing had changed there, except that the piles of paper for Ellie's attention were even higher than before.

The library looked splendid, sombre and workmanlike with computers on large desks for Thomas and his part-time assistant, while their business files had been stacked on the shelves. A rampart of books cut Mikey's smaller desk off from the rest of the room.

As Diana opened her mouth to remark that Mikey seemed to get everywhere, Ellie got in first. 'The men enjoy getting away from us women at times, don't they? How are you coping?'

'At least I've stopped being sick. I did think about aborting the infant when I discovered Evan's recovery was going to be a long-term business, but it's too late for that, and this baby is such a determined little brat, I doubt if he'd allow himself to be thrown out with the garbage.' She turned back to the hall and climbed the stairs to the first floor.

Ellie considered it was an improvement that Diana was thinking of her child as a person and not as a 'thing' any more. Perhaps she might not make such a bad mother this time round?

Little Frank's old bedroom had not been altered, except for a more grown-up wallpaper on one wall and the addition of bunk beds. Ellie explained, 'For Thomas's twin grandsons.'

Next came the room which had once been Thomas's sanctum. One wall had been papered in a warm blue and white pattern with curtains to match; the floorboards had been stripped, waxed and polished, and the furniture was light oak, with white bedding.

'Pleasant enough,' said Diana, bile in her voice. 'Though not particularly striking.'

What had she expected? Ellie said, 'This is for Thomas's granddaughter. And the end room, which was a depository for junk, has been made into a nice double bedroom with a similar colour palette. Betsey spruced up the bathroom at the end, too, with some wallpaper on one wall and a new basin. New lighting everywhere. The girls helped me, or I'd never have been able to get everything done in time.' Ellie looked at her watch. Half an hour till everyone arrived.

'You could let these rooms out for a decent sum.'

Ellie shook her head. Once Thomas's family had departed, they would put a door halfway down the corridor, to turn the end rooms into a small flat for Vera and Mikey. Mind you, no one really thought Mikey could be contained that easily.

Diana opened and closed the other bedroom doors in turn. It seemed she had something on her mind but was having difficulty in getting it out. 'I've lost track of Angelika and Freya. Do you know where they've gone?'

'Angelika was offered some work in the Mediterranean at short notice. Freya's visiting a school friend. I can give you their addresses, if you like.' She didn't add that both girls had been invited to return and live with Ellie and Thomas when his family departed, and that both had accepted.

Diana shook her head. 'Monique's dealing with their end of things. I wanted to ask you . . . No, I suppose I know what you'd say. If you put in a stairlift and altered the door frames, Evan and I could live in these rooms when he leaves the convalescent home.'

So that was why she'd come?

'No way,' said Ellie. And left it at that.

Diana twisted the rings on her fingers, hesitating, not yet ready to leave.

'Evan's getting a quickie divorce, and he still wants to marry me, but I'm not sure that I . . . . He's not going to be able to run the business for months, if at all. What do you think?'

Ellie blinked. Was Diana actually asking her advice? 'Diana, I thought you'd be rejoicing. You're going to get exactly what you've wanted all along. A husband who'll be forever grateful to you, a son you can palm off on a nanny, and control of a successful business.'

For once Diana looked uncertain of herself. 'Yes, but . . .'

Ellie wanted to say, 'No gain without pain.' But decided against it. Although true, it was too harsh a judgement. She felt a rush of loving kindness for this difficult daughter of hers. She said, 'You love Evan, don't you?'

'Yes, of course.'

Perhaps she did, in her own way, but it would not be the sort of loving and giving partnership that Ellie had with Thomas.

'Then you've got to keep that in mind. You are strong and can cope with the sort of difficult situation which would defeat other women. If you'll take my advice – which you probably won't – let Evan have his own way as much as possible, so that even in his convalescence he can feel he still counts. I'll go on praying for you.'

Diana looked as if she didn't know whether to smile, or cry.

Ellie glanced at her watch. 'That's it, then. Now, if you don't mind . . .'

She watched Diana insert herself into her car and leave . . . even as the people carrier Thomas had hired for the duration of his family's visit turned into the drive.

She threw the front door wide. 'Welcome home at last!'